continued . . .

And for Max Allan Collins

"Max Allan Collins blends fact and fiction like no other writer."   —Andrew Vachss, author of *Flood*

"Collins displays a compelling talent for flowing narrative and concise, believable dialogue."   —*Library Journal*

"No one fictionalizes real-life mysteries better."
                                             —*The Armchair Detective*

"An uncanny ability to blend fact and fiction."
                                             —*South Bend Tribune*

"Collins has an outwardly artless style that conceals a great deal of art."   —*The New York Times*

"When it comes to exploring the rich possibilities of history in a way that holds and entertains the reader, nobody does it better than Max Allan Collins."
                              —John Lutz, author of *Single White Female*

"Collins's blending of fact and fancy is masterful—there's no better word for it. And his ability to sustain suspense, even when the outcome is known, is the mark of an exceptional storyteller."   —*The San Diego Union-Tribune*

"Probably no one except E. L. Doctorow in *Ragtime* has so successfully blended real characters and events with fictional ones. The versatile Collins is an excellent storyteller."   —*The Tennessean*

"The master of true-crime fiction."   —*Publishers Weekly*

The
LUSITANIA MURDERS

MAX ALLAN COLLINS

BERKLEY PRIME CRIME, NEW YORK

This is a work of fiction. Names, characters, places, and incidents either are the product of the author's imagination or are used fictitiously, and any resemblance to actual persons, living or dead, business establishments, events, or locales is entirely coincidental.

THE LUSITANIA MURDERS

A Berkley Prime Crime Book / published by arrangement with the author

PRINTING HISTORY
Berkley Prime Crime mass-market edition / November 2002

Visit our website at
www.penguinputnam.com

ISBN: 0-425-18688-1

Berkley Prime Crime Books are published
by The Berkley Publishing Group,
a division of Penguin Putnam Inc.,
375 Hudson Street, New York, New York 10014.
The name BERKLEY PRIME CRIME
and the BERKLEY PRIME CRIME design
are trademarks belonging to Penguin Putnam Inc.

PRINTED IN THE UNITED STATES OF AMERICA

10 9 8 7 6 5 4 3 2 1

In respectful memory
of the World Trade Center victims,
who followed in the tragic footsteps
of the *Lusitania* passengers.

Though this work is fanciful, an underpinning of history supports the events depicted in these pages. The author intends no disrespect for the real people who inspired the characterizations herein, nor to take lightly the disaster that took so many lives, and marked the first instance in modern warfare where the line between combatant and noncombatant was tragically blurred.

"There's been some cover-up about the *Lusitania* . . . it was really murder."

—Edith William Wachtel, *Lusitania* survivor

"There are few punishments too severe for a popular novel writer."

—S.S. Van Dine

"So long as governments set the example of killing their enemies, private citizens will occasionally kill theirs."

—Elbert Hubbard

"NOTICE!

Travellers intending to embark on the Atlantic voyage are reminded that a state of war exists between Germany and her allies and Great Britain and her allies; that the zone of war includes the waters adjacent to the British Isles; that, in accordance with formal notice given by the Imperial German Government, vessels flying the flag of Great Britain, or any of her allies, are liable to destruction in those waters and that travellers sailing in the war zone on ships of Great Britain or her allies to do so at their own risk.

Imperial German Embassy

Washington, D.C., 22 April 1915"

Announcement appearing in New York newspapers the morning the *Lusitania* sailed

Author's Note

Using both research and literary license, the following narrative was fleshed out from a fragment that was among the few existing papers of Willard Huntington Wright (1887–1939). Wright—a trailblazing art critic and contro-versial editor of the avant-garde magazine *The Smart Set*—is better known under his pseudonym, S.S. Van Dine.

Wright had long been a caustic critic of popular fiction, but—after gaining an affection for puzzle-oriented mys-teries, while recovering from a nervous breakdown—turned to mystery writing both as therapy and as a means to climb out of a personal and financial hole. For some time, he guarded his identity behind the colorful Van Dine pseudonym; but when the Philo Vance mysteries became wildly popular, he emerged to relish and even exploit his celebrity, though he probably never completely divorced himself from the guilt attached to abandoning artistic as-pirations for the best-seller list.

Though S.S. Van Dine is little read today, Wright and his fictional detective, Philo Vance, are remembered as, first, the sensational mystery genre success of the Jazz Age, and, second, an enormous influence on the American mystery (the Ellery Queen novels began as an outright Philo Vance/S.S. Van Dine imitation).

Because I had written about the experiences of mystery writers Jacques Futrelle in *The Titanic Murders* (1999) and Leslie Charteris in *The Hindenberg Murders* (2000), I was approached by a rare-book dealer with the manuscript that provided the basis for this novel.

Despite the unimpeachable integrity of this particular bookseller (thank you, Otto), I had my doubts about the authenticity of the manuscript. According to John Loughery's fine biography of Wright, *Alias S.S. Van Dine* (1992), as his health failed, Wright "began his remarkably thorough and systematic attempt to thwart any future interest in his life story by destroying files of correspondence and early unfinished manuscripts."

Further, none of the references on the sinking of the *Lusitania* contain any mention of Wright having been on the great ship's final voyage—though Loughery indicates Wright travelled on the *Lusitania* earlier in 1915—either under his own name, or—as the fragment suggests—under the name S.S. Van Dine.

It is entirely possible that S.S. Van Dine began what he titled *The Lusitania Murder Case* as another fanciful, if fact-based, mystery. His first two Philo Vance novels, after all, were suggested by real, notorious cases—*The Benson Murder Case* (1926) was patterned upon the 1920 murder of stockbroker Joseph Elwell; and *The "Canary" Murder Case* (1927) was based on the 1923 murder of Dorothy King, the so-called "Broadway Butterfly." Perhaps *The Lusitania Murder Case* was designed as a similar roman à clef.

There is, however, evidence to suggest otherwise; that his fragmented manuscript was a memoir, not a mystery. Though Wright travels as "S.S. Van Dine," he does not disguise his identity from the reader, nor does he pretend to be the Watson-like lawyer who, as Van Dine, "writes" the Philo Vance mysteries. Nor does Philo Vance himself appear, although a fascinating prototype for Vance does.

In addition, my research indicates that Wright's description of the final voyage of the *Lusitania* is quite accurate in its facts, even to its details—and Wright did not have access to the in-depth book-length treatments of the disaster that have appeared in recent decades.

How much of the narrative that follows derives from the S.S. Van Dine fragment, and how much from my own imagination, I will leave up to my . . . our . . . readers. *The Lusitania Murders* is offered only as an entertainment, a testament to a forgotten master of the mystery genre, and a remembrance of the victims of a tragedy whose ramifications far outreached those of the *Titanic* itself.

ONE

Dinner at Luchow's

My friend H.L. Mencken—at least, from time to time we were friends—once characterized me as the "biggest liar in Christendom." So I would take no offense if the gentle reader (as Elbert Hubbard would say) discounted the tale I'm about to tell, as typical S.S. Van Dine self-aggrandizement.

On the other hand, over the years, the question I've most often been asked is how I came up with my distinctive pseudonym. The "Van Dine," I have explained, is simple: It is an elegant representation of my occasional desire to eat, a luxury that requires earning the more than occasional dollar. Some have speculated that the "S.S." represented the traditional abbreviation of "steamship," which is in part true, and relates to this tale, taking place as it does on one of the most famous—and infamous— ocean liners of the twentieth century.

Like most artists, however, I have an irresistible incli- nation toward resonance—double meanings and second levels. And while it is true that I regard my mystery novels as voyages of entertainment, "vacation reading" that encourages my patrons to board the *S.S. Van Dine* for a good trip, that "S.S." did indeed have a secondary shade of significance, which at the time seemed clever and now merely strikes me as (I shudder to admit) cute.

At the time of my ill-fated voyage on the *Lusitania,* I was in no position to travel first class; frankly, managing the fare for second class would have been a trial, and even steerage a stretch. In March of 1914, a year and two months prior, I had suffered through the indignities of second class; the food, accommodations and company were of a different order than my trip to Europe the previous spring, as editor of *The Smart Set.*

My brother Stanton—the eminent Modernist painter who pioneered the Synchromist movement—was living in London in early 1915. I had spent almost a year with Stanton in Europe—first in Paris, then London—before returning on the *Olympia* in March, leaving him to stubbornly serve his muse.

Our sojourn in Europe had been well-intentioned— Stanton sought a suitably sympathetic climate in which to paint, I to pursue writing (both criticism and fiction)—but in retrospect our timing could have been better. A continent withered by war and gripped by nationalist hysteria was hardly conducive to creativity.

In April of 1915 I began to cast about for a way to return to Europe, and convince Stanton to return stateside. But the condition of my finances—and, frankly, of my health—was less than ideal.

In some respects, though, my life was on the upswing. I had received a modest advance for my book-in-progress, *Modern Painting: Its Tendency and Meaning,* and fees for essays and reviews for various publications, *Forum* and *International Studio* among them, allowed me to move from my dismal flat in the Bronx to a two-room apartment over a store on Lexington Avenue in Manhattan. Disagreeably dilapidated though the building might be, the thirty-five dollars a month rent was friendly enough.

In addition, after a debilitating illness,* my health had recently improved. For months I had been weak and on edge, filled with hallucinations and phobias, and would surely have checked myself into a hospital if my monetary status had allowed. Instead, I ministered to myself in a singularly unromantic garret—a boardinghouse room in the Bronx—until I looked healthier and less drawn, and could come out among the civilized once again.

Perhaps a certain illness-induced gauntness emphasized my already Mephistophelian features—the receding nature of a reddish-brown hairline emphasized my intellectual stance, even if the former aspect was underscored by the devilish glint in my blue eyes and the spade-shaped if well-trimmed full beard, the upturned corners of my mustache perhaps hinting at my pro-German leanings.

Well over a decade later, my Germanophile's view might seem harmless enough; on the eve of what would be the Great War, I suffered numerous negative repercussions, due to what I admit was an intellectual's naivete. It seemed to me that reasonable men could tell the dif-

---

*Van Dine refers here, obliquely, to a drug addiction that he battled, off and on, throughout his younger years, when opium and marijuana were weaknesses of his artistic temperament. He wrote of his problem only once, in a 1917 essay for *The Medical Review of Reviews*, in which he rather farsightedly made the statement, "Drug addiction is a disease. The fact that it is self-imposed does not alter its status." M.A.C.

ference between Wagner and Kaiser Bill; that a mind fond of Mahler, Strauss, Goethe and Mann did not signify an insurgent heart.

This pro-German stance—added to my reputation as a prolific if outspoken columnist, with the boost of an H.L. Mencken recommendation—had brought me to this table. Of course it could also be said that Gavrillo Princzip made inevitable this appointment, when—on June 28, 1914, on a Sarajevo, Serbia, street—he shot and killed the Archduke Franz Ferdinand.

As a bonus, Princzip had also killed the archduke's wife, and this rash act (the archduke's assassination, that is, not Mrs. Archduke's) served to spark a war involving Russia, Germany, Austria-Hungary, France and Great Britain. Ten million lives would be lost, twenty million souls would be wounded and twenty-five million tons of shipping would be sunk.

But the war was three thousand miles away, on this warm Friday evening in Manhattan in late April of 1915; the three of us were in a bustling Bavarian restaurant near Union Square, on Fourteenth Street. Perhaps the city's best-known German restaurant, Luchow's—with its dark woodwork and baroque dining rooms with their elaborate gilt-framed landscape oils and solemn looming stags' heads—found its popularity unswayed by a growing anti-German sentiment, and remained a favorite haunt of writers, musicians and theater folk. Tonight I was dining at the invitation of publishing legend Samuel Sidney McClure and one of his associates, Edward Rumely.

We were seated at a table beneath the Wagner murals in the Niebelungen Room; I had my back to the eightpiece orchestra, which had been brought to this country by Victor Herbert, whose mediocre music they performed with all the lack of panache it deserved. Fortunately the din of dinner conversation all but drowned out the orchestra's brainlessly lilting aural wallpaper. We were drinking beer from steins, having completed our prime beef and red cabbage.

McClure was a stern-looking character, with a short blunt nose and a carelessly trimmed white mustache, his blue eyes piercing in an almond-oval face topped with a shock of gray hair; a thought-gouged crease between his eyes suggested eternal skepticism. His brown vested suit with darker brown bow tie might have been the attire of a chief clerk, not the man who invented newspaper syndication, and whose *McClure's Magazine* had taken on corruption in corporations and city government.

After all, the term "muckraker" had been coined to describe McClure's efforts, which included publishing Lincoln Steffan's "Shame of Our Cities" series and blistering exposés on Standard Oil and the United Mine Workers.

The third and final member of our little all-male dinner party was a thickset fellow in his mid-thirties who looked rather like a bulldog in a three-piece suit, a navy suit as rumpled as its wearer's homely face. This was Edward Rumely, the owner and publisher of *The New York Evening Mail*, a recent acquisition of this scion of the Rumely farm implement manufacturing clan. The family wealth may have derived from diesel farm equipment, but Edward Rumely had other ideas about making his own fortune . . . in publishing.

"I understand congratulations are in order," I said to McClure, and then lifted my stein in an informal toast toward the vested bulldog. "To both of you—for your new position, Mr. McClure, and for landing such a prestigious editor for the *News,* Mr. Rumely."

"You may not be aware, sir," McClure said to me, his voice a gruff baritone, "that I've lost control of my own magazine . . . to my 'loyal' partners, and various investors."

"I had not been so informed," I said. But I did know that S.S. McClure's reputation was that of a man of innovative, grandiose ideas . . . who lacked in business sense.

"Part of the buyout of the magazine that still bears my name," McClure said, "is a ten-year noncompetition clause."

"That applies to magazines," Rumely put in, in his knife-blade tenor, "not to newspapers. . . . Meaning I've bagged one of the biggest names in publishing to edit the *News*."

The line between McClure's eyes tensed—the bluntness of Rumely's expression understandably offended him.

"If I'm not overstepping," I said, "surely you don't *need* to work, Mr. McClure. . . ." He was approaching sixty and most certainly was comfortably wealthy.

"I *want* to work, sir," McClure said. "I need to work. Money has never been my objective—communicating progressive ideas to the public, that, sir, is my calling."

"I understand the impulse," I said. "I've hoped to educate the unwashed masses myself . . . not in political areas, where I admit a certain lack of knowledge and even interest. But in the arts—painting, literature."

"That's why we're considering you," McClure said, "for our literary editor."

"Book reviews, short essays," Rumely explained, "publishing announcements, gossip. . . ."

In those days, "gossip" meant reporting the books writers were working on, or travels they might be taking for research purposes—not peccadilloes, sexual or otherwise.

"I'm the man for the job," I said with no modesty. "I feel an affinity with you, Mr. McClure—in our shared desire to make a difference in the world. If I could persuade readers to turn from romance novels to Joseph Conrad, if I could move them to protest censorship, as pertains to Dreiser and others—"

"All well and good, sir," McClure cut in. "But you have a reputation for a sharp tongue—for sardonic, even sarcastic condescension."

"Guilty," I said with a shrug.

"I would not censor you, but I would insist that you strive to abandon any mean-spiritedness in your psyche."

"I was younger then," I said, referring to my controversial tenure at a *Smart Set*, as well as my biting *Los Angeles Times* writings, which had put me on the map.

McClure's eyes appraised me unblinkingly. "How old are you, sir?"

"Thirty-three," I said.*

He nodded, obviously glad to hear I was no longer a young pup. "This *Lusitania* voyage will be a test of your new maturity, then."

"I consider it a golden opportunity, Mr. McClure."

"Your journalistic sense of fair play will be tested."

"How well I know it. I wrote a fairly vicious piece on Hubbard in *Smart Set*."

The homespun philosopher Elbert Hubbard was booked on the *Lusitania*; I was to ingratiate myself with him and

---

*In 1915, Van Dine was twenty-eight.

do "the definitive interview" with the so-called "Sage of East Aurora" (New York). That I considered him a boob and a fraud apparently was not to get in the way of this non–mean-spirited effort.

"Though you've written of him," McClure said, "you have never met Hubbard . . . ?"

"I've been spared that pleasure thus far."

McClure's eyes tightened. "You should understand that I admire Elbert Hubbard—consider him a sort of rough-hewn genius . . . and I'm not alone. Clarence Darrow, Henry Ford, Booker T. Washington, even Teddy Roosevelt, have sat looking up at him."

Which only meant that even the best among us have our foolish streaks.

"Impressive," I said.

"Keep an open mind, sir. And do your best not to alienate your subject."

To McClure, Rumely said, "That's why we've arranged for our friend here to travel under a pseudonym. His true identity is known by Staff Captain Anderson, and he will of course carry a proper passport to present at journey's end, in Liverpool."

McClure was frowning, the line between his eyes like an exclamation point. "I dislike such deceptions."

"Modern journalism requires bold methodology," I opined. "If I were to travel under my own name, Hubbard would surely recognize it, and never grant me an interview."

"Several of the other prominent passengers," Rumely put in, "might react similarly, if they happen to know of our man's acid reputation."

McClure said to Rumely, as if I were not present, "Is he aware of the other potential interviewees?"

"I thought we would discuss that after you've taken your leave, Sam," Rumely said.

McClure had already announced that his attendance at our little gathering would be abbreviated, as he was meeting with his wife and a group of theater-goers to attend D.W. Griffith's new moving picture, *Birth of a Nation*, at the Liberty Cinema on Forty-second Street. It was said the show elevated that nickelodeon novelty to the level of art—which I sincerely doubted, though I did relish the thought of the theater's new cooling system, as stifling summer months lay ahead.

"Just so we understand each other," McClure said, his hard gaze travelling from Rumely to me. "I suppose you know that I consider myself a Progressive."

"I do," I said, and I did—from backing Teddy Roosevelt to extolling the virtues of health foods, McClure was if anything a freethinker.

"So is my friend Edward here," McClure went on, and placed a hand on the bulldog's shoulder. "We share many interests. . . . We met when my son was attending the Montessori school Edward ran for a time in LaPorte, Indiana . . . Edward agrees with my current campaign, for example, to form an international organization that would guarantee peace among all nations, world round."*

"How interesting," I said, not really caring. Politics were anathema to me.

"You see, my sympathies in the current struggle are with Great Britain . . . and Edward's are with Germany. As reasonable men who can agree to disagree, we have

---

*McClure's concept would eventually become the League of Nations and, decades later, the United Nations.

struck a bargain—the *News* will air both points of view, but ban the propaganda of both."

"I wish more newspapers would take a neutral position on the war," I said. "I'm appalled by these crude British-slanted atrocity stories—Belgium children mutilated, women raped, shopkeepers murdered . . . tasteless rabble-rousing trash."

"I agree wholeheartedly," McClure said. "But I will not tolerate a pro-German point of view, either . . . is that understood, sir?"

So that was the real heart of tonight's matter.

"I will take the same neutral stance as the *News*," I assured him.

He took a final sip from his stein. Too casually, he said, "I have learned that a book of yours is about to be published."

I shifted in my chair. "That is true."

"*The Teachings of Nietzsche?* Huebsch is bringing it out, I take it."

"Actually, sir, it's entitled *What Nietzsche Taught* . . . and much in your tradition, I seek only to guide the general reader to a better understanding of an important philosopher's much-maligned, much-misunderstood writings."

He dabbed a napkin at himself, cleansing his mouth and mustache of beer foam. "There are those who say Nietzsche is to blame, in some degree, for this war—that he was the Prophet of the Iron Fist and the Teutonic Superman . . . the enemy of common, decent people."

"Which is why my book is so important, Mr. McClure. Nietzsche wasn't interested in the acquisition of land for the state, or glory for the Kaiser . . . but in each man's ability to find within himself strength, confidence, exuberance and affirmation in life . . . a life intensified to its highest degree, charged with beauty, power, enthusiasm. . . ."

I didn't realize it, but I was sitting forward now, my voice raised somewhat, and what seemed at first an awkward silence followed . . . until McClure's grim countenance broke into an unexpected grin.

"I like the sound of that," he admitted. "And I like your spirit . . . and your mastery of the English language." He gathered his coat and hat, stood and offered me his hand, which I shook. He shook hands with his publisher, and then pressed through the bustle of waiters and patrons, on his way to see D.W. Griffith's eighteen thousand actors and three thousand horses.

We didn't even have time to rise, and Rumely smiled on one side of his rumpled face, rumpling it further, saying, "He's a rather brusque fellow, our McClure."

"Yes," I said. "But I do admire his frankness."

"Shall we have the Luchow's fabled sliced pancakes?"

"Certainly."

And we did. While we ate them, my squat companion pointed out a sort of celebrity to me—a stocky, square-jawed man in his sixties, wearing an unprepossessing black suit with string tie and a bowler hat which he left on while he ate at his solitary table.

"That's the captain of the *Lusitania*," Rumely said. "Bowler Bill himself."

"That's this Anderson I'm to check in with?"

"No. Turner's the captain, the top man, but his second in command, Staff Captain Anderson, really runs the ship. Turner's an old salt some say is past his prime . . . bit of a martinet, a taciturn type who dislikes socializing with the passengers."

"But doesn't that come with the job?"

"It does, and you'll see him from time to time—but Anderson will be your contact. The Cunard people themselves recommended we deal with him."

"We have their full cooperation?"

"Oh yes," Rumely said, and there was something sly in that smile into which he was currently shoveling pancakes, and a twinkle in his eyes that wasn't fairy-like. "We have their full cooperation for a fine set of articles— pure puffery about their famous passengers."

I was willing to write such tripe, particularly under a pseudonym. One's pride takes second place to the need for nutrition. In recent months I had, for the first time, lowered myself to the hackwork of popular fiction writing, churning out made-to-order adventure stories for pulp magazines. I had even "novelized" (what an abhorrent word) a putrid play, *The Eternal Magdalene*, into a passably literate work.

After the pancakes came snifters of Courvoisier. The sweetness of the dessert didn't really suit this follow-up, but I could never resist that particular cognac, even when ill-advisedly served.

"Who else besides the estimable Hubbard will feel the feathery brunt of my pen?" I inquired.

"Well, you'll be rubbing shoulders with some interesting passengers, there in Saloon."

"Saloon Class" was the Cunard line's designation for first class . . . ah, first class . . . if one were to be a prostitute, let it be on a soft mattress between sweetly-scented sheets. . . .

"After Hubbard," Rumely said, "your prime candidate will be Alfred Vanderbilt . . . probably the richest man on earth."

"I'll offer to take his suits to the ship's cleaner for him," I said. "Perhaps a million or two will turn up in his pockets."

The owner of the restaurant, August "Augy" Luchow— a robust gentleman whose considerable girth was matched only by his bonhomie and perhaps his handlebar mustache—was making a fuss over Captain Turner.

Rumely said, "This Madame DePage—have you read of her?"

I sipped my snifter, tasted the cognac, let its warmth roll down my gullet. "The Belgium relief fund woman? She's been too conspicuous in the press to miss, even for an apolitical lout like myself. Is she travelling the *Lusitania*?"

"Yes, she and the one hundred fifty thousand dollars in war relief cash that she's raised in recent weeks. Her motives seem sincere—she could rate a good human-interest piece."

"Anyone else?"

"Frohman'll be aboard. He's always good for a story. People love show business, you know."

Charles Frohman was the leading theatrical producer of the day—the man who brought *Peter Pan* to the stage, and Maude Adams to *Peter Pan*.

Rumely handed me a manila envelope. "There are your tickets and other materials—using the pseudonym you requested. Is the 'S.S.' a reference to steamship, or to Mr. S.S. McClure, your benefactor?"

"Both," I said. "As for Van Dine, I believe it suggests in an elegant manner the less than elegant need for nourishment."

The bulldog smiled. "Another Courvoisier?"

"Certainly. And is there anything else we need to discuss, where business is concerned?"

Rumely seemed almost taken aback. "Why, certainly—you don't think I sought you out to merely do the conventional bidding of my editor."

"Well, I—"

The publisher held up a stubby hand. "We'll have another round of cognacs, and then I'll tell you."

"Tell me what?"

He chuckled. "Why, the real reason you're boarding the *Lusitania* tomorrow, of course . . . *Waiter!*"

TWO

The Big Lucy

Before we get on with the tale at hand, in order to illuminate the nature of various deeds (dastardly and daring), some background seems advisable, regarding the Cunard steamship line's unusual partnership with the British government.

By the time the nineteenth century dragged itself reluctantly into the twentieth, German liners had become the standard for speed and luxury, which offended the sensibilities of Great Britain, that self-proclaimed "greatest seafaring nation on earth." Further, collusion between J.P. Morgan (whose White Star Line was Cunard's greatest rival) and various non-British lines (including Holland-Amerika) set the stage for domination of North Atlantic tourist trade by the upstart American line and its foreign business allies.

Lord Inverclyde, chairman of Cunard, invoked patriotic pride to convince the British government to lend the line better than two and a half million pounds for the building of a pair of new ships designed to restore Cunard—in terms of both speed and luxury—to a position of pre-eminence in the North Atlantic. Those ships, the sisters *Mauretania* and *Lusitania*, were in effect co-owned by the British government.

For this reason, the *Lusitania* was designed—its sister, too—for a dual purpose: Decks bore gun emplacements, coal bunkers ran along the sides of the hull to protect boilers from shells and deep storage spaces were fashioned for easy conversion into magazines. In effect, the *Lusitania* was a luxury liner ready to metamorphose into a battleship.*

This blurring, between commerce and combat, must be understood for the *Lusitania*'s tale to make any sense at all . . . if such is possible.

Sailing day for the *Lusitania* was the first of May, 1915, a drab, drizzly Saturday. All sailing days were bustling affairs, what with the processing of hundreds of passengers, and thousands of pieces of luggage to be lugged aboard and stored. But any time the *Lusitania* set sail (if that phrase could be loosely applied to a mighty turbine-powered ship), a throng could be expected dockside, though she had tied up there more than a hundred times, and was a familiar sight at the foot of Eleventh Street. New Yorkers had embraced the Big *Lucy* ever since that day, eight years before, when she had docked here upon completion of her maiden voyage; even the stench of the nearby meatpacking district couldn't keep them away.

And indeed an even larger than usual crowd had braved

---

*Van Dine overstates: A more fair characterization would be that the *Lusitania* was primed to become an armed auxiliary cruiser.

the growling gray sky and the sticky spring drizzle to cluster along cement-fronted Pier 54 with its massive green-painted sheds blotting out the Manhattan skyline. This was in part because an uncommon number of Americans would be boarding the *Lusitania* today, many of them women in second class and steerage—wives on their way to join soldier husbands, and nurses who had volunteered to work with the Red Cross.

But the primary reason for the dockside swarm of what might loosely be termed as humanity related to a warning from the German embassy that had appeared in virtually every New York newspaper either last night or this morning. In some of the papers, this warning had appeared side by side with Cunard's advertisement announcing the sailing of the *Lusitania* today at noon.

This notice had warned travellers "intending to embark on the Atlantic voyage" that "a state of war exists between Germany and Great Britain"; and that the war zone included the waters adjacent to the British Isles. It went on to remind would-be travellers that should they board "vessels flying the flag of Great Britain," they did so at their own risk.

Because of this, a fair share of walleyed rubberneckers had come out for a morbid good time, and a gaggle of hardboiled reporters and photographers, including newsreel cameramen, had converged upon Pier 54. Sidewalk photographers were taking shots of the looming ship with assistants yelling, "Last voyage of the *Lusitania*!" and taking down orders. Like a grotesque parody of a Broadway opening night, wide-eyed faces bobbed in the crowd to the discordant tune of burbling chatter and inappropriate laughter. Added to this were the smells of sea and oil, almost dispelling the meatpacking reek, and the sounds of a colossal ship coming to life.

As I stood dockside with my bulldog of an employer, Rumely, I was struck like a schoolboy by the immensity of the hull and the four funnels that reached higher up than my neck could crane back. And looking from left to right, one's field of vision was consumed by a black field of steel with an army of rivet heads lined up in orderly ranks.* Normally the great ship would have been festooned with flags; but today, under clouds of war, even the brass letters on the bow were painted black, and the formerly scarlet and black funnels were simply black now, to make enemy identification harder.

Impressive as the *Lusitania* was, one could hardly deem her a beautiful ship—one man's tour de force in naval architecture was another's aesthetic monstrosity. From her ventilator-strewn superstructure to those colossal ungainly funnels, the *Lusitania* was at once the largest movable object yet built by Man . . . and one of the most maladroit—a top-heavy study in ponderous bulk lacking the slim grace of the *Olympic* (and her fallen sister, *Titanic*).

"There seems to be a bit of a delay," Rumely said. His broad brow was flecked with sweat; the morning was as warm as it was damp, and his three-piece gray tweed suit was a poor choice for the time of year.

I wore a gray homburg and a crisply new three-piece

---

*The mastheads rose 216 feet; the ship was 785 feet long, extending beyond the wharf into the Hudson River (which had been dredged to accommodate her). The 10-million-dollar liner had 192 furnaces, 6 turbines (68,000 accumulative horsepower), and 2 massive boilers taking up four boiler rooms. In the hull were 26,000 steel plates held by 4,000,000 rivets. The rudder alone weighed 65 tons.

light blue suit, part of the spiffy wardrobe the *News* had sprung for me, to help me fit in with the nobs. I stroked the drizzle off my beard. "Why is that?"

"I understand the *Lucy* is taking on extra passengers from the *Cameronia*."*

"Overflow?"

"No—the British Admiralty has requisitioned her. . . . It'll probably amount to several hours, at least. Do you want to go on aboard?"

I shook my head. "I prefer to maintain my ringside seat, and allow those lines to thin themselves out. That way you can point out my interview subjects, in case the photographs you provided don't do them justice."

"Don't be alarmed by this elaborate boarding procedure," Rumely said, nodding toward the three separate lines leading to three separate gangways (for Saloon Class, Second Cabin and Third Class) where all the passengers and their baggage were being carefully inspected.

"I'm sure the documents you gave me will do quite nicely," I said. "And if they don't, you'll bail me out of the pokey."

Rumely frowned at my levity. "I hope you appreciate the seriousness of your mission."

"I do, I most certainly do." Actually, what I appreciated was the one-thousand-dollar bonus that Rumely had promised me for taking his sub-rosa assignment.

Pinkerton men and U.S. Immigration officials aided Cunard staffers in what was obviously a serious security

---

*Forty-one first- and second-class passengers transferred from the *Cameronia* to the *Lusitania*; three hundred third-class passengers were forced to wait almost a week to board another ship, the *Transylvania*.

effort. Pursers at tables screened each passenger and said passenger's luggage, then marked them (the luggage, not the passengers) with chalk before Cunard deckhands in starched white sport jackets carried the bags aboard.

Still, for all of this—and the carnival-like hawking of "final" photos and little British flags on sticks, and the handing out of leaflets quayside by men warning against travel—the passengers who had run the security gauntlet, and were now sauntering up the gangways, seemed happy and at ease. Why should the war interfere with their travel plans? Wars were, after all, the enterprise of armies— soldiers took the battlefields, while politicians negotiated, and civilians stood on the sidelines.

I was aware, however, that the passengers boarding the Big *Lucy* were at least as naive in the ways of politics as I was—or at least as I had been, prior to signing on as Edward Rumely's journalistic spy.

The evening before, after S.S. McClure had left us alone, Rumely had informed me that I had been chosen for this job because of my pro-German sympathies. I had explained that while I considered Germany a diverse and culturally progressive modern state—and not the British-concocted caricature of the press—I had no interest in politics.

And Rumely had only smiled and said, "Well, I am content that you are, at least, aware of the preponderance of British propaganda, and the need for balance."

I really wasn't interested, but he was picking up the check, so I said, "That's certainly true."

"Are you aware of the recent scandal on the very pier from which you'll be sailing?"

I admitted I was not, and Rumely, in some detail, told of German cargo ships that were trapped in port by British ships lying in waters outside the three-mile zone. In violation of President Wilson's neutrality proclamation, a group had been supplying food and fuel to those British ships.

"I have credible reports," Rumely told me, "that the Cunard line itself is involved in this criminal effort."

"Really," I said, and tried to put some indignation into it.

"Further reports indicate that the Cunard line is using its passenger liners to transport contraband—including ammunition, weapons and perhaps even high explosives."

"Mr. Rumely, that would seem patently ridiculous—the *Lusitania* is a passenger ship, not a freighter . . ."

"Exactly why Cunard hopes she will be given a free pass by German U-boats. And there are other reports that the *Lucy* is heavily armed—three- or possibly even six-inch guns."

"Wouldn't these be apparent?"

"Not if they were effectively disguised in some fashion."

I was beginning to see what Rumely expected of me. "You'd like me to ascertain whether these big guns exist . . . and whether guns and ammunition are secreted away in the cargo hold."

"Exactly . . . and, of course, you must conduct the interviews Mr. McClure has requested."

"And how will Mr. McClure react if I come back with a story of American collusion with the British in smuggling contraband through the war zone?"

Rumely's expansive face expanded further in a wide smile. "For all his pro-British leanings, he will be delighted—he made his reputation on publishing exposés. You, of course, will have stumbled upon these facts innocently, in the course of pursuing your shipboard interviews."

I said nothing; the likelihood of arranging an interview with Alfred Vanderbilt in a cargo hold seemed distant, but the promise of a trip to Europe to fetch my brother—plus a handsome check—made mentioning this seem imprudent.

Now Rumely and I were dockside, well-positioned to watch as reporters buttonholed prominent passengers who waited in the security line, the war threat having temporarily made equals out of all men. One of those queued up was, in fact, Alfred Vanderbilt himself . . . travelling with a valet but without his wife or other family members. Judging by the familiarity of their conversation, Vanderbilt and the slender fellow in line behind him were friends.

In what I would take to be his mid-thirties, Vanderbilt had a handsome oval face characterized by thick dark eyebrows and a dimpled ball of a chin. The slightly built multimillionaire presented a breezy appearance in his charcoal pin-stripe suit, blue polka-dot foulard bow tie and jaunty tweed cap.

The reporters pelted him with questions about the danger of taking this voyage, and he laughingly replied, "Why worry about submarines? We can outdistance any sub afloat."

"Is this trip business or pleasure, sir?" one reporter called.

"I'm attending a meeting of the International Horse Show Association. And that's all I have to say, gents."

While Vanderbilt was known to be happily married (to his second wife), he had long been a popular figure at sporting events; but some said his love for fast horses, and fast cars, was matched by a fondness for fast women.

It was no surprise that these reporters might assume the European trip would include discreet appointments that were not exclusively with horse breeders.

"You'll have your work cut out for you with that one," Rumely said. "Alfred doesn't like to talk to reporters. He's had some unhappy experiences with the press."

Before long the reporters were descending on a squat, even frog-like figure in a black double-breasted suit with a stiff collar and dark felt hat; he leaned on a cane, which made him seem even shorter. Something in the cheerful expression on his moon face appeared forced—was he in pain, I wondered?

"That's Charles Frohman," Rumely said, but I had already guessed as much.

This was the legendary Broadway producer, the so-called "Napoleon of the Drama." I put him at around sixty years.*

"What's wrong with him?" I asked Rumely.

"Articular rheumatism. He had a bad fall, some time ago, and has never been the same since. Yet he makes these pilgrimages to London, twice a year."

A reporter was asking, "Are you afraid of the U-boats, Mr. Frohman?"

The producer grinned, a pleasant smile on an ignoble face. "No—I only fear IOU's."

Another reporter called, "Going to check out the current crop of West End productions, sir?"

"Yes—in particular, *Rosy Rapture* at St. Martin's Lane—we'll see if it's Broadway material."

---

*Frohman was forty-seven.

Another chimed, "Is it true you've secretly married Maude Adams?"

He seemed genuinely embarrassed as he shook his head. "If only I were so lucky—I'm afraid this cane is my only wife."

I said to Rumely, "Seems like a decent sort."

Rumely nodded. "By all accounts, he is. . . . That fellow there, with the black bushy beard, that's Kessler."

In a well-cut brown suit with darker brown bowler, the sturdy-looking, forty-ish Canadian wine merchant—known as the Champagne King—carried a brown valise so tightly his knuckles were white.

The reporters had questions for him, too.

"What sends you to Europe under this threat?"

"Business and pleasure," Kessler said, a smile flashing through the black thatch that obscured much of his face.

"Which do you enjoy more, Mr. Kessler?" another journalist asked, good-naturedly. "Making money, or spending it?"

I knew from materials Rumely had provided me that Kessler loved to throw extravagant dinners and parties, particularly in Europe.

"That's all part of the same process," the bearded wine magnate said, with another grin.

"What's in the bag, George?" a reporter asked, with impertinent familiarity.

The grin disappeared and Kessler said, "My clean underwear," and turned away from the reporters, his good humor turned to irritation.

But the press boys didn't seem to mind; Kessler was a minor celebrity compared to another man who'd just fallen into line.

In a wide-brimmed Stetson, an oversize blue velvet

bow tie and a knee-length, loose-fitting duster-type tan overcoat, Elbert Hubbard (like Kessler) stood clutching a valise—a battered-looking leather one—waiting his turn next to his handsome wife, Alice, modestly attired in a blue linen one-piece travelling suit and straw hat. Hubbard was knocking on sixty's door, and his wife was perhaps ten years younger. They both had brown, graying, shoulder-length hair.

The reporters were thrilled to see the eccentric home-spun philosopher, and Rumely didn't bother identifying the man to me, because Hubbard's picture had been unavoidable in the press over the years, particularly after the success of his article "A Message to Garcia."

"Fra Albertus!" one of the reporter's cried, invoking a painfully precious nickname the so-called author had bestowed upon himself. As far as I was concerned, self-published books and magazines, and homely little stories and supposedly wry aphorisms, didn't an author make.

"Yes, friend?" Hubbard said, smiling beatifically at the reporter, who was one of half a dozen swarming around him like flies near something a horse had dropped. "How may I help you?"

"Aren't you afraid of the U-boat threat, Mr. Hubbard?"

"To be torpedoed," he said, "would be a good advertisement for my pamphlet 'The Man Who Lifted the Lid Off Hell.' "

"You mean the Kaiser, don't you?"

"I do. William Hohenzollern himself. I intend to interview Kaiser Bill, you know."

"You can't interview him," another reporter put in, rather snidely, "if the *Lucy* sinks."

Hubbard lifted his shoulders in a theatrical shrug. "If they sink the ship, I'd drown and succeed in my ambition to get in the Hall of Fame. After all, there are only two respectable ways to die: one is of old age, the other is by accident."

The reporters were writing down each glorious word. How I despised this middle-brow malarkey.

"I believe the drizzle has stopped," Rumely said.

"Perhaps—but not the drivel."

A brass band had begun to play, drowning out both Hubbard and the reporters; and even John Philip Sousa was a relief by way of contrast.

The reporters gathered around one last passenger, though with the band blaring, we couldn't eavesdrop on the questions. I was probably too awestruck to have listened, in any event, because the passenger the reporters were clamoring around was a beautiful dark-haired, dark-eyed woman of perhaps forty, graceful, lithe, dignified, in a black dress with occasional white frills and a black bonnet with white feathers. Accompanying her was another tall, shapely woman, a little younger—in her mid-thirties, possibly—in a shirtwaist costume of tan cotton pongee with white linen collar and cuffs and, startlingly, no hat.

Rumely identified the beauty in black as Madame Marie DePage, the Special Envoy to the United States from Belgium. The wife of Antoine DePage, the Belgian Army's Surgeon General, Madame DePage had spent several months in America raising money for her husband's Red Cross-sponsored field hospital.

"She raised one hundred fifty thousand dollars," Rumely reminded me.

"With that face, even I would have made a donation. . . . Who's her friend?"

"No idea."

Madame DePage's female companion had high cheekbones and dark blonde hair and pale blue eyes—a striking combination of strength and femininity. She was almost as arresting as Madame DePage herself, and I found her even more fascinating—or was that just her anonymity?

All five of my prime subjects for interviews were standing in the distinguished line, the reporters having gone off trolling for other prey, when a Western Union delivery boy seemed to materialize, and move among them. The band covered up his questions, but he was clearly seeking the recipients of the wires.

Then all five—Vanderbilt, Frohman, Kessler, Hubbard and DePage—were curiously opening up the little envelopes, probably expecting a cheery bon voyage from a friend . . . though I could not imagine the mutual friend that might have sent telegrams to these five. Of course, Western Union may have had missives from five separate senders and they were just delivered at the same time. . . .

And yet all of their reactions were the same! Frowns of disgust—even the sweet, positive-minded Sage of East Aurora, Elbert Hubbard himself, scowled. In fact, he wadded his telegram up, and hurled it to the cement.

No—wait . . . I'd been wrong: Six telegrams had been delivered. Vanderbilt's dark-haired slender friend had also received one, and he and Vanderbilt were shaking their heads, discussing what was obviously a mutually shared distaste for what they had just read. Only Hubbard, however, had discarded his telegram, the others folding theirs and sticking them away, into suit or pants pockets.

The line was moving forward now, and I shook hands with Rumely, and gathered my single suitcase, and got into the back of the queue. No one seemed to notice me pick up the wadded telegram Hubbard had discarded.

Nor did anyone seem to notice when I unfolded it like

a crumpled flower to read: FRA HUBBARD—LUSITA-
NIA TO BE TORPEDOED. CANCEL PASSAGE IM-
MEDIATELY IF YOU VALUE YOUR LIFE.

It was signed, rather melodramatically (and redun-
dantly, I thought), MORTE.

THREE

A Self-Confident Fool

Off the coast of Scotland, the day before the *Lusitania* left port, one of the Kaiser's submarines sent a British coal-carrying steamer to the ocean's floor. In the Dardanelles, fierce fighting was afoot; and Britain and her allies were bombing German towns while warships attacked U-boat bases. And yet the passengers aboard the *Lusitania*—my innocent self included—seemed to feel immune from the conflict.

Even with the journalistic espionage I intended to carry out, I found myself lulled into peacetime complacency by the Big *Lucy*'s lavishness. Despite my criticism of its unlovely top-heavy exterior, I could only applaud the elegance of the ship's internal beauty, from public rooms to accommodations; I had travelled numerous times on so-called luxury liners, but truly Cunard had set the standard with the *Lusitania* (and, presumably, with her sister, *Mauretania*).

This was obvious from the moment I boarded through

the first-class entrance on the Main Deck. The entryway area—where a flock of ship's crew (stewards overseen by a purser's clerk) checked names off a list, dispensed room keys and gave directions—had a light, airy feel. The floor was tile, white with black diamond shapes, the furnishings white wicker, the woodwork a blazing white with golden touches, and scarlet brocade-upholstered settees were built into the walls. Potted ferns shared space with floral arrangements; there were so many flowers aboard the ship, the sweetness in the air was almost overpowering, like the visitation area of a funeral home whose current attraction was a popular fellow indeed.

As we all waited our turn with the stewards and purser's clerk, the only annoyance was an overabundance of children, not all of whom were well-behaved, despite the best efforts of nannies; tiny shod feet echoed off the tile floor like gunfire, shrill little voices tearing the air. Oh well—this was to be expected. Cunard's advertising bragged of the safety the Big *Lucy* provided mothers and children.*

"I wouldn't worry, if I were you," a rich alto voice almost whispered in my ear.

I looked to my left, where that tall hatless blonde female in the tan cotton pongee, Madame DePage's friend, stood next to me. At the moment, her strong, handsome face tweaked itself with a smile, and her blue eyes had a twinkle; tendrils of her piled-high hair seemed to have a mocking life of their own. While no physical giant, I am certainly not a small man, and it was startling to look

---

*The passenger list of the *Lusitania* included 129 children, 39 of whom were infants.

directly into the eyes of a woman on my own level.

"Pardon me?" I said.

"The kiddies," she said, a corner of her mouth turned up, in sweet irony. "The ship provides numerous play-rooms and nurseries. . . . In the days to come, you'll be little troubled by having them underfoot."

I could only return the smile. "Am I really that easily read?"

She gave me a tiny shrug. "Most people's features are a map of their inner thoughts."

"And I'm one of those?"

"Perhaps."

I gave her half a bow. "S.S. Van Dine, madam. Who do I have the honor of providing me with this minor humiliation?"

She gave me her hand, and my fingertips touched hers. "Philomina Vance," she said. "May I ask what the 'S.S.' stands for? You don't look terribly like a steamship."

"That at least is a relief. It's, uh, Samuel."

"Is that the first 'S' or the second?"

"Well, uh, it's the, uh, first, of course. The other 'S' is quite unimportant."

Another shrug. "Well, I'm going to call you Van."

"You have my consent. And I will call you Miss Vance."

"Anything but Philomina." She flashed another smile, no irony at all now—but the eyes still twinkled. "You know, Van, I think we're going to be great friends."

"Really? And why is that?"

"Any man with the nerve to wear that Kaiser Bill beard in these times is either extremely foolish or enormously self-confident. And I like self-confidence."

"But what if I prove a fool?"

"Oh, I like a good laugh, too. Either way, I should come out swimmingly."

Then we reached the stewards, and went our separate ways. It took her rather longer to go through the rigmarole than I, because she seemed to be doing it for Madame DePage, as well as herself—though, strangely, the lovely and mysterious Madame DePage was nowhere to be seen.

Wearing their ornate grillwork doors like family crests, a pair of elevators—that is "lifts," this was a British ship, after all—awaited to take Saloon passengers to Decks A and B, and their accommodations.*   Since few people travelled alone on a transatlantic voyage, most of the cabins were designed for two or more occupants; but one of the handful of single cabins had been thoughtfully booked for me by my employer, Mr. Rumely. My cabin was on B Deck, on the portside of the ship, and the lift brought me to the deck's entrance hall, where additional elegance awaited—white woodwork, Corinthian columns, black grillwork, wall-to-wall carpeting, damask sofas, more potted plants, further flowers. Offices opposite the lift curved around a funnel shaft.

Sun was filtering in through windows and down the stairwell, as I took a left off the lift past the wide companionway (as shipboard stairways insisted on being called) and then a right down the portside corridor, which bustled with other guests finding their bearings, often

---

*The *Lusitania* had seven main decks, lettered A through F, highest to lowest, with the Hold Deck at the bottom. A Deck was also known as the Boat Deck; B Deck as the Promenade Deck; C Deck as the Shelter Deck; D Deck as the Upper Deck; E Deck as the Main Deck; and F Deck as the Lower Deck.

aided by bellboys in gold-braided beige uniforms. Moving past doors of various cabins on my right, and two expansive suites of rooms on my left, I found my cabin perhaps halfway down the corridor, at the juncture of a short hallway to my left, a single window at its dead end sending mote-floating sunlight my direction.

The cabin was on the corner of the corridor and the small hallway, and was a palatial cubbyhole without, unfortunately, a view onto the sea. What it did have was rather amazing, considering the limitations of space: a wrought-iron single bed, a washstand with hot and cold running water, off-white woodwork, electric lighting, a wardrobe and a bureau with mirror—better appointed, by far, than my Lexington Street apartment, and heaven compared to that boardinghouse room in the Bronx.

As there was no closet, I transferred the contents of my suitcase into the bureau drawers, and slid the empty bag under my bed. I was sitting on the bed, wondering when we'd be leaving port, when a gong clanged, making me jump—first of the "All Ashore" signals. I checked my pocket watch: half past eleven.

Even a man of sophistication can enjoy the simple pleasures of the spectacle of a great liner shoving off, so I made my way to the portside of the Boat Deck. In the corridor, the aftermath of good-bye parties coming to a close was evidenced by people hugging and kissing, those leaving expressing a wish to be going along, even as the "All Ashore" gongs continued to reverberate. The aroma of food being cooked announced in its unique way that the voyage was about to begin: The first meal was in preparation.

On deck, passengers were lining the rail, and I found a place for myself just beyond the first-class promenade

with its hanging lifeboats, toward the bow of the ship—
the area called the forecastle, from which the bridge could
be made out easily. So could the sight of visitors streaming down the gangways; why did the image of rats abandoning a sinking ship pop into my mind? Far too trite a
thought even to have.

Deckhands who had traded in their crisp white sport
jackets for turtleneck sweaters and heavy, seaworthy
windbreakers, performed a thousand small tasks beyond
the average passenger's comprehension; this whirl of activity, more than anything else, announced that the great
ship was coming to life.

Cargo hatches were battened, and bells rang out as officers rushed up gangways with last-minute paperwork in
hand, bills of lading and cargo consignments and such.
The pilot's H flag was hoisted from the halyard of the
signal bridge, and on the narrow stern of the control
bridge the American flag flapped, while upright streamers
of myriad other flags ran up and down the fore and aft
masts, lending a gay ambience worthy of a cruise ship.
Less festive, even ominous, was the black smoke belching
from the fat exclamation points of the black-painted funnels.

After the floral fragrance of the public areas of the Big
Lucy, the deck presented olfactory reminders that this was,
indeed, a ship. In addition to the coal smoke, engine oil
and grease smells, and the pungent whiff of tarred deck-
ing and the nastily mysterious odors emanating from scup-
pers and bilges, the bouquet of salty sea air provided an
ever-present reminder that this was—despite the Cunard
line's best efforts—a steamer, not a luxury hotel.

On the dockside sightseers and friends seeing off passengers threw confetti, and waved hats, hankies, miniature

American flags and, when all else failed, their hands. I did not wave back: I didn't know any of them, and Rumely had long since disappeared back into the reality of Manhattan.

"You really are a grouch," an already familiar alto voice said, next to me.

I couldn't suppress the smile as I turned to her, those loose tendrils flying like little blonde flags of her own in the breeze.

"Just because I don't behave like a schoolboy," I said, "waving at a bunch of strangers, doesn't make me a grouch."

"No. I am sure there are other factors."

I laughed, once. "Miss Vance, are you following me?"

"Why, do you mind?"

"No," I said forwardly. "The sooner a shipboard romance begins, the better, I always say."

She arched a brow; her eyes were an impossible light blue, eyes you could gaze straight through to the core of her . . . a core consumed, at the moment, with mocking me. "Is that what you think this is? The beginnings of a romance?"

I shrugged. "We only have a week. And, after all, you like my beard."

She raised a finger. "No—I said I liked the self-confidence it indicated—that you're a man who goes his own way. If I could have my way with you, I'd cut that beard off."

"If I could have my way with you, I'd let you."

She did not blush, but she did turn away so I would not see just how broad her smile was. And when she turned back to me, the smile had lessened but was very much still there. "You are a rogue, Mr. Van Dine."

"I thought you were going to call me Van."

"I should call you a horse's S.S."

And I laughed again—more than once. "I like you, Vance."

"No 'Miss'?"

"I don't think so. Whether a shipboard romance develops or not, I believe you were right the first time."

"How's that?"

I half-bowed. "We are going to be great friends."

Below, burly stevedores were hauling the creaking gangplanks onto the pier, really putting their elbow grease into it. Hawsers thick as a stevedore's arm were cast loose from bollards, splashing into the slip's scummy waters before the sailors drew the ropes up onto the decks.

Leaning on the rail, I asked her, "May I inquire what's become of your companion, Madame DePage? I gather you're travelling together."

She nodded past me, looking up, and I followed her eyes to the bridge; on the deck beneath the row of windows, Captain Turner—all arrayed in his gold-braided finery, looking rather more distinguished in his commodore's cap than he had in his bowler at Luchow's—was holding court with five of his most distinguished first-class passengers.

Gathered about him in a semicircle were Miss Vance's companion, Madame DePage, impresario Frohman, the "Champagne King" Kessler, and the richest man on any ship, Vanderbilt, as well as his lanky dark-haired friend, whose name I had not yet ascertained. The group consisted of every illustrious passenger who had received one of those mysterious telegrams—with the exception of the homespun Elbert Hubbard.

Miss Vance gave me a look that I understood at once

to mean we should move closer, which we did, until we were near enough to overhear Turner's remarks to his guests.

But it was Frohman who was speaking at the moment, the half-crippled producer leaning on his cane with seemingly all of his weight. "Tell me, Alfred—is it true you cancelled your passage on the *Titanic* the night before she sailed?"

The frog-like Broadway czar's tone was genial enough, but the question had a certain edge.

Vanderbilt, with the face of a somewhat dissipated boy under that jaunty cap, said, "It's true—I had a feeling about it."

Kessler asked, "Any premonitions this time?"

The multimillionaire shrugged, and the crusty captain put a hand on Vanderbilt's shoulder, and gestured down toward where Miss Vance and I stood . . . but he was really invoking the swarm of passengers clustered along the rail. He said, in a blustering way (which was easier for Miss Vance and me to hear than the previous exchange), "Do you honestly think all these people would have booked passage on the *Lusitania* if they thought they could be caught by a German submarine?* Why, that's the best joke I've heard all year, this talk of torpedoing!"

Captain Turner laughed, and so did Vanderbilt. I ex-

---

*Even with the *Cameronia* passengers, the *Lusitania* was underbooked. While second class was over capacity with 600 passengers, third class had 367 bookings out of a possible 1,186; and first class had 290 where 552 could be accommodated. Still, Turner was in a sense correct, as the 1,257 aboard represented the largest number of passengers on a single crossing since the start of the war.

changed glances with Miss Vance—neither of us was smiling, much less laughing.

The same could be said for Madame DePage, who—in a musical voice touched with that accent shared by France and her native Belgium, so fetching in a woman, so obnoxious in a man—said, "I do not find this war a subject fit for the . . . joking."

The smiles vanished from the faces of Vanderbilt and Captain Turner, both men apologizing.

"I am concerned not for me myself," Madame DePage said, her pretty dimpled chin lifted, "but for the wounded in this tragic atrocity." The latter word, divided by her accent into four lilting syllables, had a poetry at odds with its meaning. "If this ship, she goes down, t'ousands will suffer in hospital."

Madame DePage was referring to the $150,000 she had raised; this implied the cash was on board with her—a dangerous state of affairs even in peacetime.

"I have to say I share madame's concern," Vanderbilt's slender friend said. "These warning telegrams are most alarming."

I had thought that was the reason for this little gathering—for the captain to reassure his guests. But he was a ham-handed old salt, wretchedly awkward with people.

Still, he tried his best: "Mr. Williamson, I'm sure, when we trace them, these messages will be the work of some publicity hound. Please . . . my friends . . . think nothing of these things."

The captain was gesturing with one of the telegrams.

Vanderbilt said, "I'm sure it's just someone's idea of humor. A tasteless joke."

"Germany could concentrate her entire fleet of subs on this ship," Turner blustered (this seemed a strange thing to say, by way of reassurance), "and we would elude them."

"That's quite a statement, Captain," Frohman said.

"I have never heard of the sub that can make twenty-seven knots—and we can."

"Flying that American flag will help," said Vanderbilt's friend, whose name apparently was Williamson.

Since America was not at war with Germany—and with the *Lusitania* repainted as she was—hiding behind the Stars and Stripes seemed a good way to deceive a U-boat commander. But it had been tried before, and the White House had complained to Cunard.

Turner did not respond to Williamson's remark, and merely patted backs and gave out assurances that the warning telegrams were of no import, easing the group off the small raised deck with invitations to join him at his table for meals, if they liked.

"Someone was missing from that little gathering," I said.

"I know," Miss Vance said.

I arched an eyebrow at her. "Really? And who do you assume that person to be?"

Matter-of-factly, she replied, "Elbert Hubbard. He received one of those warning telegrams, as well."

"Is that what they were referring to? Warnings they received?"

Miss Vance informed me coolly that Madame DePage had received a telegram warning her that the ship would be torpedoed—signed "Morte," death.

I shrugged. "Perhaps the Sage of East Aurora didn't receive a warning—perhaps a legitimate telegram came in to him at the same time these warnings arrived for the others."

She shook her head. "I doubt that—not when he reacted to it in such disgust. He crumpled it and tossed it to the ground, you know."

"Is that right? Well, again, perhaps its contents were displeasing to him without it having been one of these warnings. Perhaps someone wired Hubbard to inform him of what a complete nincompoop he is."

She smiled a little. "I think he's a great man."

"You do not."

"Well . . . a good man. A well-intentioned man."

"That's something wholly other than 'great.' "

Now she shrugged. "Well, I suppose we'll never know what was in that telegram Mr. Hubbard received."

"I suppose not."

"Not unless you share it with me, Van." She smiled at me, the eyes atwinkle again. "After all, you did pick it up."

I would not like to know what my expression looked like: Surely my mouth was agape and my eyes were wide and I appeared more the fool than a self-confident man. I realized that my masculine charms had not inspired this fetching wench to seek out my friendship, after all—she had seen me pick up the discarded telegram, open and look at it, and had sought me out, in her wily surreptitious female manner. I was beginning to suspect she was a damn suffragette.

"Could I see it?" she asked sweetly.

"See what?" I asked, but my bantering was limp. I took the telegram from my suitcoat pocket and handed it to her.

"So Hubbard was warned, too," she said, studying the crumpled paper.

"Why, are you a detective?"

THE LUSITANIA MURDERS 41

Both eyebrows climbed her fine forehead and she asked innocently, "Do I look like a detective?"

"No . . . but then, I don't believe I look like a fool, yet apparently I am one. And here I thought you wanted to be my great good friend."

"I do," she said nicely, apparently genuine, as she handed back the telegram. "Van, I'm just a good friend of Madame DePage, accompanying her, looking out after her interests."

A low hum began to emanate from deep within the ship, growing into a muffled roar; the ship's four steam turbines began their rotation, and giant propeller blades made a muddy froth of the Hudson River.

I glanced at my pocket watch: twelve-thirty. All delays, all doubts, all fears be damned—we were finally pulling away, as the Big *Lucy* gave off three throaty blasts from her mighty bass horn.

"Shall we have lunch," I asked, putting away my watch, "and discuss this further?"

But she was gone—Philomina Vance had disappeared into the crowd on deck.

And I stood there alone, strangely sad as the big ship—like a massive building pulling away from its foundations—groaned away from the dock. A brass band on deck was playing one song ("It's a Long Way to Tipperary"), the band on the pier another ("God Be With You Till We Meet Again"), and somewhere a chorus was singing "The Star-Spangled Banner." Shouts of farewell tried to climb over that cacophony only to be drowned out by the bellow of steam whistles.

Soon a trio of tugboats puffed up to the much larger vessel to nudge and cajole her bow, easing her around till she was pointing downstream. It didn't take long for the faces on the dock to turn indistinguishable, and finally even the skyline of Manhattan was just a blur of brick.

"Would you like to have lunch with me?" that delightful alto intoned.

I turned toward the sound, hopefully, but tried not to show eagerness; she was again at my side, not a hint of guile in those clear blue eyes.

I said, "If you're not a detective, you must be a magician."

She smiled gloriously. "And why is that, Mr. Van Dine?"

"Because of these vanishing acts you pull off."

She shrugged and offered me her arm. "You'll just have to hold on to me, then."

That sounded wonderful.

And I took her arm, like the fool I am, and went off for lunch with her, convinced no more ulterior motives lurked within that pretty blonde hatless head.

If I were a lesser writer, I would at this point say: *little did I know . . .*

But of course, we all know I'm above such things.

FOUR

Warm Welcome

We took luncheon in the Verandah Cafe. Most passengers were availing themselves of the opportunity to get their first look at the ship's fabled domed dining room; but Miss Vance said she preferred to save that treat for this evening. Though the day remained overcast, this shipboard outdoor cafe held a certain airy appeal for both of us, and the relative privacy was attractive, as well.

The cafe was on the Boat Deck, past a lounge area rife with rose-upholstered wall seats and chairs, and even a marble fireplace; the tones of white and gold continued to prevail. The cafe was at the after-end of the deck, a twenty-by-forty* area with a white ceiling and dark-wood pillars open to the first-class promenade. The floor was parquet, the furnishings a mix of wood and wicker, with little potted trees whose stick-thin trunks rose to bushy explosions of green.

---

*Twenty-four-by-fifty.

We sat at a small round table whose white linen table-cloth was at odds with the casualness of the clientele, mostly men in caps with legs crossed, smoking cigarettes, reading newspapers. Miss Vance and I were the only mixed couple—and among the few patrons having lunch-eon.

I had a plate of dainty deviled-ham sandwiches with their crusts trimmed off—apparently here in first class, the upper crust preferred no competition; and Miss Vance partook of a cup of beef broth. We both had tea, although my lovely companion took hers iced.

"How is it that you became acquainted with Madame DePage," I asked, with an offhandedness that I hope disguised my rapt interest. "If I may be so bold."

"You may." The breeze was doing wonderful things with those blonde tendrils. "The madame and I are not friends, although we are friendly. I'm a paid companion."

"Ah. A secretary?"

She offered me half a smile, half a shrug. "Something along those lines."

"Madame DePage must be a generous mistress."

An eyebrow arched. "Why is that?"

I offered her a complete shrug, invoking both shoul-ders. "To book you Saloon passage."

It was common practice for servants and others attend-ing first-class passengers to have rooms in second class (though rarely in third).

"Actually," she said, between sips of iced tea, "I'm sharing quarters with Madame DePage."

"Is that right?"

"Yes it is. She has one of the Regal Suites.* The other, I understand, is Mr. Vanderbilt's."

I nibbled a corner off a sandwich. "My little cabin is just down the hall from one of the Regal Suites—is yours portside or starboard? On the left or right, that is."

She smiled a little. "I know my portside from my starboard, sir—our suite is on your side of the ship."

Perhaps that would prove convenient, I thought. But I was also struck by the way she had referred to the suite so possessively—"our suite"—which was somewhat less than a subservient attitude . . . not that there seemed to be much in the way of subservience about Miss Vance.

"And how long have you been a writer, Van?" she asked casually.

I froze between bites and put down my sandwich. "I don't recall mentioning that I was."

"Aren't you?"

"Truthfully . . . yes." I looked unhesitatingly into those remarkable eggshell-blue eyes. "I'm aboard on a journalistic assignment. In fact, you might be in a position to help me out."

She cocked her head. "Really? How so?"

"I'm hoping to interview the travelling celebrities . . . and your mistress, Madame DePage, certainly qualifies."

With a tiny wave of a gesture, she said, "That shouldn't prove difficult. The madame is friendly to the press—she has a point of view she's most anxious to communicate. I would be happy to pave the way for an audience."

I grinned at her—toasted her with my teacup. "Most generous of you, Vance."

---

*The pair of Regal Suites, on either side of the Promendade Deck, catered to the crème de la crème of transatlantic travellers; each suite offered a dining room, two bedrooms, a bath and toilet, and sitting rooms for maids and valets.

"My pleasure . . . but I must say I'm a bit surprised you're a reporter. I would have taken you for an author of fiction, or perhaps literary criticism."

"Why not a poet?"

She was studying me the way a scientist looks at something smeared on a slide. "I don't sense the romantic in you . . . at least not in the conventional sense. You have an acid eye, of a sort that would seek expression more directly than in that elliptical way a poet might employ. . . . Besides, I don't believe poetry would strike you as a manly pursuit."

Miss Vance was remarkably insightful—although I had written some small amount of poetry, in my time—but I was wondering how she had gathered so much about me in so short a span.

"Vance," I said, frankly exasperated and not a little impressed, "how did you arrive at the conclusion that I was *any* kind of writer?"

Her lips twitched with amusement. "Well, Van, you're a very well-groomed gentleman—your beard is immaculately trimmed . . ."

"Thank you."

"But on your right hand, you have ink under your nails . . . either from a pen and/or the messy ribbon of one of those beastly typewriting machines."

Reflexively, I looked at the nails of my right hand and, to my dismay, she was quite right.

"In addition," she said, "at the dock you were observing passengers in a manner that indicated you were either, one, an agent or police official, private or government; or, two, a writer intent on observing human behavior. In retrospect, I should have noticed that you were keen on only the celebrities standing in line, which would have sent me in the direction of journalism."

This seemed quite a remarkable observation to me, and I said as much.

"Further," she said, keeping right on with it, "your attire reflected money and a sense of style, and yet was brand-new—"

Now I had to interrupt. "Certainly it's not unusual for a passenger about to board an ocean liner to dress in recently purchased apparel. What woman doesn't buy a new 'outfit' for a trip?"

"Well, Van, you're not a woman—"

"Thank you for noticing."

"But your freshly purchased apparel, added to the other facts, spelled *writer*."

"Why?"

"Writers, even the most successful of them, lead a relatively solitary existence, and most often work at home. It's characteristic of the professional writer to be rather . . . indifferent where fashion is concerned."

Understanding, I said, "But a writer who's attending a special event . . . a play, an opera, a wedding . . . will certainly go out and buy new apparel."

Her smile indicated she liked that I was following her line of logic. "Yes. But this, added to these other seemingly insignificant details—topped off by your extraordinary gift with language—led me to risk sharing with you my assumption that you are, indeed, a writer."

Maybe she was a detective, after all.

"Well, I am a writer," I said, "and a damned good one, if you'll forgive my frankness."

"I like your frankness, Van. By the way, what's your real name?"

Again, she had startled me.

"How . . . why . . . ?"

She smiled and made a breezy gesture with her left hand. "The initials 'S.S.' for a man on a steamship voyage—could anything be more absurd? And when I asked you what the initials stood for, you had to think about it! You don't strike me as a man whose limited mentality does not include a ready retention of his own name."

I could only laugh; she had me!

But I told her, for reasons of my own, I needed to keep my real name to myself; she would have to be content with my pseudonym.

"I guess I don't mind, terribly," she said. "But perhaps I was wrong—perhaps you aren't a writer."

"Oh?"

"Yes . . . mayhap you're a German spy."

I almost choked on my tea. "Please . . . in time of war, that's not amusing."

Still, her expression was one of amusement. "Ah, but America is not at war."

"Ah, but . . . we're not in America any longer. In fact, on this ship, we're in Great Britain."

She nodded. "An astute observation."

A burly officer—in the typical white cap and navy gold-braided blazer—was swaggering down the promenade; he had broad shoulders, a shovel jaw and an amiable manner. I had never seen the fellow before, but he smiled and nodded at me, as if we were old friends. On the other hand, the officer was nodding and speaking to other passengers, who lined the rail, so maybe I was imagining things. . . .

"Do you know that gentleman?" Miss Vance whispered.

"No."

"He seems to know you."

And indeed the officer was striding over to us. I touched my napkin to my lips and stood.

"Mr. Van Dine?" the officer said, his voice a tenor, somewhat surprising coming out of such a formidable figure. He had dark bright blue eyes and rather bushy eyebrows, and was extending a sturdy hand.

Shaking it, I said, "I'm afraid you have me at a disadvantage, sir."

He had a firm grip, but had stopped short of showing off about it.

"I'm sorry—you were pointed out to me, on deck," he said. That struck me as odd: No one knew me to do that!

He was introducing himself: Staff Captain John Anderson.

And now I understood—this was the contact aboard ship Rumely had told me about, the Cunard employee aware of my real name, and that I was a journalist aboard to write flattering articles about the ship and its passengers.

I introduced Miss Vance.

"We're honored to have Madame DePage with us," Anderson said to her. He had the faintest cockney around the edges of an accent he'd obviously worked at to make acceptable to the upper-class passengers. "She's a great lady, with a fine cause."

"I'm so glad you feel that way," Miss Vance said, not sounding terribly sincere.

"Would you sit down with us?" I asked him, politely.

Anderson seemed almost embarrassed, as he said, "I didn't mean to interrupt, Mr. Van Dine. I'd hoped to catch you after lunch, so I might show you around a little."

Miss Vance said, "We're quite finished with lunch, Captain Anderson."

"Well, I'm certainly free," I said, "if you'd care to take time away from your duties to bother with me."

"Not at all. I'm anxious to. . . . Miss Vance, would you care to accompany us?"

"You're very kind," she said, rising, "but I need to join Madame DePage. She likes to write her correspondence after lunch."

"Can I escort you to her?" I asked.

"No . . . I'm a big girl, gentlemen. I'll find my way."

And the individualistic Miss Vance nodded to us, and moved off down the promenade, or actually up—she was heading toward the entryway where an elevator or stairs could convey her to her employer.

"Interesting woman," Anderson said.

"Fascinating."

"Probably a suffragette," he sighed.

"Probably," I said. "But then, no one's perfect."

Anderson suggested we sit for a moment, and we did. He told me he hoped to help me arrange interviews, and offered to do whatever he could to make my access to the ship and its passengers as complete as possible, and my voyage a pleasurable one.

"We're grateful to the *News* for this opportunity," Anderson said, "to show potential passengers that this war scare is no reason to avoid travel."

"Well, that's a wonderful attitude, and quite the opportunity for a journalist. . . . And I'm happy that you seem willing to give me a sort of Cook's tour, as I do want to write about the ship itself, and not limit my work to these celebrity interviews."

Anderson's smile was wide and infectious. "That's good news, Mr. Van Dine. Shall we start?"

Of course, Anderson wouldn't have been as cooperative if he knew I was here to search out contraband; so I worked hard to make a friend of him. It's not a pretty thing, but money was involved—and, anyway, if the Cunard line was using passenger ships to transport war materials, the practice should be exposed. Passengers—like myself, about whom I cared greatly, after all—would be at risk, if this indeed were happening.

The tour I received was certainly complete, and the company entirely amiable—though I did not press Anderson with overtly prying questions, and neither did the good staff captain duck any of my queries . . . even those of a more sensitive nature.

"What about these rumored guns supposedly hidden on deck somewhere?" I asked him, about midway in our tour.

"Like most rumors," Anderson said, half a smile digging a hole in one cheek, "there's a certain basis in fact . . ."

I tried not to reveal the inner excitement I felt at this revelation.

". . . but the reality is rather less sinister, as I will demonstrate."

At the appropriate moments during my tour, the staff captain pointed out to me four deck platforms—two forward, two aft—with mountings awaiting three- or six-inch guns. Either caliber would require dockside cranes, Anderson assured me, and such weapons could hardly be camouflaged, "much less hidden."

This disappointed me, but I instinctively believed Anderson—his frankness seemed obvious, and his character appeared lacking in guile. (Nonetheless, in my spare time,

I prowled every foot of deck space above the waterline; peering beneath any recess or overhang, checking under every winch, I saw no guns mounted or unmounted.)

Though Anderson's affable candor impressed me, I did not yet feel comfortable enough with him to broach the subject of contraband—that, I felt, might come later. I would make it a priority to establish a friendship with the man, in hopes of learning more.

Anderson definitely was the man to whom I needed to get close: He admitted that "the internal distribution of the cargo" was very much his responsibility.

"And I do not take that responsibility lightly," he assured me. "Faulty cargo planning can materially affect the trim of the ship, you know."

"Indeed," I commented, though truthfully I had not a clue.

Surely I could have asked for no more friendly nor knowledgeable tour guide. Anderson, anxious to impress the press with the Cunard line's superiority, began with the fabulously luxurious public rooms of Saloon class, which might have been lifted bodily and set down on the ship out of some splendid hotel or exclusive London club. In addition to the description-defying dining room (about which more later), these included a reception room and various lounges, as well as music, reading-and-writing and smoking rooms. In addition, the ship offered a barbershop, a lending library, a photographer's dark room, a clothes pressing service, a separate dining saloon for valets and maids, and even a switchboard for its innovative room-to-room telephone system.

I don't consider myself easily impressed, but I felt as wide-eyed as a schoolgirl, strolling acres of deep carpet through first-class lounges extravagantly appointed with plush armchairs, marble fireplaces, grand pianos, rich drapes and expensive (if dull) oil paintings. A man of impeccable taste such as myself, marooned for months in cheap flats and ghastly garrets, could only wonder at this oasis of late-Georgian elegance, this world of silk waistcoats, gold watch chains, double-staffed settees, mahogany paneling, carved maple-topped tables and wrought-iron skylights.

Since I was travelling first class, Anderson did not bother showing me a sample of the sumptuous cabins. But I quickly became as impressed with the size of the ship as I had been with the luxury of Saloon class—the damned thing seemed to go on forever, interminable corridors with their polished linoleum floors and a dizzying profusion of white, red and blue lights marking exits, fire extinguishers, washrooms, pantries and other shipboard appurtenances, all within a maze of decks and companionways, towering masts and funnels and, of course, self-important people, some of them passengers, others stewards or crew members, the officers with their gold braids and medal ribbons seeming to wear perpetual expressions of faint disapproval.

Anderson was a pleasant exception to the latter, and I felt his genial nature was not due merely to my status as a member of the press. We passed between first, second and third class with no change in his attitude of friendliness toward passengers—a young man in ill-fitting clothing in steerage, seeking a new life in America, got the same nod and hello from Anderson as a Vanderbilt or Kessler.

Now and then, however, the staff captain would show

a sterner side, if he encountered a crewman whose dress or bearing was not up to snuff. We paused for three or four of these dressing-downs.

Moving along from one of them, Anderson sighed and said, "It's a problem, it is."

"What's that?"

He arched an eyebrow. "Off the record, sir?"

"Certainly. My goal here is to build up, not to tear down."

"We are rather desperately understaffed,"* he admitted. "And some of the staff we have is, frankly, not up to snuff."

"That doesn't sound like Cunard's style."

"It isn't. But the Royal Navy has scooped up many of our best crew, for the war effort. Finding able-bodied seamen for this trip was a chore, I must admit."

"You don't seem entirely satisfied with the result."

"I'm not. There are crew members aboard who've never sailed other than as a passenger."

This was the staff captain's only negative remark of the tour, and I must say the meticulous craftsmanship of the ship's construction carried over into the second and third classes. The public rooms of second class—from dining saloon to smoking room—could have been taken for those of the first class of almost any other ship sailing the North Atlantic. Plainer in style (white remained, gold did not), the public rooms were large and well-appointed; the example of a stateroom—a four-berth—that Anderson saw fit to show me was only a small step down from my own.

---

*Of the seventy-seven positions he had attempted to fill, Staff Captain J.C. Anderson managed only forty-one.

If the Second Cabin staircase may not have been as grand as the one in Saloon, the structure could only be deemed impressively handsome, on its own terms.

Third Class was no dark, cramped hold stuffed with human bilge, rather a functional if austere succession of bare-bones public rooms—the dining room was like a gymnasium with tables—that made no attempt to fool passengers into thinking they were in a fine hotel or country home. Massive painted expanses of steel bared the ship's every rivet, every bolt; but the spartan cabins were both spotless and spacious, and on the bunks were bedspreads bearing the distinctive Cunard crest—a lion rampant with a globe.

"That's a handsome touch," I said.

Anderson grinned and shook his head. "I'm afraid that's not intended to dress up the cabin, Mr. Van Dine. . . . We mean to discourage passengers from helping themselves to the bedding, when they head to shore."

The passengers I saw in Third Class, however, were not of the stereotypical sort one might expect in steerage—no tired, poor, huddling masses. No, these travellers seemed to be an Anglo-Saxon lot, Britons mostly, but a good share of Germans, too, skilled or semiskilled workmen. These were practical men, with limited funds, interested not in Grand Staircases and electric elevators and smoking rooms, but clean quarters and edible food and cheap passage.

The degree to which all of this had been thought through by the ship's designers could be seen in the very columns throughout the ship—in Saloon, they were (as has been noted) Corinthian; in Second Cabin, an elegant Doric; and in Third Class, the cleanly simple Ionian.

Though I could hardly be shown every nook and cranny, Anderson's tour of the Big *Lucy* was surprisingly complete.* On the lowest deck, from the periphery, I witnessed the care and feeding of the liner's huge furnaces, courtesy of men in dungarees and boots and blackened faces, using rags knotted round their necks to occasionally wipe their faces, somehow thriving in a cavern of blistering heat and blinding coal dust.

Anderson pointed out the engineers and firemen and stokers and trimmers—the "dirty gang," he dubbed them— and over the satanic roar he explained the jobs of each; but I couldn't make sense of it, just as I couldn't understand how any man could consign himself to such a hell, in trade for mere existence. It took only moments for the scorching heat and the sticky coal dust to compel me to request that we end this portion of the tour.

Part of me knew I should have pressed for a view of the cargo holds down here—this was where, my employer Rumely had speculated, any contraband would be kept— but I preferred to allow Anderson to escort me out of this hades, with the goal of eventually returning to the heaven that was Saloon Class.

Before completing our tour, Staff Captain Anderson— having shown me around the various classes of the ship—

---

*As he reports it, Van Dine has organized the tour in a fashion that suits his literary intentions; but he perhaps gives a false impression of the geography of the ship. The upper decks, A and B, were shared by the first and second classes, and Decks C and D were shared by the first, second and third classes. Only Deck E was exclusively third class (cabins only). Segregation of classes was accomplished in various ways; the Saloon dining room on D Deck, for example, was separated from the Second Cabin dining room by a network of galleys and pantries.

suggested we conclude on Deck C, the Shelter Deck, where many of the services and facilities of the ship were located.

"A liner is like a city," Anderson said, "and we have the same sort of needs as any modern metropolis."

I was rather tired of this process by now, but not wanting to be rude—and cognizant of the need to stay in the captain's good graces—I put up with a mundane survey of various offices, the seldom-used brig, the hospitals (male and female) and of course the dreaded nursery.

The latter included a children's dining saloon, and we had moved thankfully through that madness of magpies and were heading down a short corridor that opened onto the Grand Entrance and the elevators, when voices behind a door marked STEWARD'S PANTRY caught my attention.

The voices were speaking in German (one of my several languages), and—though the closed door muffled it, somewhat—I distinctly heard: "We should hide the camera."

As I paused, touching his sleeve, Anderson turned to me quizzically, and I whispered, "Do you employ Germans on your staff?"

Several voices behind that door were audible now, speaking in German, but too soft to make out the words.

Anderson gave me a sharp look, and motioned for me to stand to one side, which I did.

Then the staff captain opened the door on three men in stewards' whites, huddled within the small pantry, surrounded by shelved canned goods and other foodstuffs. They were young men—a skinny tallish brown-haired one, a shorter broad-shouldered very blonde fellow and a rather average one, whose hair shade was somewhere between that of his companions—and two of them froze, chatter ceasing. The shorter one had his back to Anderson, and as he turned, he began, in German, "About time—"

But Anderson was clearly not who these fellows were expecting.

And the wide-eyed fellow who had just swivelled indeed held in his hands a camera.

Before Anderson could pose a question, the man with the camera barrelled at him, thrusting him out of the doorway and against the corridor wall, staggering the staff captain with both surprise and power.

The brawny blonde fellow, clutching his camera, moved right past me—or tried to: I stuck my foot out, and he tripped, diving gracelessly into the linoleum, his precious cargo flying. I fell upon him, inserting a knee in his back and looping an arm around his neck, incapacitating him.

From the corner of my eye I witnessed Anderson deliver a fist to the chin of the skinny one, who'd come scrambling out after his compatriot's break for it, knocking him back into the pantry, presumably into the other fellow (this I adjudged from sounds, as I could not see that action from my vantage point).

Reinforcements seemed to appear immediately, including the master-at-arms, whose name was Williams, and a steward named Leach—the pantry was his province, and the young man was shocked to find it crawling with German stowaways.

For that, apparently, was what the trio was—and spies to boot, if the camera meant what it seemed to.

The master-at-arms took my prisoner off my hands, and hauled him back to the pantry, where soon all three were locked inside, awaiting further decisions.

The first one came from Anderson, who said to Williams, "Fetch the ship's detective."

Breathing hard, I said, "I wasn't aware the ship had a detective."

Anderson explained that no detective was on staff; Cunard hired Pinkertons and sometimes made arrangements with travelling Scotland Yard or New York Police Department men. On this trip, however, it was a Pink.

"You've already met her," Anderson said, eyes atwinkle.

And I didn't need the deductive powers of Philomina Vance to figure out whom he meant.

FIVE

Tourist Trade

Within five minutes, Miss Vance had arrived, still fetchingly hatless and attired in tan cotton pongee. Her first request was to gain access to the pantry, behind the closed door of which the three stowaways were at the moment stowed.

"Did you search the pantry," she asked Anderson rather sternly, "before confining them?"

"No," he said, taken aback by the query. "Should I have?"

"There is no telling," she said, her manner as coolly professional as a doctor examining a patient whose symptoms were troubling, "how long this trio had been left to their own devices in there."

She meant the pantry.

"That's true," Anderson admitted.

"They had plenty of time to secrete a weapon or even an explosive device. You may have just thrown Brer Rabbit into the briar patch, Captain."

I have to give Anderson credit: Some men wouldn't have taken such criticism, coming from a woman; but the staff captain was a bigger man than that.

"You're correct," he said, shaking his head. "I was a fool. . . . Williams!"

The master-at-arms, short but sturdy with dark eyes and dark thick eyebrows, snapped to; he had the confiscated camera in hand. "Yes, sir."

"Get your revolver."

The dark eyes flared, but the man said, "Yes, sir."

"Handcuffs, too."

"Yes, sir."

Miss Vance was nodding approvingly.

We were clustered in the compact hallway, a group of men providing a court for this commanding woman. In addition to myself and the staff captain (and the now absent Williams), steward Neil Leach—a brown-haired, blue-eyed, pasty-white fellow in his middle twenties with crooked front teeth and an eager manner—stood on the periphery.

"Who is allocated to this pantry?" Miss Vance asked.

Leach spoke up. "I am, ma'am. . . . Actually, I'm in charge of the children's dining saloon—this is their pantry."

She nodded. "And do you keep a supply of stewards' uniforms in there, along with foodstuffs?"

The hint of sarcasm-laced accusation in her tone was not lost on Leach, who blushed and began to fluster. "Why, no, ma'am, of course not . . ."

Anderson stood up for the lad. "A supply closet is a few steps from here, Miss Vance. And various stewards' offices are all in this area of the ship."

"That's right, ma'am," Leach said, still flushed. "And

our sleeping quarters, all of us stewards, are only one floor down . . . just forward of where we stand."

"Mr. Leach," Anderson said to the shaken steward, "perhaps you should get back to your duties."

"Yes, sir."

The sound of children making their usual squall indicated Anderson's decision was a wise one.

When Leach had gone, Anderson said to Miss Vance, "I can vouch for Mr. Leach. His uncle is a good friend of mine."

Miss Vance seemed unimpressed.

Anderson went on: "The boy's a law student—he got stranded on vacation in New York, and I'm helping his uncle, or rather young Neil, to get to England to take his final examinations."

"That's all well and good," she said. "But these stowaways were waiting in your trusted steward's pantry, wearing stewards' uniforms themselves."

"For pity's sake, Miss Vance," Anderson said, clearly exasperated. "His father's an English judge."

Anderson could not understand that Americans like Miss Vance (and myself) were not as impressed with pedigrees as the English.

"Is Mr. Leach an experienced hand?" she asked.

"No—this is his first voyage." Anderson explained to her what he had to me: that he was short-staffed, that many able-bodied seamen had been shanghaied, in effect, by the Royal Navy.

"Then we'll keep an eye on young Leach," she said. "After all, these three got aboard somehow. . . . Where's your brig?"

"On this deck, aft," Anderson said. "Down near the hospital rooms."

"How many cells?"

"One large cell, four bunks."

She nodded her approval.

"What did you mean," I asked, coming in off the side-lines, "they may have explosives?"

"It's entirely possible," she said, "that spies such as these, in addition to using their camera to take pictures, say, of the rumored guns aboard—"

"There are none," Anderson interrupted, obviously peeved.

"They wouldn't know that, Captain," she said. "In any case, spies who had taken their incriminating pictures, with the aid of greedy crew members, might well plant a bomb aboard a ship like this one, and then—stowaways and crew conspirators, alike—jump ship."

"What, in the middle of the Atlantic?" Anderson asked, as if all of this seemed patently preposterous.

"No," she said calmly. "Just off the shore of Ireland . . . close enough to be picked up by rowboat, or even to swim for it."

Anderson had nothing to say to this all too plausible theory.

"They could have already placed their explosive," I pointed out.

She brushed a blonde tendril from her face, as if she were impatient with it—or was that with me? "Yes—but I doubt they've engaged any timing device, as yet. Too many uncertainties about exactly when we might arrive."

It was obvious Anderson was taking all of this seriously now. He said, "You omit one rather dire possibility, Miss Vance."

"And what would that be?"

"Perhaps they aren't planning to wait until they near

shore. Perhaps they have already planted their device, and set their timer . . . because they intend to go over the side in a lifeboat, and be plucked from the seas by a U-boat."

I frowned. "That's a bit romantic, isn't it?"

But both Anderson and Miss Vance gave me sharply sober looks that said otherwise.

"With all due respect," I said, "surely you're leaping to unfounded conclusions."

"These are not conclusions, Mr. Van Dine," the female private detective said. "They are possibilities . . . all too credible, I'm afraid."

"But this is a passenger ship," I insisted. "I've seen for myself that there are no guns aboard." I looked imploringly at Anderson. "Please tell me the *Lusitania* is not transporting munitions!"

"We are not," he said. But then he added, "We do have limited materials that might be considered contraband, by some . . ."

That was a fascinating admission; under other circumstances, I would have been grateful for it.

" . . . but the point is, the Germans are desperate to halt the export of munitions and other war supplies to Britain and her allies. Just because this ship is not at this moment doing so, that doesn't remove the threat of such in the future . . . or of the *Lusitania*'s ability to be easily converted into a battle cruiser."

"Disabling a British steamer of this size," Miss Vance said, shaking her head somberly, "would be most desirable for the Germans . . . making this ship an obvious target for saboteurs."

I was pondering that disturbing fact—and it seemed a fact to me now, not just an opinion—when Master-at-

Arms Williams returned with his revolver. He seemed nervous, his forehead beaded with sweat.

Miss Vance held out her hand, and smiled sweetly at him, as if accepting a dance at a ball. "May I?"

Williams looked curiously at the staff captain, who said, "Go ahead—she's the ship's official detective, after all."

She took the revolver into her graceful, ungloved hand, and the bulky weapon seemed shockingly at home there. She even smiled down at it, as if welcoming an old friend.

"When I have the drop on them," she said to Anderson softly, almost a whisper, "I'll stay in the doorway. You and Mr. Williams and Mr. Van Dine rush in and quickly search the men, head to foot—pat them down for weapons."

Startled by my inclusion in this raiding party, I asked, "And if I should find any?"

She beamed at me and the blue eyes sparkled. "Why, remove them."

I nodded dutifully.

"Unlock the pantry, Captain," she said, so lightly it didn't seem the command it was. "Stand aside, everyone. . . ."

Anderson positioned himself nearest the door, Williams fell in after him along the corridor wall and—at Miss Vance's gestured command—I tucked myself next to the door along the wall on the opposite side. The staff captain used his key in the lock, then pulled down the handle and shoved the door open.

Miss Vance was smiling—something delightfully demented in that smile, I might add—as she stood at the open doorway, aiming the gun in at them, like a stickup artist robbing a stagecoach, an image that suited what she said: "Put 'em up, boys!"

Then she took a step back and, almost imperceptibly, nodded in a manner that sent Anderson and then Williams and, yes, me scrambling into that cramped pantry.

The three stowaways stood crowded together, but with their hands high and their eyes on the fierce, pretty (and pretty fierce) woman in the doorway. I took the one nearest me, the dark-blonde average fellow, and "patted him down" (as Miss Vance had put it), finding no weapon. Anderson did the same with the brawny blonde one, whom I'd earlier tripped up; and Williams was checking the skinny tall dark-haired stowaway, who seemed the youngest of the trio, and the most anxious.

No guns or knives or anything resembling a weapon was found.

Nor was any identification or even personal items, for that matter.

Williams handcuffed the stowaways—hands behind their backs, Miss Vance suggested, to prevent any "Houdini nonsense"—and Williams (to whom the distaff detective had returned the revolver) and Anderson led them off, the captain saying he would return, shortly.

That left Miss Vance and myself alone in the corridor, just outside the now-vacated pantry.

"And here I was, so terribly impressed with your deductive powers," I said.

She arched an eyebrow, smiled half a smile. "Aren't you, anymore?"

"No. You didn't deduce I was a writer—you've known my identity all along! You've been working with Anderson from the start."

"I have been working with the staff captain," she admitted, "but he hadn't told me about you. I didn't learn your identity until I went to ask him about you ... when we were on deck together, remember, eavesdropping on that conversation regarding the threatening telegrams?"

"I see ... but that took place *before* you dazzled me with your deductions. And you told Anderson where he could find me—that's how he knew I'd be in the Verandah Cafe, because that's where you led me, by the ring in my nose."

She wasn't at all chagrined; her laughter was gay—the woman was really enjoying herself!

"You're not a bad detective yourself, Van," she said. "I think we'll make a good team."

"Really? And what if I have no desire to play Watson to some liberated female's Holmes?"

Her smile softened. "I don't need a Watson, Van—but I could use a partner."

I was still slightly miffed. "Is that so?"

"Yes—you have Anderson's ear, and his trust. I'm a woman ..."

"I noticed."

"... and that limits my sphere of influence, no matter what my expertise. He did well at first, but ultimately he became defensive ... you agree?"

I nodded. "He doesn't like to have the reliability of his crew challenged."

"Yes, because it calls his judgment into question."

Again I nodded. "His ego, his vanity ... you might say his *male* ego and vanity. It's not a rational response, because the good staff captain as much as admitted to me he's had to scrape the bottom of the barrel, putting this particular crew together."

"Right. So I would ask you to cultivate your friendship

with the captain. And in the meantime, I will cable back to New York for my home office to check up on some of these crew members."

"The Leach boy, you mean."

Her eyes tightened, but her brow remained satin smooth. "Yes—and Williams, too. Both arrived at the scene almost instantaneously, I gather."

"That's true. And the apparent ringleader, that blonde with the camera, said 'About time,' when Anderson barged in on them."

She thought about that. "As if," she said, "they were expecting someone . . ."

"A crew member?"

"That would seem a strong possibility. They spoke in German, Van?"

"Yes."

"And you speak the language?"

"I do."

"What else did you hear?"

" 'We should hide the camera.' The same speaker, I should say."

She nodded, then glanced at the pantry. "I'll need to search this cubbyhole of theirs." She turned to me. "You're a journalist, and you speak German. I would like you to conduct the interrogation of the prisoners."

"Isn't that Anderson's call?"

"Yes—but, with your permission, I'll request that of him, and I'm sure he'll comply."

I shrugged. "Certainly. I'm all too glad to be of service—particularly if will help keep me from being blown to particles."

She offered up a tiny, dimple-inducing half-smile. "That does seem a worthwhile incentive."

"May I ask you a question, Miss Vance?"

"Of course, but, please, there was nothing false about our friendship—I am still 'Vance,' and you are still 'Van.' "

"All right, Vance . . . are you or are you not Madame DePage's companion?"

"I am her bodyguard, you might say. She's travelling with a great deal of money."

I frowned. "Isn't it in the ship's safe?"

"There is no ship's safe—accommodations for valuables are available in the cargo hold, but Madame DePage considers that inadvisable. She believes . . . and I must say, so does the Pinkerton agency . . . that Cunard's offices harbor German spies."

"And what is the source of this information?" I asked, picturing Pinkerton's usual rabble of street-corner informers.

"The British Consul General."

"Oh. . . . You don't mean to say Madame DePage's hundred and fifty thousand in war relief funds are in . . . your suite?"

"I believe I've said quite enough . . . but I hope I've demonstrated my belief and faith in you, Van."

She had; I was complimented and, as far as it went, she could trust me.

"Then how is it," I asked, "that you're also the ship's 'official' detective?"

What she said next confirmed something Anderson had mentioned earlier.

"Cunard has no ship detectives," she said, "in the manner, say, of a ship doctor. . . . Instead, they've found a way to conserve on this expense. Their policy is to subcontract a detective already planning passage, sometimes trading the cost of tickets for the detective's willingness to be on call. I believe on the last passing, a Scotland Yard man filled the bill . . . but frequently, it's a Pinkerton man."

"Man?" I asked.

"So to speak," she said.

Anderson was approaching. He was still a few feet away when he said, "I have another favor to ask, Mr. Van Dine."

"Anything to help."

As he reached us, the staff captain was slightly out of breath; had there been a tussle? "We aren't travelling with a translator, and I don't know of any crew member who speaks German."

Or at least one who would admit to it. . . .

"So," Anderson continued, "I wondered if you'd be so kind as to serve in that capacity. We need to question these blokes, after all."

I glanced at Miss Vance, who said, "What a splendid idea, Captain."

He smiled, liking her approval, enjoying the illusion that he was in charge.

"In the meantime," she said, "I will investigate here."

"Investigate how, Miss Vance?" he asked, perhaps a touch suspicious.

"Well, I'll begin by searching this pantry," she said, "to see if they've cloistered any weapons or explosive devices."

Anderson frowned. "If you find any of the latter, how do we proceed?"

She lifted an eyebrow. "Do you have an explosives expert on board? Anyone on the crew with experience along those lines?"

"I can check, Miss Vance, but I don't believe so."

"Well, then we'll have to settle for my limited expertise in that area."

Anderson's eyes frowned. "And if your expertise isn't sufficient?"

"Then you might wish to cover your ears," she said pleasantly.

After an exchange of wide-eyed expressions, the captain and I repaired aft to the brig, on the starboard side. As we walked, we conversed.

"I've demanded their names," Anderson said, meaning the stowaways, "and their intentions . . . but either none of them speak English, or they're feigning ignorance."

"What will you do with them?"

"Well, we could hand them over to the next inbound ship . . . we should be reaching the *Caronia* any time now."

That was the blockading cruiser, with whom a customary mail stop was made.

"Is that wise?"

He shrugged as he walked. "I must admit I would prefer to take them to England for interrogation . . . we're on English soil, legally speaking, making them spies in a war that America is not fighting."

"Excellent point. And I would suggest holding on to them has yet another benefit . . ."

And I shared a particularly nasty, crafty thought with Anderson, who grinned.

"Excellent thinking," he said. "When you question these rotters, be sure to drop that little bomb on them."

"Oh, I intend to."

The brig was next to the separate hospital rooms for males and females. The chamber was about twice the size of my cabin, and the entry area of the white-walled glorified cubicle included a desk and chair (the confiscated camera was on the desktop), with a wall of bars with a jail door separating the rest off into a cell. Two bunks were on either side, with an exposed toilet and a little sink giving them running water but no privacy, or for that matter dignity—not that they deserved either.

Still in their stolen stewards' whites, the three stowaways were not taking advantage of the bunks—two of them milled about, the tall skinny one and the fellow of average build, both tossing the occasional wary glance at their apparent leader, the burly blonde one, who stood staring at us sullenly.

"This is Mr. Van Dine," Anderson said to them curtly. "He speaks your damn language, so there will be no excuses now."

Anderson told me he would leave me to them—he wanted to see how Miss Vance was coming along with her investigating—and he departed. Williams sat at the desk, swivelled toward the prisoners in their cell, the revolver in his hand—a melodramatic touch, it seemed to me, with our spies under lock and key, but a certain point was made.

Positioning myself a foot or so from the wall of bars, I spoke to them in German. "Who are you, and what is your purpose?"

The blonde leader shook his head when the other two seemed eager to reply to the comforting sound of their own language.

"I don't mean you any harm," I said. "I'm not a member of the crew—I am merely a journalist who speaks your mother tongue."

The burly blonde perked at this, and said, "We are impoverished tourists."

"Tourists?" I asked.

"Yes—college boys who came to America looking for a good time."

They seemed a little old for that and I said so.

The blonde said, "We were foolish. We spent all our money on girls and whiskey. Now to get back to Europe, we have to sneak aboard. And we were caught."

"Wearing stewards uniforms."

He shrugged. "We found them and put them on. We hoped to blend in."

"Speaking nothing but German?"

Another shrug. "We are foolish boys out on a lark. We made a mistake. You have heard the expression, 'reckless youth'?"

I smiled. "Do you really think this story will hold up under British interrogation?"

The blonde said nothing, but his two cell mates stared at him with anxiety oozing from their pores.

"You see, Staff Captain Anderson has to quickly decide," I said, "whether to bundle you boys back to the U.S.—for the next few minutes that remains an option— or to deliver you into the hands of the British secret service."

The blonde shrugged. "You imply we would prefer to return to America. But we boarded to go to Europe. We will explain ourselves when we arrive. We're not spies."

"No, no, you're college boys . . . and I'm just a journalist who doesn't even know how Britain executes saboteurs. Do you happen to know—for my story? Is it the rope, or firing squad?"

The skinny one turned pale; he staggered over and sat on the lower bunk and put his face in his hands.

"We are foolish college boys who stowed away," the

blonde leader said. "We have nothing else to say."

"Fellows," I said amiably, "I told you I'm a journalist. What you don't know is that I work for a pro-German publisher. I was sent here to ascertain whether there are guns and munitions aboard this ship."

That got the blonde's attention; the other two, as well, the skinny one lifting his face from his hands.

"If you have discovered that information," I said, "I will report it to my editor . . . and if you are frank with me about your identity, I will do my best to convince Captain Anderson that you should be sent back to America."

The skinny one was on his feet, moving toward his leader. "Listen to him, Klaus!"

Klaus, the blonde, shot his skinny comrade a look that froze the man.

Then the blonde said, "If we were spies, we would not have had time to find out such things."

"I see. What about explosives?"

This startled even the blonde, though he showed it less than the other two.

"Have you had time to deploy an explosive device?" I amplified.

The average fellow said, "Klaus, he's friendly . . . he is on our side."

"Shut up," Klaus said. Then to me: "We are college boys. We are not who you assume us to be."

I shrugged, and dropped my bomb, as promised. "All right. But this is what my recommendation will be to Staff Captain Anderson: Keep these three imprisoned; if they *have* set an explosive device, with a timer, they may decide to talk, after all . . . as the clock ticks away."

The blonde sneered at this, but the other two were

clearly upset, each going to a bunk at either side of the cell and flinging themselves there, turning their faces to the wall. They might have been sobbing.

"We are not fools," Klaus said.

I glanced first at the skinny fellow, then at the average one, and said, "Well, you aren't, anyway."

I turned and told the master-at-arms that I was going to join Captain Anderson at the pantry, and Williams said he would keep an eye on the prisoners. I quietly told him he might want to put the revolver away now; embarrassed, he agreed, and set the weapon on the desk, next to the confiscated camera.

As I exited, Steward Leach was coming my way down the corridor. "What have you learned? Are they spies?"

I paused and looked into the eager, concerned eyes of the pasty young steward. "They are Germans with a camera and a bad cover story. Short of having 'spy' written in ink on their foreheads, I'd say the evidence is conclusive. . . . Shouldn't you be tending to the kiddies?"

He grinned, baring his yellowish crooked teeth. "Luncheon is over. The brig is part of my watch—I need to check in with the master-at-arms, and see what he requires of me. . . . Eventually those bastards will need food and water."

"Might I suggest the crusts the cooks cut off your sandwiches," I said. "As for the water, throwing them overboard might suffice."

When I reached the pantry, Anderson and Miss Vance were in the corridor outside the little room. Anderson turned eagerly to me for a report, and I told him that the blonde leader—Klaus—claimed they were college boys who'd run out of money and were stowing away home.

"Tourists!" Anderson said disgustedly.

"Well," I said, "they did have a camera."

Miss Vance said to me, "Speaking of which, I found a bundle of photographic plates hidden at the rear of a lower shelf."

"What else did you discover?"

"No weapons . . . no explosives. The only other items were three stacks of clothing, hidden behind some boxes—their street clothes, dock worker attire."

"That might indicate they had just changed into the stewards' uniforms," I said thoughtfully, "when we caught them. . . . Does that also mean they hadn't yet committed any acts of sabotage?"

Anderson shook his head. "They had plenty of time to hide a small pipe bomb."

I frowned. "What sort of bomb?"

Miss Vance completed Anderson's information. "A piece of pipe no larger than a healthy cigar that could ignite any ordinary substance, coal or wood, and not leave a trace."*

"We'll search the ship," Anderson said. "Discreetly but thoroughly."

"What a wonderful idea," I said with dry sarcasm.

But Anderson and Miss Vance had made it obvious how easy it would be to miss a tiny but deadly bomb.

To brighten the mood, I told Anderson of the threat I'd left the stowaways to ponder.

---

*A typical example would be a piece of hollow lead tubing with a circular disc of copper dividing it into two chambers, one filled with pitric acid, the other with sulfuric acid; a wax plug at either end would make the mini-firebomb airtight. The thickness of the copper disc could act in effect as a timing device, determining whether within days or hours when the acids would meet, and combust.

"Did you sense they might have placed such a device?" Anderson asked.

"I couldn't say—the ringleader is too collected to read, and the other two are so anxious they also defy assessment."

"That's unfortunate," said Miss Vance.

"I do believe it might be worthwhile," I said, "for me to question our little group periodically—the leader is a stalwart type, but, as I say, the other two are weak . . . promisingly so."

Miss Vance complimented me on this offering, and said to Anderson, "Could you have that camera and these plates taken to the darkroom, for development? That would seem a good place to start."

Anderson agreed.

"Of course," I said, "if you come up with some wonderful panoramic shots of the Manhattan skyline, we may have to reconsider. We may be hosting three innocent tourists, after all."

"Somehow I doubt that," Miss Vance said.

As did I. As did I.

SIX

After-Dinner Treat

All around the ship, stewards were knocking on cabin and stateroom doors, checking to see if the dark curtains had been drawn in compliance with wartime blackout regulations; I was spared this minor indignity only because my cabin did not look out upon the ocean. I was not, on the other hand, spared another indignity, that of snapping, buttoning and hook-and-eyeing myself into the monkey suit required of those men wishing to eat in the *Lusitania*'s fabled dining room.*

Tonight, after all, marked this first social event of our voyage. Throughout Saloon class, ladies were no doubt squeezing their forms, whether dainty or not, into evening gowns that had been long since selected with painful care

---

*The author's aversion to formal evening wear relates to his disdain of traditional, imposed values, not to any preference for casual attire; Van Dine was in fact something of a clotheshorse with a fashion sense both fastidious and stylish, particularly after his mystery-writing success.

to compete with the elegance of the white-and-gold palatial dining room that awaited them.

And in the ship's galleys, larders, bakehouses and confectionery kitchens, a battalion of cooks, bakers, butchers and scullions would even now be applying finishing touches to the voyage's initial and typically elaborate meal, served by the *Lucy*'s regiment of waiters.

I had been invited by Miss Vance—with the generous approval of Madame Marie DePage—to dine at the DePage table tonight; I was to meet them in the dining room. Taking the lift down to D deck, and the main floor of the saloon, I was guaranteed the full effect of the most talked about restaurant on the seven seas. And I was not disappointed.

The First Class Dining Saloon was like a gigantic ornate Easter egg filled with the crème de la crème. The two-tiered white chamber, trimmed in the usual gold, was overseen by an enormous alabaster-and-gilt dome whose ornate plasterwork and oval panels, depicting cherubs after Boucher, would have been the envy of many a cathedral. Fully five hundred patrons at once could be served here, between the circular balcony of the upper tier (à la carte) and the main floor (table d'hôte), which was as wide as the ship itself. Marble Corinthian columns, circular tables with linen cloths and shining silver and glittering crystal, rose-tapestry swivel chairs, an immense mahogany sideboard . . . Cunard had spared no expense to provide a regal ambience for its first-class passengers.

A Strauss waltz floated down from the balcony, courtesy of a subdued orchestra, and despite the room's size and the number of patrons therein, the combined table conversation was a murmur, not a din, the occasional clink and clank of silver and china merely percussive touches. Waiters glided from table to table with a grace usually confined to dancers, as diners entered the palatial saloon, taking it all in with wide eyes, the upper class gawking like hicks at the county fair.

I spotted the theatrical impresario Frohman, entering opposite me; he was relying heavily on his cane, followed by an entourage of half a dozen men and women, including two well-known and attractive actresses, Josephine Brandell and Rita Jolivet. The group was disturbing the decorum of Strauss and quiet conversation by speaking in the boisterous, self-centered manner typical of theater people.

Moving past the slow, loud group, bushy-bearded George Kessler—the Champagne magnate—swaggered over to a small table where a middle-aged man with a younger wife held a seat for him. Perched between two of those gold-crowned columns, at a table for eight, were Madame DePage and her party, including Miss Vance, who had thoughtfully saved the seat next to her for yours truly.

I went immediately to Madame DePage, who graciously rose to offer me her dainty hand, which was ensconced in black lace—her entire ensemble was black, her evening gown heavy with beads and lace, a black feather rising from a small hat . . . all in all, a peculiar cross between the funereal and the gay.

I accepted her hand, almost (but not) kissing it as I half-bowed, saying, "It's a great honor, Madame DePage. I admire very much your humanitarian efforts."

The dark-haired, dark-eyed beauty—her skin was like cream, her lips pursed in a perpetual kiss—lowered her head in a small bow of her own. Then her eyes lifted to mine, sparkling as she said, in her lilting accent, "Miss

Vance says you're a charming fellow, Monsieur Van Dine. And you wish to interview me for your newspaper?"

"I do, Madame—at your convenience."

"I will be delighted. It will be pleasant to speak of the serious matter. . . . Men, they die, they suffer, while we do the frivolous thing, inside of this . . ." She searched for a word. ". . . bubble."

"Bubbles are notoriously fragile, Madame."

"Oh, yes they are. It is a . . . illusion, our safety. The world, she is at war."

"I understand your point of view, Madame. But international law does not allow a ship like this one to be fired upon, until it has been searched and munitions or guns discovered."

"And then?"

I shrugged. "Then the enemy can fire away."

"And what of the passengers?"

"Oh, they must be removed."

"Ah, but passengers can be 'removed' in various ways, n'est-ce pas?"

I smiled and lowered my head in capitulation.

The lovely philanthropist made introductions. Seated next to her was Dr. James Houghton, a distinguished-looking gent in his middle forties, who was travelling to join Madame DePage's husband as his assistant at the hospital at La Panne. Seated opposite them were a slender, bird-like but not unattractive woman in her later forties and a much younger man, possibly thirty or at most thirty-five, who seemed nonetheless to be her sweetheart. The woman was Theodate Pope, daughter of a car manufacturer in New England somewhere, and her bright-eyed soul mate was Edwin Friend.

"So you're a journalist?" the bird-like Miss Pope asked, in a breathy, high-pitched voice. Her beaded gown was a light green satin.

I had at this point taken my seat at the far end of the table, next to Miss Vance, lovely in a blue satin the color of her eyes, every tendril of the blonde hair neatly up, complemented by a small hat with a large darker blue feather. This put me next to Mr. Friend, as well.

"That's right," I said, seeing no reason to amplify, though the designation "journalist" obviously did me little justice.

The woman persisted. "Have you any interest in the paranormal?"

"Psychic phenomenon, do you mean? I'm afraid I have little patience with superstition, Miss Pope."

Her friend Friend chimed in. "Ah, but this isn't superstition, sir—it's science. That's why we're going to England, you see."

I didn't see, nor did I particularly care to.

But Miss Pope was saying, "Edwin and I are pursuing our mutual interest in psychic science. We've arranged to confer with the members of the English Society for Psychical Research!"

That last had been delivered so triumphantly I was obviously expected to cheer or at least provide an ooh or an ah. Instead I merely nodded, and said, "Well, I wish you both luck."

This response disappointed them, but it achieved my desired effect: They turned away from me, to their own company, and throughout the evening spoke enthusiastically and incessantly to one another about spiritualistic matters.

Miss Vance whispered, "You handled that well, Van."

I looked into the china-blue eyes, wishing I might live there—no pleasanter place could be easily imagined. "Did I, Vance?"

Still speaking so low that only I could hear her, she said, "You dispensed of them without insulting them— it's nice to know your acid tongue can be reigned in."

From the balcony the strained strains of "The End of a Perfect Day" wafted unsettlingly down, replacing Strauss with the inexplicably popular treacle of songwriter Carrie Jacobs Bond.

"The orchestra certainly knows how to kill one's appetite," I said to Miss Vance.

And a familiar male voice nearby blurted: "How wonderful! One of my favorite tunes, by my favorite composer!"

Elbert Hubbard had arrived. Pausing just behind us, the homespun excuse for a philosopher was escorting his wife, Alice, apparently in search of a table. Mrs. Hubbard was slender and not unattractive, in a scrubbed sort of way, though the woman seemed ill at ease in her chocolate-color satin evening gown, which had been in style once. Hubbard wore the required tuxedo, but one of his trademark floppy silk ties flowed down over his white shirt front, in seeming protest. With his shoulder-length gray-touched hair—so much like his wife's—he cut a distinctive if bizarre figure in the midst of so much conservative wealth.

Then he noticed Madame DePage, who had turned to smile and nod to him. They were apparently acquainted— or at least had been introduced, at some point—because Hubbard and his wife went to her like iron shavings to a magnet.

"Marie," he said, "how lovely you look. . . . I hope you

can find time, on this voyage, to sit with me and exchange ideas and thoughts."

"I would be delighted, Fra Hubbard," she said.

I was dismayed to think so intelligent a woman could be swayed by this master of middle-brow blather.

"I am afraid I would have little to discuss," Madame DePage said frankly, glancing about the room with mild distaste, "with these rich."

Hubbard shrugged and his thick locks bounced on his shoulders. "Men are rich only as they give, Madame— you are the rich one in this room. He . . . or *she* . . . who gives great service gets great rewards."

"Someone should follow him around," I whispered to Miss Vance, "and sew that stuff on samplers."

She gave me a reproving look, but her eyes were laughing.

Madame DePage introduced the Hubbards to Miss Pope and her young lapdog, and the bird-like female inquired as to the great Hubbard's opinion of paranormal research.

"My opinion is favorable," he said. "The supernatural is the natural not yet understood."

That brightened Miss Pope's eyes like a Hallowe'en pumpkin whose candle had just been lit.

But then Hubbard moved on—he seemed incapable of real conversation: He was strictly in the aphorism business. And his wife hadn't said a word, merely a pleasant appendage of his. They made their way to a table beneath the orchestra, which had just begun playing another Carrie Jacobs Bond number, "Just-a Wearyin' for You," a for-lornly lachrymose affair that had Hubbard looking sky-ward, as if God Himself were responsible for this dismal dirge.

"Why would a man so determinedly sanguine," I asked

Miss Vance, speaking of Hubbard, "be prone to such simple-minded sentimental slop?"

Miss Vance just looked at me. "Perhaps I was wrong."

"About what?"

"Your ability to control that tongue of yours."

I smiled. "You seem to have an abnormal interest in my tongue, Vance."

Another woman might have blushed; Miss Vance merely smiled wickedly and said, "That remains to be seen. . . . Have you noticed that Captain Turner is at the head of the captain's table?"

"Why, is that a surprise?"

"It's well-known that Bowler Bill rarely makes such an appearance—he delegates the social duties to Staff Captain Anderson."

I nodded. "And Staff Captain Anderson is conspicuous in his absence."

She nodded back. "Supervising the search of the ship, no doubt."

"Shouldn't the ship's detective be accompanying him?"

She frowned, shook her head, letting me know that—even in a hushed conversation like ours—mentioning her function as the *Lusitania*'s dick was undesirable.

Still, she answered my question. "I'm travelling with Madame DePage—and I dine with Madame DePage."

Glancing at the centrally placed captain's table, I noted that—of the celebrities aboard, specifically those who'd received warning telegrams—only Vanderbilt and his friend Williamson were sharing Turner's company. I asked Miss Vance if she recognized any of the other diners at the coveted central table, and three of them proved to be shipbuilders; a tall, dignified woman in a dark gown was (Miss Vance said) Lady Marguerite Allan, wife of Sir

Montagu Allan, heir to a Canadian shipping concern, whom Lady Allan and her precociously lovely teenaged daughters were sailing to meet in England.

Vanderbilt and Williamson were listening to Captain Turner's every word as if seated at Socrates' knee; everyone at the table was fawningly attentive to the captain, who was taking a game stab at playing the genial host.

"Amusing, isn't it?" I said to Miss Vance. "If old Bowler Bill weren't in that gold-braided uniform, say a plain blue serge suit, those people wouldn't look twice at him—he'd just be another provincial with a queer north-country twang."

Miss Vance glanced over and she laughed a little. "Cruel but true . . . and the wealthier they are, the more attentively they listen."

"Look at Vanderbilt hang on every word, as if Bowler Bill were Admiral Nelson himself."

"On the other hand," she said with a shrug, "the *Lucy* is possibly the most famous ship in the world . . . and Turner *is* her master."

I granted her that. "He's the highest authority we have. Our very lives are in the hands of that old salt."

That seemed to trouble Miss Vance, who—after a pause—asked, "Do you know how the captain reacted when he heard of the stowaways?"

"Outrage?"

"Hardly. He showed no surprise at all—merely said in his forty-five years at sea he regarded stowaways as just another shipboard nuisance."

"Like Elbert Hubbard," I said, "or an orchestra prone to playing Carrie Jacobs Bond."

That also made her laugh a little, and then we were examining the embossed card that was this evening's menu. Under a gilt wreath encircling the Cunard flag, a superb bill of fare included oysters on the half shell or hors d'oeuvres followed by soup, and a choice of fish ranging from deviled whitebait to *Supreme de Barbue Florentine*, with entrees including braised gosling, sauteed chicken, and haunches of mutton. For a man who'd been reduced to living on coffee and sandwiches (that Bronx rooming house was still a too vivid memory), such fine cuisine would make a welcome change.

Between courses, Madame DePage announced she'd be attending a concert in the music room, after dinner, and would be pleased if anyone at the table would care to join her. The Royal Welsh Male Chorus was aboard, it seemed, returning home after touring the U.S. and Canada.

"The Welsh, you know," she said, that charming accent almost making the offer palatable, "are a race of singers marvelous."

Everyone nodded and said they would love to join her . . . with the exception of myself, who stayed mute, and Miss Vance, who said, "It's been rather a long day, and I'm afraid I'm quite fatigued—would you mind terribly if I retired to the stateroom?"

Madame DePage didn't mind at all.

So I walked Miss Vance to the Regal Suite, which was so near my regal cubbyhole, when she presented me with a pleasant surprise. "I was hoping," she said, "you might join me for an after-dinner drink."

"I would love to. If madame won't mind . . ."

Her smile was wide and her eyes were narrowed. "Madame will be consumed with the concert for an hour, at least. And my bedroom is quite private, even has a door of its own, opening onto the hallway . . . should Madame DePage cut her musical evening short."

This was all quite agreeable to me and I said as much. This lovely Pinkerton agent was making a splendid case for the independent, modern woman.

We did not enter through the suite, rather going directly into her bedroom, which was larger than my cabin, and included a sitting area with a rose-color sofa. That's where we sat and chatted and sipped snifters of brandy (she disappeared into the outer suite only long enough to fetch our drinks).

She wanted to know about me, and I told her that I'd been the editor of a prestigious magazine, but my reign had been truncated, because the publisher had lacked courage and foresight. I could not tell if she recognized the names of the authors whose work I'd bought—James Joyce, Joseph Conrad, D.H. Lawrence, Ezra Pound, a sampling—but she seemed impressed with my intensity if nothing else.

I made it clear that journalism was a means to an end— not just for money, rather to gain passage to join my brother in London, and convince him to come home.

"Your brother is one of these modern artists," she said, clearly fascinated.

"Yes, and an important one—a leading Synchromist. As for myself, I'm working on a book on modern art, which'll present an entirely new aesthetic. Listen, am I boring you?"

She was half-turned and gazing at me steadily, an arm resting along the top of the sofa. "Not at all—I'm interested. I love the impressionists, but I must admit I've not warmed yet to the modernists."

I was bowled over by this! She not only had wonderful

blue eyes and a remarkable figure, but a *mind....*

Exhilarated, I said, "Do you understand what I mean when I say that one can stand in front of a great painting, and feel the same incredible emotional effect as hearing a fine symphony, brilliantly performed?"

Her eyes flared. "Oh, yes! That is exactly how I feel, standing before a Mattise, or Cézanne."

"You see, art is judged by the wrong criteria—with too much concern for literary content and moral values ... not an emotional, visceral response. Don't be afraid of modern art, Vance! It's not so much revolutionary as it is evolutionary...."

And we talked for perhaps half an hour on this subject, or rather I talked, before I realized I had to know who this fascinating woman was.

"How is it," I asked, "that a female Pinkerton agent has such refined tastes, and a mind keen for discussion of aesthetics?"

She granted me one of those half-smiles. "I wasn't born a detective, Van.... I'm afraid I had an even more disreputable profession prior to joining the Pinkertons."

Her father had been an upper-middle-class businessman in Chicago who worked with Potter Palmer, making "a killing" rebuilding the city after the 1871 fire. The family frequently attended plays, and Philomina grew up fascinated by the theater. She had appeared in school plays, and participated in local amateur theatrics, before pursuing dramatics at private schools.

Still, acting seemed inappropriate for a young woman of her station ... until her father lost everything in the depression of the early 1890s, dying of a heart attack, leaving the family destitute. A theatrical agent who had scouted the budding actress in local amateur and school productions had taken Philomina on, and she quickly achieved some success in the Chicago theatrical scene.

"When I met my husband," she said, "I was just starting to play leading roles."

Husband?

"You see," she said, "Phillip was a Pinkerton agent himself, investigating a group of swindlers called the Adam Worth gang. Have you heard of them?"

I had.

"At any rate," she continued, "Pinkerton was looking for female agents, particularly ones that could intermingle with upper-class society . . . and not just as a maid or servant. My theatrical background was perfect—disguises are part and parcel of the Pinkerton approach."

"Did you leave the stage?"

"Yes, I was achieving some notoriety in the Chicago theatrical scene, but the financial rewards were frankly slender . . . and I had a mother and two sisters to support."

"And the Pinks paid well."

"They did and they do . . . and I worked for a year before I married Phillip, though I think I fell in love with him the day we met. You see, he loved me, really truly did, in an unconditional way that is rare . . . he didn't care that we couldn't have children . . . an illness in my childhood . . . anyway. Phillip was killed two years ago, in the line of duty. Shot by a damned thief."

"I'm sorry," I said, and I was: as much as part of me was relieved to hear her husband was no longer on the scene, the pain in her eyes seemed all too palpable. "Did they find the bastard?"

She didn't blink at my language. "I found him. And killed him."

That called for another round of brandies, which she kindly fetched.

Leaning back on the sofa, snifter in one hand, her other hand on my arm, she said, "Since then I've worked part-time for Pinkerton . . . on a case by case basis. You see, I've begun acting again . . . meeting Mr. Frohman is a hidden agenda of mine, taking this assignment, I must admit."

Lost in her eyes, I said, "I would love to see you perform."

"I thought you might," she said, and kissed me.

Soon the lights had been dimmed, and we kissed and petted on the sofa, like teenaged spooners.

"Are you married, Van?" she asked.

"Does it matter?"

"Yes it does . . ."

"I'm divorced."*

"So you're a man of the world."

"As you're a woman of the world."

"And we need partake of no pretense."

"Not by my way of thinking."

It took a while to get out of all those clothes, but we managed, and the wrought-iron bed for one accommodated two, nicely, particularly since sleep was not what we had in mind.

Nonetheless, afterward she did fall asleep in my arms, clinging close, and I dropped off, as well, into a contented

---

*Van Dine was separated, though not legally; his wife, Katherine (and their daughter, Beverly), were living in Los Angeles, waiting for Van Dine to "establish himself in the literary world" and send for them. He did eventually divorce Katherine.

slumber. Madame DePage must have returned at some point, but I did not hear her come in, out in that adjacent suite. Something else, later, did wake me—I was not sure what, I merely sensed noise, perhaps a commotion in the hall—and I slipped from the bed and gathered my clothing.

I held my pocket watch near the sliver of light from the hallway door and saw that it was five minutes after two a.m. After getting back into the monkey suit in a rather half-hearted, half-buttoned fashion, I bent over the bed and kissed the slumbering goddess.

She smiled and murmured something, and fell back into a deep sleep.

I left her bedroom feeling giddy as a schoolboy with a new crush. Miss Vance was a lively, sophisticated woman, and I could hardly have hoped for a better partner in a shipboard romance . . . let alone for said romance to have blossomed so quickly, so fully.

So distracted was I that I almost tripped over the corpse that lay on its side in the hallway.

SEVEN

First-Class Murder

When she replied to my knock, Miss Vance peered through the cracked door and at first seemed as confused as she did sleepy; then, seeing it was me, she smiled in a lazy, half-lidded manner that normally would have struck me as quite endearing.

"Miss me already?" she almost drawled, opening the door a bit, her curvaceous form barely concealed in her camisole.

"Put something on," I told her. "There's a dead body in the hallway—and I suspect foul play."

She said nothing, her lethargy replaced at once by alertness. Leaning out into the hall, she saw—a few paces down, toward my cabin—the slumped figure of what appeared to be a ship's steward.

Frowning, she asked, "Is that—?"

"It's not a steward I killed, coming out of your room, to save your virtue. . . . No indeed."

"The ringleader," she said breathlessly.

Klaus, the burly blonde stowaway—still in his stolen stewards' whites—lay on his side on the shining linoleum, his blue eyes staring at nothing, his expression one of disappointment and surprise . . . a common enough one, at the point of death, I should think. Who among us won't be naively disappointed, and bitterly surprised, when the inevitable arrives?

She sealed herself within her quarters, and I returned to the body. At this time of the morning, the corridor was otherwise deserted. Kneeling over the man, I noticed a wound in his back, a blossom of crimson, still dripping.

I remembered the vague sense that there'd been a commotion outside the stateroom—that had been, after all, what stirred me from my slumber. I'd quickly dressed and exited, so if that commotion indeed had resulted in the violent death of the blonde stowaway, this was a freshly created corpse . . . born within the past ten minutes or less.

Proving that a woman could indeed dress as quickly as a man (should the situation call for it), Miss Vance emerged in a simple blue-gray gingham morning dress— well, this *was* morning, after all—with collar and cuffs of dotted lawn and a rather loose skirt. She looked nothing like any detective I ever heard about.

Or such was the case until she knelt next to me, eyes narrowed, unhesitant to achieve a close proximity to the corpse.

"Have you touched anything?" she asked.

"Somehow I managed to resist. Is that a bullet wound?"

She leaned in, her pretty nose damn near touching the blossom of blood. Then she drew back, her eyes meeting mine and holding them. "No—that's a knife wound. Possibly a hunting knife—judging by the width of the tear in the fabric . . . nearly two inches."

"Couldn't the cloth have been torn in the struggle?"

She shook her head. "I don't believe there was a struggle—this is the classic example of a man stabbed in the back."

I disagreed—telling her I had heard a to-do in the hall. Surely this was the result of a scuffle escalating into tragedy.

She shrugged. "Perhaps there were two other men . . . two assailants, let us say. One is arguing with our late friend here, facing him, and the other is behind him."

"I see—one keeps him busy, the other stabs him in the back."

"Or one is arguing with the victim, and as the argument seems about to get out of hand, the accomplice ends the discussion with a two-inch blade of steel."

She stood and so did I.

"Of course," she said, "what immediately comes to mind is his two friends—the other stowaways."

"Yes! If Klaus escaped the cell, so must have the others—and there was tension between them . . . I witnessed it."

Nodding, she said, "The other two seemed more likely to cooperate, to talk—wasn't that your opinion, after interrogating them?"

"It most certainly was. . . . Shouldn't we alert Staff Captain Anderson, or perhaps Captain Turner himself?"

"We should. But I'd like a few moments, here, at the scene of the crime . . . before too many well-meaning fools come tromping through."

I was doubtful this was wise. "We may have two stowaways at large, remember—one of whom is armed with a hunting knife."

"Van, I scarcely think they'll be trying to take over the

ship with it—they are probably seeking a new hiding
place, not looking for another victim."

Miss Vance requested that I stand near her doorway,
and she returned to her quarters and emerged moments
later with a magnifying glass.

I had to laugh. "How Sherlock Holmes of you!"

"What may seem a cliche in Conan Doyle," she said,
"is a valuable tool in real detection. . . . Physical evidence
has put many a guilty neck in the hangman's noose."

The detective in gingham knelt to examine the linoleum
in the area of the corpse, an activity that took several
seemingly endless minutes.

Finally she turned toward me, her eyes glittering in a
predatory fashion. "Droplets of blood," she said.

Walking along, half-bent over, gazing through the magnifying glass, she followed a trail of tiny scarlet globules.
She stopped at the mouth of the short corridor next to my
cabin.

"Come," she said, motioning to me. "Hug the wall, as
you do."

I joined her—and there on the floor, halfway down the
short corridor so near where I slept, was a black-handled
hunting knife, smeared crimson. Blobs of blood trailed
toward where it lay. Miss Vance said this indicated the
knife had been flung there—by the murderer.

Gesturing back down the hall, toward the corpse, she
said, "The murderer walked along with the bloody knife
at his side—probably held out, a ways, to prevent getting
any blood on his clothing. Then, seeing this corridor, im-
pulsively pitched the murder weapon away."

"Then this was not a carefully calculated affair—rather
a killing by impulse?"

"Yes—but by a person carrying a deadly blade. That

indicates some forethought of foul play. . . . Now it's time to contact the good staff captain."

Within five minutes Anderson had arrived, looking remarkably crisp in his gold-braided blue jacket with cap, for after two in the morning, anyway.

"Sorry to have disturbed you," I said. Miss Vance had made the call. The master-at-arms was on his way, as well.

"I'd just returned to my cabin," he said, his expression wide-eyed yet business-like as he surveyed the corpse on the linoleum, "having dispatched a second group of crew members to continue the search of the ship. We've found nothing thus far."

"Until now," Miss Vance said, with a redundant gesture toward the corpse. She quickly filled Anderson in, leading him for a look at the discarded knife that lay on the floor of the adjoining short corridor.

"I would like to take that weapon into evidence," she said. "While I'm limited, I do have a kit with me that includes fingerprinting works."

"Good Lord," Anderson said, "what if you find prints on the handle? What would you compare them to? Would you have us fingerprint everyone on shipboard?"

"If need be. However, might I suggest, for the present at least, that we not advertise this matter."

Anderson sighed in relief. "I'm very pleased to hear you say that. As soon as possible, I would like to arrange for the body to be taken to the ship's hospital."

Miss Vance nodded. "Splendid idea, Captain—I would like the ship's doctor to have a look at the body. I would also like to examine all of the late stowaway's effects."

This was agreeable to the staff captain, who requested the use of Miss Vance's phone.

"We'll get the doctor up here," Anderson said, "and a stretcher, and remove the deceased to a comfortable bed."

"I'm sure he'll appreciate that," I said.

A voice said, "Good Lord," which seemed to be the exclamation of choice here in the corridor; the master-at-arms, Williams, had arrived. The short, sturdy fellow had come from the direction of my cabin, and he stood a respectful distance from the dead man, gazing down with mouth and eyes agape, his thick dark eyebrows pushing his forehead into his scalp.

No one greeted the master-at-arms—it didn't seem warranted.

"The captain will have to be woken, too," Anderson said to no one in particular, rubbing his chin, apparently contemplating the various phone calls he would need to make from Miss Vance's room.

"Mr. Williams," I said to the master-at-arms, "who was guarding the stowaways?"

"No one," he said with a shrug, still gazing at the corpse.

"And why is that?"

Anderson answered for him. "They were locked in the cells, and the brig itself is kept locked. No one sees them except the steward who brings them their supper."

"Which," I said, "would be Mr. Leach."

With a nod, Anderson said, "I have to make my calls," and was turning toward Miss Vance's door when I spoke again.

"That's all well and good," I said, "but shouldn't a priority be to check the status of those cells? Until we do, we won't know for certain that all three stowaways are at large."

Anderson glanced back at me, trying unsuccessfully to

conceal his annoyance with my amateur's question. "Mr. Van Dine, if the ringleader is dead in first class, it's reasonable to assume the door to the cell has been unlocked . . . and, if so, that all three went through that open door."

"Two open doors," I reminded him. "To escape, both the cell door and the outer door had to be unlocked. I would suggest you have a security breach—some crew member may be in league with these Germans."

Now he turned all the way around and did not hide the annoyance in either his expression or his voice. "Sir, my men—"

But I cut him off: "Consist of whomever you were able to round up from loose ends, with all the able-bodied seaman serving the Royal Navy."

The staff captain sighed—he twitched a non-smile, which was as close as he could allow himself to acknowledge the truth of my statement.

An awkward silence hung between us, until Miss Anderson said, "Mr. Van Dine has a point about the brig— I suggest he and I go down and check out the scene, until you can arrange for our dead stowaway's removal."

The frustrated Anderson agreed to this, and went into Miss Vance's room, the door of which had been left ajar.

Prior to attending to our task, Miss Vance took care of another one.

"Do you have a handkerchief I could borrow?" she asked me.

I said certainly, and gave her one.

Stepping around Klaus, she returned to the short corridor, disappeared down it, and quickly returned holding the knife by its bloody tip, her fingers shielded from the blood by my handkerchief. She took it into her cabin, deposited it somewhere, and returned to the hall.

Williams was on one side of the corpse and Miss Vance on the other, when she asked pleasantly, "Are you still carrying that revolver we shared earlier?"

Williams blinked; those thick dark brows seemed only to emphasize a certain vacuity about his eyes themselves. "Why, yes, ma'am." He patted his jacket on the left side, where indeed a bulge indicated something heavy resided there.

"Might I borrow it, please?" she asked, as if requesting another hanky.

His forehead furrowed, but then he shrugged and said, "Certainly, ma'am."

And he removed the revolver from his pocket, and passed it across the corpse to Miss Vance. There was something terribly unsettling about the one-handed ease with which she managed the weapon.

Though our destination was merely a floor down, we took the elevator, on which the pistol-packing Miss Vance posed several questions.

"You suspect someone among the crew, Van?"

"Don't you?"

"Do you suspect someone specifically?"

"Mr. Leach and Mr. Williams have the easiest access to the brig—the steward in charge of food service, and the master-at-arms."

She nodded, but the tightness around her eyes seemed not to agree.

"What bothers you about that theory?" I asked.

"A clever criminal would not lay the blame so near his own door."

I shrugged. "Perhaps he isn't clever—does either Leach or Williams strike you as a mastermind?"

"No . . . and that's what troubles me. But I've already

cabled my home office, and they'll both be thoroughly investigated within forty-eight hours."

We exited the elevator into the Shelter Deck's Grand Entrance area, with its potted ferns and wicker furnishings. Without the usual milling of people, the ship seemed like a big empty house we were haunting, our footsteps echoing off the floor as we headed into the First Class Saloon, where the tables were already covered with fresh linen, china and silverware, ready for breakfast service. This tabernacle of a restaurant seemed absurdly vast, when only two people were in it, and we hurried across as if we were thieves trying not to get caught—that Miss Vance had a gun in her dainty fist only served to emphasize this sense.

We moved aft down a corridor with a galley on one side and pantries on the other; the hospital rooms, with the brig at the far end, were down a corridor to the left, bisecting the ship. The brig door was closed, but—when Miss Vance tried it—unlocked. The lovely detective seemed about to go in, when I inserted my arm between her and the door.

I shook my head. Even if she was the one with revolver, I would go in first. I was still, technically at least, the man here.

Opening the door quickly, I moved inside the same way, with Miss Vance and her gun following close. While I had not been expecting anything, really—other than perhaps an empty cell—what we did view was certainly not on either of our mental lists of possibilities.

The other two stowaways were still inside the cell, though the barred door yawned open. They were asprawl on the floor—the tall, skinny, brown-haired one to the left, the average fellow with lighter brown hair on the right. Even from just inside the room, the dark red—almost black—splotches could be seen on their white stewards' jackets, over either man's heart, like badges of blood.

Miss Vance and I exchanged troubled looks, and she entered and knelt over either man. Strangely, she leaned near and sniffed the open mouths of each corpse, as if checking their breath for the scent of something . . . although neither had any breath left, obviously.

She rose, and stood there surveying the carnage, pistol at her side.

"Knife wounds?" I asked.

She nodded and exited the cell, approaching me; I was standing near the unattended desk. "What would you say happened here, Van?"

I walked toward the cell, looked in through the bars, studied the position of the bodies, and tried to reason it through.

"Think out loud," she suggested.

"Well, perhaps the knife . . . does it appear, from the wounds, to be the same weapon? The hunting knife in the corridor?"

She nodded.

I began again. "Perhaps the knife was smuggled in to them by a comrade among the crew . . . or possibly, somehow, they managed to sneak that weapon past the searches of their persons, unlikely as that might seem."

"Continue."

I offered a sigh, a shrug and the following speculation: "I would say Klaus and his stowaway associates had a falling-out—when I interviewed them, signs of such a conflict were apparent. My guess is that these two wanted to cooperate with the shipboard authorities, possibly reveal not only the nature of their mission but where . . . perhaps . . . a ticking bomb might be found aboard."

Her expression indicated my reasoning seemed sound enough to her.

Encouraged, I went on. "So we have three stowaways and one knife—with two stowaways at odds with their leader. A struggle ensues, and one of them stabs Klaus in the back . . . but Klaus is a tough, brawny exemplar of the fatherland, and, though wounded, he manages to take that knife away, and stab his assailant . . . and then he stabbed the other would-be traitor, and left them to die."

Miss Vance sighed; she began to pace. "This presumes that Klaus could have survived such a wound long enough to get to that first-class corridor."

"Relatively speaking, it's not that far away—one floor up."

Still pacing, she said, "We'll ask the ship's doctor his opinion, based upon examination of the wound . . . but the blood droplets, and the apparently discarded knife, seem at odds with your theory."

I raised a lecturing finger. "Perhaps you've read the evidence incorrectly . . . meaning no disrespect to your professional standing. Perhaps that trail of blood led in the opposite direction you assumed—perhaps it was Klaus who discarded the bloody knife, and staggered down the hall, in the direction of your room, his wound leaving a trail of liquid rubies for you to find."

"And the commotion you heard in the hallway?"

I shrugged rather elaborately. "Klaus succumbing to the wound . . . losing his balance . . . falling unconscious, like the deadweight he had become, to the floor."

She smiled. "That's not bad, Van. . . . Very nicely deliberated. But you may be falling into a trap of sorts."

"How so?"

Her eyes tightened. "I believe these bodies were *meant* to be interpreted as the aftermath of a falling out amongst our stowaways."

"This is somehow staged? How do you 'stage' murdered men? They're really dead, after all."

"Oh, they're dead all right. . . . Step inside that cell, Van. Take a closer look."

With another shrug, I did as she suggested, and followed her lead and knelt over the skinny corpse, who—upon examination from this proximity—revealed an interesting further fact.

"His skin is a rather dreadful shade of light blue," I commented.

"If you take a look at his friend," she said, "you'll see he shares the same condition."

I did, and he did.

"Now sniff around his mouth," she prompted.

I was with the smaller of the pair, the darker-haired corpse, whose mouth—like his vacant eyes—was open.

"Hmmm," I said, and rose, doing my best to hide my revulsion at the examinations I'd just been asked to make. "I would characterize that scent as . . . well, it is familiar."

"Almonds," she said. "Bitter almonds."

I exited the cell and approached her, where she stood near the desk. "You're the detective—what's the significance of that?"

"Well, I'm a detective, and we would need a doctor, willing and capable of performing a full scientific postmortem examination, to confirm my suspicion. But those symptoms—the blue-tinged skin, the scent of bitter almonds—would seem to indicate cyanide poisoning."

I tried to process this information. "These men were poisoned, as well as stabbed?"

"I would say they were poisoned . . . and stabbed after their deaths, to cloud the issue."

Now I was the one pacing. "But what can it mean?"

"I am not certain. But I have a suggestion that you may reject."

I stopped and planted myself in front of her. "Let's hear it."

She raised a cautionary palm. "Let's keep our speculations to ourselves. No, on second thought . . . you *share* your first impression of this scene of the crime, with Staff Captain Anderson, and anyone else from the ship's staff who might ask your opinion."

"Why on earth? Your analysis, bizarre as it is, makes a hell of a lot more sense."

She walked to the cell and looked through the bars at our dead stowaways. "If those men were poisoned, it was by someone on the crew—possibly Leach bringing them food, or Williams, or someone else with access to this brig . . . Anderson himself, included. I would not like to alert our suspects, at this point, that we have these suspicions."

"I see. . . . You wish to give them a false sense of security."

Nodding, she said, "Yes, and as the only trained investigator aboard this ship, I am up against a murderer who is very likely also a German spy . . . a clever murderer, able to manipulate evidence in a most confusing manner. There may be, as you have indicated, a ticking bomb on this ship at this very moment . . . and I prefer to stay one step ahead of our prey, while seeming to be several steps behind."

I saw the sense of this, and agreed to be her accomplice in cover-up as well as crime solving.

We heard some noise in the corridor, and stepped out to have a look—Williams and another crew member were carrying the deceased Klaus, covered by a white sheet commandeered from somewhere or other, down the corridor. A slender dark-haired, flush-cheeked boyish fellow in his early thirties—wearing a brown suit and no tie, indicating perhaps haste in dressing—was unlocking the door of the room next to the brig.

Anderson rounded the corner, picking up the rear of this little procession, and as the rosy-cheeked fellow opened the door, and the stretcher disappeared inside what was obviously one of the hospital rooms, the staff captain approached us outside the brig.

"So far," Anderson said, "no sign of the other two stowaways."

"I would have to disagree," I said, and I gestured rather grandly to the open door of the brig.

Anderson stepped inside, and then exploded, delivering several salty phrases, before turning to apologize to Miss Vance, who had followed him in. I was just behind her.

Now it was Anderson thinking aloud, and he came to the same conclusion that I had: A falling-out among the stowaways had led to the "winner" of the struggle managing to stumble to first class, discard his knife, and stagger to his death.

"That's a reasonable explanation," Miss Vance said.

"And," Anderson went on, adding a detail that frankly had not occurred to me, "I can tell you why he chose first class to die in—he was making for the lifeboats, to lower one and make his escape."

Miss Vance was frowning. "Could one man manage that?"

The staff captain dismissed that with a wave. "Possibly not, but he would have to try, wouldn't he? That would be his only possible means of escape! . . . Let's have the doctor have a look at these two."

Anderson stalked out, and Miss Vance and I exchanged lifts of the eyebrow.

I said, "One man might not be able to lower a lifeboat and escape . . ."

"But," she completed, "a man with an accomplice aboard the ship could certainly manage it."

"Even so, Anderson's wrong—the lifeboats are adjacent to first class, all right . . . but on the Boat Deck, another floor up. And the corridor Klaus died in is forward of not only the brig but the elevators—what was our stowaway doing in *that* corridor?"

Miss Vance was smiling at me, and there was nothing predatory about it. "Nicely observed," she said.

Moments later Anderson escorted into the brig the slender baby-faced fellow wearing the thrown-on brown suit. The staff captain made his introductions—this was Dr. John F. McDermott, the ship's physician.

McDermott must have read my mind—or perhaps my expression—because he said, "I know I look young. . . . I've only been practicing for a year. But I was not last in my class, I assure you."

He was also not first, or he would have said so.

As McDermott entered the cell, and crouched over first one, then the other victim, Anderson said to us, "Our longtime ship's doctor, a wonderful old boy named Dr. Pointon, James Pointon, couldn't make the voyage, this time."

"Rheumatism," McDermott said, from within the cell, as if this is what had killed the two stowaways. "Dr. Pointon is suffering from a rather severe case, and I'm just filling in."

"Quite a competent lad," Anderson assured us, meaning McDermott.

But Miss Vance gave me a look that told me she hoped the opposite was true: that this young pup would not recognize what that "wonderful old boy Dr. Pointon" might have—the symptoms of cyanide poisoning.

"Just like the other fellow," McDermott said, emerging from the cell. "Stabbed to death."

The faintest smile flickered over Miss Vance's lips.

"Of course," I said, "the other fellow was knifed from behind."

McDermott nodded, approaching us. "Yes, on the left, between his ribs, piercing his heart."

"Wouldn't death have been instantaneous, in such an event?" I asked.

Miss Vance frowned at me—which was disconcerting, since she still had that gun at her side.

The young doctor said, "Normally I might say so—but since your stowaway managed to walk out of here and reach the next floor, before he collapsed . . . obviously not. The history of medicine is filled with such strange anomalies."

What a pleasure to learn of the history of medicine from so experienced a source.

"Dr. McDermott," Miss Vance said, "when you've stripped the clothing from the deceased next door, I wish to have a look at the body, and at the effects."

"Certainly." He turned to Anderson. "We're lucky we didn't have any more deaths tonight—we only have three

beds in the male hospital. . . . Could you have them transported for me, Captain?"

Anderson nodded, and the boyish doctor said polite
good-byes and that it was pleasure to meet us, "even under such circumstances," and returned to a patient his
inexperience could not harm.

"Mr. Van Dine . . . Miss Vance . . ." Anderson's expression was grave. "Even more than before, I must urge
your cooperation."

"Why, of course," I said.

Miss Vance merely nodded.

Anderson went on. "These murders must remain con-
fidential—I wish neither to alarm the passengers, nor im-
pede any investigation you might deem necessary, Miss
Vance."

"I believe this is a wise course of action," she said.

A voice from the doorway interrupted the conversation.
"Begging your pardon."

It was McDermott; his expression was perplexed.

"Captain Anderson, there's something you should see
. . . Miss Vance, as ship's detective, I believe you'll find
this of particular interest."

Though I had not been invited, I joined the little group
as they followed the young doctor to the infirmary next
door, where the next surprise in this extraordinary affair
awaited us.

EIGHT

Cold Storage

At first Dr. McDermott's discovery seemed anticlimactic, following as it did the discovery of German stowaways and a parade of foul play that extended from the brig to first class. (Later Miss Vance shared with me her fear that the inexperienced doctor had finally noticed the blue pigmentation and almond odor, and had belatedly put two and two together . . . a morsel of math she could well do without.)

The ship's infirmary, male apportionment,* was a blindingly white room—neither chamber nor cubicle—where the naked corpse of Klaus the ringleader lay face-

---

*Existing blueprints of the *Lusitania* indicate two hospital rooms for men and one for women, side by side on the shelter deck, mid-ship and somewhat aft. The brig, however, is not indicated on these plans, though it is clear from numerous sources that the ship indeed had a brig, which (according to Van Dine, at least) was one of those two hospital rooms designated for men.

down (apparently so that the knife wound could be examined) on a hospital bed along the left wall. On a counter opposite the doorway, beneath various cabinets, in front of rows of lidded glass containers of an innocuous variety—cotton balls, throat depressors and gauze—was the pile of the late stowaway's clothing . . . which is to say, his commandeered clothing, the stewards' uniform.

But next to the pants and shirt and undergarments were a pair of heavy brown shoes and darker brown woolen socks. These would have seemed as undramatic as the other apparel were not for young Dr. McDermott's presentation of a slip of paper, about four inches by four inches, which had been folded up, until the doctor examined it.

"This," the baby-faced physician said, "was in the deceased's left shoe . . . under a loose flap at the heel."

Protocol might have deemed Anderson the first party to examine this discovery; but Philomina Vance stepped forward and snatched it from the young man's fingers, startling him.

"It's a list of names," she said, scanning quickly through narrowed eyes. "A very interesting list of names, at that. . . ."

The doctor was nodding. "That's why I came running— I may be new in this job, but I certainly recognize our foremost passengers when I see them."

She handed the list to Anderson, at whose side I stood; he made no effort to withhold its contents from me, in fact openly shared the scrap of paper with me.

The names, in no apparent order, were Charles Williamson, Marie DePage, Charles Frohman, Elbert Hubbard, George Kessler, and Alfred Vanderbilt. Next to each name was a number.

I looked at Anderson curiously, and he anticipated my question: "Cabin numbers."

Miss Vance asked, "And those are, in fact, the correct designations?"

Anderson nodded. "This isn't just a list of our most famous, prestigious passengers . . . but a inventory of where to find them."

"What can it mean?" the doctor asked.

Anderson glared at the young man. "That is not your concern, Doctor."

"Well, I didn't mean to—"

"Your job is to deal with the dead, and to keep mum about it. Understood?"

The young doctor nodded, his cheeks crimson.

I had a feeling an irritation had been building in Anderson due to Miss Vance's take-charge demeanor, and the poor wet-behind-the-ears doc had taken the brunt . . . the staff captain being too much of a gentleman to dress down a woman, who was after all the ship's official detective.

Anderson turned to Miss Vance, but as he spoke, his eyes flicked to me occasionally. "I have alerted the captain, and he has requested an update, and audience with both of you."

"When, pray tell?" Miss Vance asked pleasantly.

"He should be ready for us, now . . . Doctor. Carry on."

The doctor swallowed, said, "Yes, sir," rather meekly, and attended his dead patient.

Soon we were moving through the deserted, cavernous first-class dining saloon, three abreast. Miss Vance, perhaps sensing a growing aggravation in Anderson, said nothing. I, of course, threw caution to the wind.

"What do you make of the list?" I asked. "Why room numbers?"

Anderson's expression was blank. "I would hesitate to speculate. . . . Miss Vance, have you a thought?"

Seizing the opening, she said, "It could be a list of targets . . . assassination targets."

That, frankly, had not occurred to me, and it stopped me momentarily in my tracks; but I quickly caught up with them—Anderson hadn't missed a beat, this dire possibility apparently having dawned on him, as well.

"It would certainly be demoralizing to the British government," Anderson said, "should such important parties be lost while under our protection."

"You can't be serious," I said. "The Germans don't want the United States in your damned war! Why, killing the likes of Vanderbilt and Hubbard and the rest, that would incite Americans to the point of hysteria."

We were in the Grand Entrance area now, that bulwark of wicker and ferns, the elevators and staircase opposite us.

Anderson had flinched at the phrase "damned war," but his response did not indicate any offense had been taken. "Politics is Greek to me," he said. "Still, I doubt your country would go to war over such killings; but the embarrassment to Great Britain, I should say, would be most devastating."

On the elevator, Miss Vance said to Anderson, who stood between us, "Assassination isn't the only purpose that list might hold."

Anderson looked sideways at her, brow knit. "Can you tell me another?"

"These are rich people—don't forget, I'm here in part to guard Madame DePage's charity chest, which is itself a small fortune. Perhaps that list is meant to direct these stowaways . . . posing as stewards . . . to those cabins—for plunder."

The elevator deposited us at the Grand Entrance of the Boat Deck, where more wicker and ferns awaited. Anderson paused there, his patience obviously wearing thin.

"Miss Vance," he said, "these are spies—German spies."

Her smile was cheerfully professional. "And may I remind you that the darkroom found nothing at all on their camera plates?"

This was the first I'd heard of that; but I didn't see it as significant: We'd merely captured the espionage agents too early for them to indulge in their information gathering.

Anderson said something of a similar nature to Miss Vance, who replied, "Why do you assume theft and sabotage are mutually exclusive concerns?"

The staff captain's eyes tightened and his head titled to one side—this was an interesting question.

She continued: "Why not commit espionage and/or sabotage, with a side dish of thievery. . . . If they were planning to wait until near the end of the voyage, off Ireland, our three 'tourists' may well have been picked up by members of the IRA, who are in collusion with Germany, after all."

Miss Vance never ceased to amaze me. I said, "You mean they could be funding IRA efforts to aid the German cause?"

"They could. Or they could be saboteurs taking advantage of their proximity to so much wealth, to do their country's foul bidding even while feathering their own nests."

I nodded. "Perhaps it had been offered as an incentive, in undertaking a perilous task?"

"Perhaps."

Anderson seemed weary. He was really not up to this level of deliberative assessment, and I felt anything further Miss Vance offered would fall on deaf ears. What the staff captain said next confirmed my suspicion.

"With all due respect," Anderson said to her, "I must request that you refrain from sharing with the captain any of these far-fetched theories."

"I thought he'd requested my presence," she said, "for me to make a full report."

Anderson twitched a humorless smile and shrugged. "Use your own judgment, then."

The captain's suite of rooms took up the forward end of the Boat Deck, adjacent to the raised officer's house on the navigating bridge. Anderson knocked on the middle of three unlabelled doors and a deep voice from within bellowed, "Come!"

We entered.

This was a day room—even if it was three in the morning—with white walls relieved by oak wainscotting and the occasional framed nautical print and a ship's wheel clock; the furniture was Colonial and the effect spartan. A round maple table with four chairs was central, and on the table was a tray with tea service.

The old boy—though in his late fifties, he seemed nearer seventy—was smoking a pipe and pacing; he was wrapped up in a dark blue dressing gown, which somehow conveyed a military bearing, an effect undercut by his white pajama trousers and brown leather slippers. His thinning white hair was mussed from sleep—he had not bothered to brush it, apparently—and his jutting jaw, flat nose and slitted eyes combined to convey distinct grumpiness.

"Thank you for coming," he said to us, his tone at odds with his words. There were no introductions, no ceremonial handshakes. He simply gestured to chairs at the round table, and offered everyone tea—"Coffee would defeat sleep," he said, "and we do hope to have some yet, tonight, don't we?"

No one pointed out to him that night was long since gone; but everyone accepted his generous offer and Miss Vance volunteered to do the serving, which Captain Turner took her up on, with a gruff, "Thanks."

Turner's big blunt-fingered hands lay on the table like fists waiting to happen, the pipe in one of them; the smoke smelled no worse than burning refuse. His grizzled countenance seemed to accuse, even as his words claimed otherwise: "I want you people to know I appreciate your efforts."

"Thank you, sir," Anderson said.

Miss Vance and I thanked him, as well, and sipped our tea.

"These are dangerous times," the captain said, "and I don't take them lightly."

Had anyone suggested he had?

"I have a boy serving in France," he said. "Artillery officer. And my other boy is in the Merchant Marine . . . also an officer."

There was an implied "of course."

"Seems to me I've spent my life racing Cunard ships against these . . . Germans," he was saying, pausing for a few puffs of his pipe, as if stoking his personal boiler. "Their *Deutschland . . . Kronpriz Wilhelm, Kaiser Wilhelm II,* even this new one, *Kronprizessin Cecile . . .* hah!

My girl *Lusitania* has shown them all her stern."

Miss Vance and I smiled politely; Anderson, too.

"Now here we are racing their goddamned U-boats," he growled, shaking his head. To Miss Vance he said, "Pardon a sailor's salt, ma'am."

"Don't think of me as a woman," Miss Vance said, making an impossible suggestion. "I'm a Pinkerton agent, Captain—and your ship's detective."

The weathered face smiled, but the cold eyes indicated his true opinion of Cunard having hired a female detective.

I risked a question. "How much danger *are* we in from U-boats, Captain?"

"None." He puffed the pipe. "Even at our reduced speed, we'll have no trouble outrunning them."

"Reduced speed?"

One shoulder shrugged, and contempt curled his upper lip, a bit. "The powers that be have ordered me to get by on three of my four boilers—to save coal, and to suit our reduced crew. That takes our top speed down from twenty-six knots to twenty-one . . . cruising speed from twenty-four to eighteen."

"Still, no steamer cruising at even that speed has been torpedoed yet," Anderson said, with an unconvincing off-handedness, shifting in his chair.

"That's reassuring," I said, but it would been more so without the "yet."

Anderson locked eyes with me and said, "Mr. Van Dine, you do understand we've taken you into our confidence. Normally we wouldn't share such information quite so casually . . ." And here the staff captain shot a look at his superior officer. ". . . in front of a newspaper man."

But this point seemed lost on the old boy, who rattled on, "Anyway, even if we were struck by a torpedo, we'd never sink . . . not with our watertight bulkheads."

"That's reassuring, as well," I said.

Anderson had a dazed expression.

"And if we should sink," Captain Turner said, with a fatalistic shrug, "the sinking would be so slow, we'd have plenty of time to get the passengers away in the lifeboats."

"This is all encouraging information," Miss Vance said, "but might I be so bold as to inquire how it relates to the murders of these stowaways?"

Turner sighed smoke, then gestured with the pipe in hand. "My understanding is that they aren't 'murders' at all—it's a falling-out among spies, and they've killed each other, and we're all the better off for it."

Her eyes wide, Miss Vance said, "I suppose that's one way to look at it."

"Young lady," the captain said, "it's the only way. The passengers on this ship, God bless them, came aboard despite alarmist talk of U-boats and sabotage and war. I do not want them unnecessarily burdened with further trepidation."

"Captain," she said, setting her tea cupdown with a clatter, "these men may have an accomplice on your crew—it's no secret the *Lusitania* had to settle for second best, and worse, in assembling—"

"That's a gross exaggeration," Anderson said, bristling.

I was surprised she had broached this—but I noticed she continued to guard her hole card carefully: the cyanide poisoning of the two stabbed cell mates.

Turner patted the air with his pipe in hand. "Let her talk. Let her talk."

Crisply she said, "Someone had to help smuggle those

men aboard. And when the stowaways were captured, perhaps that same someone butchered all three, to cover his tracks."

"Suppose he had," Turner said. "Suppose we have a greedy boy who invited those Krauts aboard. . . . If so, he's no spy, he's no German, just . . . a greedy boy. He's killed our spies for us—our passengers are hardly in any danger now."

Miss Vance seemed stunned by this response, as well she should have been: Its absurdity was worthy of Lewis Carroll, and the captain did after all vaguely resemble Alice's walrus.

"Captain," I said, trying to do my part, "a new piece of troubling evidence has come to light—Mr. Anderson? The list?"

Anderson showed Turner the list from Klaus's shoe, and the captain frowned and asked us what significance we gave it.

Miss Vance presented the two theories—an assassination agenda, or a blueprint for shipboard robbery. Turner listened, entertaining himself with sips of tea and puffs from his pipe.

Then he made an expansive gesture with one hand, saying, "How does this change anything? Don't we still have three dead Germans, who can neither kill nor steal? Don't we still have passengers who deserve to make this crossing without undue trepidation?"

No one had answers to any of that.

So Turner went on: "And here is what we'll do. Those bodies will be moved from the hospital to a refrigeration compartment on the lower deck. . . . See to it, Anderson, that these cadavers are kept quite separate from the beef, mutton, vegetables and so on."

News of that might upset the passengers more than German spies!

"Yes, sir," Anderson said. "We'll store them in ice, sir."

"They have to make the full journey, after all," Turner said, "before we turn them and this entire situation over to the British Secret Service."

Anderson nodded toward Miss Vance. "Our detective has taken the knife in question into her personal custody."

"Well, that's fine," Turner said.

"She has with her fingerprinting equipment, sir."

Turner frowned, pipe in his teeth. "How does that help the situation?"

Miss Vance said, "If I find fingerprints on the knife, I can compare them to our three dead stowaways. If prints belonging to a fourth party are present, we probably have a murderer aboard . . . possibly a crew member."

"What are you suggesting?"

"Well," she said, and she was keeping her tone strictly business-like, "we would fingerprint the crew, to make comparisons."

Turner's eyebrows climbed his forehead. "Ye gods, how long would that take?"

"It can be done gradually, when they're off duty. It's tedious, but easily accomplished . . ."

Those eyebrows were still high. "And if there's no match among the crew?"

She shrugged. "Fingerprinting the passengers might be beyond my capability, under these circumstances . . . but I can assure you the British authorities will not allow anyone off this boat before they themselves have taken this measure."

Turner was shaking his head. "I don't see how I can allow this . . ."

"Captain," Miss Vance said tersely, "you have no choice."

His eyes and nostrils flared. "Oh, don't I? Are you running the ship now, young lady? Is 'detective' a rank above 'captain,' where you come from?"

She was sitting rather stiff-backed. "As a Pinkerton operative, sir, I am an officer of the court. If I have knowledge of a crime, it is not only my duty, but my legal responsibility to report it."

Anderson said, "No one is suggesting that this crime not be reported!"

Gesturing with his pipe in hand, smearing the air with smoke, Turner said, "We're not talking crime, Miss . . . uh, Vance. This is an instance of espionage, and it's a military matter, not a criminal one."

"That's for others to judge," she said.

Turner's pale face began to turn a peculiar shade of purple. "The captain is the only judge on the high seas, my dear . . . and you are sorely trying the patience of the captain."

"Meaning no disrespect, sir, I was hired by Cunard, not by you. I answer to Cunard, to Pinkerton . . . and to the law. I will cooperate with you in every way—both Mr. Van Dine and I have already pledged our confidentiality to Staff Captain Anderson. We have no desire to alarm the passengers, or even the crew . . . in fact, our investigation will proceed more effectively under a similar cloud of secrecy."

"Your 'investigation,' " the captain curtly said, "will consist of checking that knife handle for fingerprints. When you have a result, come to me."

"Yes, sir," she said.

Turner's beady gaze swivelled in my direction. "I've

talked freely in front of you, Mr. Van Dine—and I know it's made Mr. Anderson nervous."

"No need for anxiety," I said. "My intentions are honorable. My goal is to conduct interviews with various passengers—that is all."

That those passengers were the same ones listed on the scrap of paper in the dead man's shoe I did not point out.

Anderson said, "Mr. Van Dine assures me he intends to portray our ship in the best possible light."

Sitting back, puffing his pipe, Captain Turner said, "Very good—Miss Vance, I would like you to help arrange these interviews . . . perhaps starting with your charge, Madame DePage."

"Certainly, Captain."

Turner rose. "Now I would suggest we all try to catch a few hours of sleep. . . . I can tell you that's what I plan."

After a brusque good-bye, we found ourselves back in the hallway.

Anderson confronted his ship's detective. "Most of that was entirely out of line, Miss Vance."

She stood up to him, her nose inches from his. "Let me ask you a simple question, Captain Anderson—how will you feel if one of your passengers turns up murdered?"

He reared back. "Why would—"

But she pressed forward. "And, afterward, it's learned that you and the captain were unconcerned that a killer was at large on this ship . . . that no attempts were made to find him?"

His eyes were wide. "The . . . the stowaways are dead. The danger is past."

"Are you quite sure? Are you certain you know why that list of prime passengers was found in the dead spy's shoe? Do you truly think a man who'd been stabbed in the heart found his way to the next floor before dying?"

Anderson couldn't seem to find any words with which to respond.

"I know you're just trying to do your job," she told him, backing off. "And I'm doing mine. . . . Now, I still have work to do. Unlike Captain Turner, I doubt I'll be 'catching' a few hours sleep."

"Nor will I," Anderson said. He sighed. "I meant no offense, Miss Vance . . . if I spoke out of turn . . ."

"No apology needed. This is an unusual situation—we're all finding our way, as best we can. But if I might be so bold . . . think for yourself, Captain Anderson."

"I don't understand . . ."

She nodded toward the door of the captain's suite. "You'll have to: That salty old bastard doesn't have a brain in his head. . . . Good evening."

Anderson looked as if he'd been poleaxed, and Miss Vance walked quickly down the corridor, and I followed her. We took the stairs, not the elevator, to our floor one deck below.

And then we were walking along the empty corridor where, not long ago at all, a corpse had resided on this very linoleum.

"I'm going to examine that knife handle for prints," she said, at her door.

"Do you need my help?"

"No, thank you. It's a one-person job." She touched my cheek; her flesh was cool. "Get some rest."

I thought about kissing her, but it didn't seem befitting, somehow. So I blew her a kiss instead, and walked down to my room.

I had washed up, and climbed first into my nightshirt

and then beneath my covers, when a sharp knock at the cabin door startled me.

Answering it, I found Miss Vance there—her eyes wide, her face white—and she brushed by me, and sat on my bed. She was in quite a state.

"It's gone!" she said.

I sat next to her—she fully clothed, me in my night-shirt—and asked, "What is gone?"

Her eyes flashed at me. "The knife, you fool—someone took it from my room."

"My God—then there *is* a murderer on the crew!"

She sighed. "Not necessarily—a passenger could have bribed a passkey . . . and, remember, Anderson was concerned about my fingerprinting the crew and/or the passengers, even before Turner brought it up."

"You mean, he could have had someone remove it, just to prevent that inconvenience?"

"Yes . . . these British boneheads have some very peculiar ideas about propriety."

I put an arm around her, and she fell against me—even a strong woman like this could go soft from defeat.

"What good would it do to make accusations?" she wondered aloud. "Suppose they agreed to search the ship—you know damn well that knife has been pitched overboard, long since!"

I could only agree. "What does that leave us? In the eyes of Turner and Anderson, this incident is closed . . . at least until we reach Liverpool, and the British authorities are brought in."

She sat up, eyes brightening. "Has it occurred to you that the late Klaus may have found his way to first class because he had an *accomplice* there?"

"Well, no . . . but why would anyone in first class be

an accomplice to German stowaways . . . ?"

She was smiling, tightly. "That is what we must find out, Van."

"How?"

"By talking to our most likely suspects . . . who I believe are the same names on that list found in the stowaway's shoe."

I was frankly bewildered. "What makes *them* the most likely suspects? Before, you said they were potential victims—either of assassination, or robbery . . ."

"I still consider that a strong possibility. Perhaps the name of the real mastermind was mixed in with the targeted victims to encourage ruling that person out as a suspect."

"You're saying Vanderbilt or Madame DePage might be German spies, or at least in league with them? Or that imbecile Hubbard . . . ?"

But she was on to her next possibility: "Or maybe it was a list of targets *plus* the name of their shipboard contact, in first class! Right down to the cabin number!"

"Vance, is that really likely?"

She cast that glittering predatory gaze on me again. "However you look at it, these same six names have turned up twice: first, in those warning telegrams; next, in a list that was in the dead stowaway's possession . . . which directly ties those six people to that murdered man."

"I suppose it does. But how?"

"That," she said, "would seem to be the question . . . and since you have to interview them anyway, who besides S.S. Van Dine will have a better opportunity to find out?"

And to seal the bargain, she kissed me.

NINE

C'est La Guerre

The alarm clock that woke me was a powerful bellow, like the mournful cry of some mythical sea beast—in reality, of course, the ship's foghorn. I'd made arrangements to meet Miss Vance for the second breakfast sitting, and could well have rolled over and gone back to sleep; but the events of the day previous had been so intense, that when I'd awakened, so had countless thoughts and myriad questions.

After toiletries that included a refreshing shower and a trimming of my beard, I dressed in a gray houndstooth-check suit and walked out onto the wide sheltered promenade, which was lined with deck chairs, none currently in use. In fact, I seemed to have the rail all to myself as I gazed out where the endless expanse of ocean should be, seeing instead an impenetrable whiteness. The ship's foghorn—half roar, half moan—blew its melancholy warning out into the swirling nothingness, and no doubt keen eyes on the bridge were at this moment searching for any sign of another ship, whose dark blur might loom abruptly, and perilously, out of the shroud of fog.

The great ship might well have been suspended in mid-air, a misty hand gripping her all around and underneath, freezing her in place. Though the ship may have seemed motionless, surely it had not stopped but only slowed*— soon the *thrump* of the bow cutting through a wave put the illusion to rest.

The otherworldly, almost surreal atmosphere gave me a chill, though the weather was mild enough—weren't murders enough? Must Nature herself conspire to make the *Lusitania* a ghost ship?

Such thoughts were forgotten, however, when (perhaps an hour later) I repaired to the First Class Dining Saloon, where I joined the lovely—and astonishingly refreshed-looking—Miss Vance. She again was boldly hatless, and her attire striking, her Gibson-girl figure nearly done justice by the dark green satin dress with yoke-style over-blouse and much lighter green high standing collar and sleeves.

Once more our tablemates were Madame DePage and her colleague Dr. Houghton, and (across from them) Miss Pope and her young paramour, Mr. Friend. Again, I had gone directly to Madame DePage to thank her for allowing me to join with their little group.

---

*Van Dine's sense that the liner had reduced speed was correct, though by mid-morning of Sunday, May 2, the fog had cleared, and the order for "full astern" again was given. By noon, the *Lusitania* had logged only 501 nautical miles, putting her south of Nova Scotia—meager progress for a ship that had once set a record of 617 miles in a day. With a reduced number of boilers operating, and the battery of 192 furnaces only three-quarters fired, the ship was capable of little more.

"Please consider yourself one of us," she said, "for the remainder of the voyage."

I asked if we might sit down for that interview today sometime, and she said most certainly—would this morning in the music room, at eleven, be convenient? It would. After a few other morning pleasantries, the three couples—Miss Vance and I comprising the third—fell into their private conversations.

These conversations were limited, however, as the ship's banquet of a breakfast took up much of one's attention. We chose between fruit or fruit juice, followed by a selection of oatmeal, grape nuts, malted milk or hominy; then kippers, turbot, lemon sole or Yarmouth bloaters; eggs to order or sauteed calf's liver; and Cumberland lamb or Wiltshire bacon and Cumberland lamb, with a side of baked apples or pancakes. About that point a waiter offered from a tray of cold cuts an array of ham, beef, smoked ox tongue and capon. And there of course were oatcakes, toasted muffins and scones . . . with tea, coffee or cocoa. For those disappointed in such light fare, special orders of steak, mutton chops or chicken were available from the grill.

I ate heartily, despite my knowledge of the corpses sharing the cold storage compartments, and so did Miss Vance, whose pragmatic nature continued to impress.

"Are you planning to attend the morning's divine services?" Miss Vance asked me, between nibbles of scone.

"My mother and father were deeply religious," I said, and took a sip of coffee before continuing. "Sober citizens and devout churchgoers. . . . They saw to it that in my youth I attended enough services to last my lifetime."

"Captain Turner's conducting the services in the main lounge," she said, a twinkle in her eyes. "No doubt asking for blessings on the king and all those at sea."

"A religious service as served up by Bowler Bill surely would have its rewards, as entertainment if not theology."

Across from us, Miss Pope was discussing religious matters as well, in her own unique way—specifically, the glories of Sir Oliver Lodge, the spiritualist.

"I would imagine," Miss Vance said, "that as little as the captain likes rubbing shoulders with passengers, the Sunday service must seem one of those 'perils of the sea' to which the prayer books allude."

Keeping my voice a near whisper—the orchestra was silent at breakfast, the only music the chatter of conversion and the clink and clank of china and silver—I said to her, "I believe we need to make amends to Staff Captain Anderson."

Miss Vance nodded. "Yes—things grew tense last night. Perhaps I made an inappropriate remark or two."

"In my view, you were all too easy on these Cunard clods . . . but we need Anderson on our side, to help our other interviews. Don't you think that steward Leach should be questioned? And Master-at-Arms Williams?"

With a thoughtful frown, she said, "I do . . . but not just yet. I consider them . . . and for that matter, Mr. Anderson himself . . . suspects."

I was buttering a muffin. "I assume that is why you withheld certain information from Anderson and Captain Turner last night . . . information of a bluish, almond-scented variety."

Nodding again, she said, "If one of them is either a murderer or an accomplice to the stowaways—"

"Or both," I cut in.

"—or both . . . then better to give that unknown party a false sense of security. After all, we're stuck on this

boat for the better part of a week—no one's going any-
where, just yet."

"Particularly not the stowaways," I said, as those conversing—and feasting—around us remained blissfully unaware of the tragedy and danger in their midst.

Perhaps an hour later, Miss Vance and I were walking
on the open-air promenade on the Boat Deck—the fog
had been replaced by bright morning sunshine, touching
the vast shimmering blue with golden highlights—and
quite by accident encountered Staff Captain Anderson.

The square-jawed, burly Anderson was aft of us, and
had not yet seen us, being otherwise occupied—he raised
a silver whistle to his lips and blew a shrill command.
Miss Vance and I glanced at each other curiously, and
positioned ourselves along the rail, watching. A handful
of crew members suddenly appeared from here and there,
like ants sensing sugar at a picnic, climbing into life jackets to which they affixed badges with the number fourteen
on them.

The lifeboats were slung from davits above the rail,
turning their portions of the generously wide Boat Deck
into narrow walkways.* Right now those crew members
were clambering up and into the hanging lifeboat—boldly
numbered fourteen—which swung a little during the
course of the exercise. Soon the sailors were sitting

---

*Crew drills on the *Lusitania* invariably alternated between the same
two emergency boats, Number 13 and Number 14; lowering the boats—
a tricky procedure—was not part of the drill. Hard-sided lifeboats on
the ship numbered twenty-two, odd numbers hanging starboard, even
hanging portside; stored in cradles underneath these conventional boats
were twenty-six "collapsibles," folding boats consisting of a shallow
wooden keel with canvas sides.

straight and trim within the suspended boat.

Then Anderson blew his whistle again, and the sailors leapt from the boat onto the deck and disappeared like those same ants scurrying back to their hills.

We approached Staff Captain Anderson, who seemed to frown just a little when he saw us, but I could not be certain.

We both bid him good morning, and I said jovially, "You look surprisingly well-rested, after such a long night."

My remark seemed to put him at ease, and he said good morning to us, adding, "It was indeed a long night, Mr. Van Dine. . . . However, the two of you look none the worse for wear, I must admit."

I patted my stomach. "If I can survive all this food . . . Miss Vance and I were just walking off a hundred or so courses of breakfast."

A simple soul, Anderson beamed, proud of his ship and the service it delivered to its passengers. "We do try to keep our guests well-fed. People have come to expect a steamer to be a floating gourmet banquet."

"The *Lusitania* fills that bill easily. . . . What were you up to, there, Captain? If you don't mind my asking."

"Oh, I was conducting a lifeboat drill."

"It's all very well drilling your crew," Miss Vance said, already risking the staff captain's enmity, "but why aren't you drilling the passengers?"

His affability remained. "Captain Turner doesn't consider it necessary for passengers to take part in these drills."

I said, "What's your opinion?"

"Cunard doesn't pay me to have opinions on subjects that the captain has already formed one about."

Miss Vance was shaking her head. "With all this talk of U-boats and torpedoes, I should think a drill would provide the passengers comfort and reassurance."

Now the strain was showing in his tightening features. "Captain Turner does not care to have the passengers unduly alarmed."

The subject seemed closed, so I inquired about Anderson helping me with certain celebrated passengers.

"I'm sitting down to talk with Madame DePage this morning," I said. "Could you possibly arrange for another interview or two for the afternoon?"

"Certainly. Any preference of order?"

"None."

"Consider it done."

"Thank you."

Miss Vance decided to press her luck, and asked if she might make a small suggestion.

"Of course," Anderson said, but not terribly enthusiastically.

"Would you please have the rooms of Mr. Leach and Mr. Williams thoroughly searched? Preferably without their knowledge."

"I've already done so."

Miss Vance brightened at this news. "Splendid. And?"

The staff captain shrugged. "Nothing untoward was discovered. And we've heard nothing from you on the fingerprinting subject—what have you discovered?"

"Oh, the process is a slow one," she lied. "I won't know whether that blade has prints for several days."

"I see," he said, seemingly accepting that absurdity. He tipped his cap. "Do please keep us informed. . . . Mr. Van Dine, I'll leave word with the switchboard about those interviews."

I thanked him, and he strode aft, disappearing through a doorway.

"Interesting fib," I said to her, with a smile.

"I was studying him as I spoke," she said soberly. "He betrayed nothing."

"Probably because he had nothing to betray."

She sighed. "Probably."

We walked amidst the affluent passengers of Saloon Class, on deck decked out in their Sunday finery, fresh from divine services, derbies and boaters on the men, the chapeaus on their ladies no more elaborate than your average wedding cake. The wide open-air deck, narrowing when a davit-slung lifeboat interrupted with a reminder of reality, was the avenue down which these swells strolled in a manner seemingly oblivious to the hazards of ocean travel during wartime.

The *Lusitania*—like any great ship—was a city unto itself, almost a world unto itself; but I could not keep my mind from taunting me with the knowledge of three murders recently committed under the uninformed noses of these Sunday saunterers.

Time came when Miss Vance and I retired to her cabin, where we went over in some tedious and repetitious detail the facts and experiences of the day (and night) previous. I will not bore the reader with this, and admit no new insights were garnered. But it seems to be human nature to beat a dead horse, or in our case, a murdered trio of stowaways.

The First Class Lounge and Music Room, where my interview with Madame DePage took place, was aft of the Boat Deck's Grand Entrance, an enormous* chamber ri-

*Sixty-eight feet by fifty-two feet.

valing the domed dining saloon in elegance.

Decorated in a late-Georgian style, panelled in inlaid mahogany, the lounge boasted its own domed ceiling with ornate plasterwork surrounding stained-glass panels through which sunlight filtered during the day (with electric bulbs to light the night). An apple-green color scheme unified the floral carpet with cushions and drapes, and marble fireplaces bookended the chamber forward and aft, over which were elaborately framed enameled panels of dignified if dull landscapes. For all its size, the lounge created coziness through arrangements of its satinwood and mahogany furnishings, which included easy chairs and overstuffed settees and tables just large enough for cards or snacks.

In a corner of the lounge, near a grand piano that bore silent witness, Madame DePage—in stylish black again, with a hat bearing one black feather and a white one— sat regally in an arm chair with Miss Vance on her left and me on her right.

The dark-haired, dark-eyed beauty was the only person beside myself and certain crew members aware that Philomina Vance was the ship's detective—and that Miss Vance's role as her travelling companion was something of a ruse. Still, guarding the funds Belgium's lovely envoy had raised for the Red Cross was a significant part of the Pinkerton agent's assignment.

Nonetheless, we had decided not to share with Madame DePage the true facts, regarding the existence (much less the demise) of the stowaways. Miss Vance and I were, on the one hand, complying with the wishes for confidentiality of the two captains; but, also, Marie DePage was a possible suspect as an accomplice to the Germans, if not their murderer; and, in any event, an undeniable key figure in the affair.

She had, after all, received one of the warning telegrams, and her name had been on the chief stowaway's list.

Which meant she may have been targeted for robbery—or even death—by the late saboteurs.

I was armed with a pencil and a secretary's spiral-bound notebook, dutifully taking down the rather stale "news" the charming, charismatic woman was sharing with me.

"I tour your beautiful country," she said, her accent turning syllables into poetry, "for two month."

She meant "months," of course, but such lapses in her otherwise admirable mastery of English only made her seem all the more charming.

"This effort was for the Belgian Red Cross," I said, pencil poised.

"*Oui*—my husband, Antoine, is Surgeon General of the Belgian Army, and director of the Queen's Hospital at La Panne. That is where I find this passion."

"At the hospital, you mean?"

The dark eyes flashed, and so did a lovely white smile. "Yes—I visit the wounded soldier there, talk to them, write letters to their family for them. Soldier from both side! German boys, too. One say to me, 'Madame, why do you write for me? I am your enemy.' And I say, 'To me you are just a wounded boy who needs help.' They are all . . . you know the expression? *Enfants perdus?*"

I did. Lost children—soldiers sent to certain death in war.

Despite her smile, her eyes had welled with tears, and Miss Vance handed her a handkerchief.

"You must excuse me," Madame DePage said, dabbing at her tear-pearled lashes. "You see, my son, Lucien, he is seventeen. I have just learn, a few days ago, that he has . . . join the army."

Miss Vance turned to me. "That's why Madame De-Page booked last-minute passage on the *Lusitania* . . . to see her boy before he goes to the Western front."

This apparently was why no better arrangements had been made to transport the $150,000 in cash she'd raised for war relief, than for her to transport those funds herself . . . with the help of the Pinkerton agency.

I politely listened—and made a record of—her impassioned description of her impoverished, war-torn country. But I was confused.

"Hasn't Belgium already fallen to Germany?" I asked, chagrined that something so important to her was so vague to me.

"All but this leetle small tiny corner of my country," she said liltingly, "in the northwest . . . that is where our hospital is." She glanced around the opulent room, where wealthy travellers lounged, playing cards, conversing, having a bite to eat between shipboard repasts. "It is hard to be here . . . in such luxury . . . *c'est-à-dire,* to have enjoyment while others suffer."

"People like these," I reminded her, meaning the rich passengers of the ship, "made generous donations to your cause."

According to an article I'd read in the *News*, her final and very successful stop had been on Fifth Avenue, where she spoke to a wealthy bunch called the Special Relief Society; and the J.P. Morgan Company was one of her fund-raising tour's chief sponsors.

"Please do not misunderstand, monsieur—in Pitts-

burgh, in Washington, D.C., the response . . . the gener-
osity . . . it was tremendous. The people of your country
have large heart . . . liberty, they love. But the big conflict
of this war is still in the future. The worst fighting, yet to
come. We must foresee the coming slaughter, and be prepare to help the t'ousands of wounded, friend or foe. . . .
I tell my American friend . . ."

She meant "friends."

". . . this war, in the night, like a thief, it will come for
you." She shrugged. *"C'est la guerre."*

"Madame," I said, "as a friend . . . I hope I might consider myself such?"

"Ça va sans dire!" she said, which meant, "that goes
without saying."

"And this is not for publication—merely comes from
my own personal interest and concern. . . . Have you received any threats of any kind, during your stay in America?"

She frowned, shook her head. "No . . . the letters, they
have all been on my side . . . usually with money in them,
I am please to say."

"No malicious phone calls, either, at the hotels or
homes where you stayed?"

"Nothing . . . not even from the pro–German-American
. . . and I know there are some."

Strangely, it occurred to me at that instant that I was
no longer as pro-German as I'd been the day before! Encountering saboteurs aboard the ship on which one is sailing can do that to a person.

"Though the Allied cause is in my heart," she was saying, "I am a neutral because of my work. . . . I do not
discuss the atrocity, to stir passion for the people to open
their heart and wallet. No, I speak only of the suffering

of boys on both side, of the starvation of the noncombatant in this tiny strip from Nieuport along the Yaer to the
French frontier . . . ten mile wide, forty mile long."

"Madame, I know you feel great compassion for the
boys fighting on either side of this conflict."

"*Bien entendu* . . . but of course."

"Prior to boarding, were you approached by any young
men to aid them in returning to their homes?"

"I do not understand."

"German boys, stranded in America . . ."

She shook her head again. "This would be a good place
for them, America, where they would have no guns to
shoot at the Belgian boy."

That had seemed unlikely, her aiding the stowaways;
but I'd had to inquire, however elliptically.

Trying again, I asked, "Has anyone approached you on
the ship, and struck up an acquaintance? By this I mean,
someone you had not met previously."

She shrugged. "On shipboard, this happen all the time.
You yourself, monsieur, this describes."

That was true. But I pressed on: "I mean someone unknown to you prior to boarding, who has made some effort to get close to you."

A new friend, taken into the madame's confidence,
might well have robbery in mind.

Thoughtfully, she said, "I had not met before Miss
Pope—but I knew of her, hear of her, we have the mutual
friend. . . . She is an architect, you know, a designer of
library, a leader of the party Progressive."

And a lunatic who believed in spooks and fairies.

"Anyone else?"

She nodded. "There is a Dr. Fisher—Howard Fisher.

He travel with his wife's young sister, a Miss Connor, Dorothy Connor."

Fisher, she said, wanted to help his British brother-in-law establish a hospital in France.

"They say they would like to join forces with my husband at La Panne," she said.

"But you'd never heard of them before. And they are first-class passengers?"

"*Oui.*"

I wrote down their names. Later I would ask Miss Vance to investigate them, to which she readily agreed.

"I've focused on your war efforts," I said. "Is there anyone on the ship that you knew previously—someone out of your personal life who you did not expect to see? Anyone with a grudge?"

"*Au contraire* . . . but for my friend Dr. Houghton, who go to assist my husband at La Panne."

"How long have you known Dr. Houghton?"

"A few week—he is from a town in New York . . . Troy."

"He sought you out?"

"Yes—at one of the rally where I raise the money."

I had already jotted the good doctor's name down, and would request Miss Vance investigate him, as well.

"These question," she said, and her eyes were amused and yet her aspect remained one of *tristesse*, "they are not for your newspaper, no?"

"No." I glanced at Miss Vance for help.

"Madame," the lady Pinkerton said, "Mr. Van Dine and I have become good friends . . ."

The regal woman smiled. "Perhaps he is the man I hear in your room last night?"

This astonished both of us, but Madame DePage only

laughed, the weight of the war finally disappearing from her shoulders. "I am French. Do you think I would judge you? . . . You know the expression *le coeur a ses raisons que la raison ne connait point?*"

The heart has reasons of which reason knows nothing.

Suddenly I wondered just how friendly she and Dr. Houghton had become, no matter how dedicated she might be to her husband and his cause.

"*A la belle étoile,*" I said, "who knows what harmless time might pass, aboard a ship like this?"

Madame DePage smiled, eyes atwinkle, nodding her approval of starry nights and shipboard romance.

"Mr. Van Dine and I have become friends," Miss Vance said, trying again—and this was the first time I'd seen this calm and collected woman show any sign of embarrassment, "and he is helping me investigate. We believe a ring of thieves may be aboard the ship."

She did not mention that the members of this ring—at least, the three German stowaways—were in cold storage.

"I see," Madame DePage said. "And you seek the *faux bonhomme*? The false friend, who tries to become close?"

"Yes," I said. "Even a crew member who you might find in your room, seemingly quite innocent. . . . Ask yourself, does he belong here? Is he serving some ship's purpose, or his own?"

The lovely envoy nodded and smiled. "Your concern is appreciated, monsieur. But I think the . . . Miss Vance, what is the word? . . . The precautions we have take, this will make the effort of any thief foolish. . . . And now I must bring our conversation to a close. I wish some time in my suite before luncheon—can you believe it is almost time to eat again?"

She rose, bid us bonjour, and Miss Vance and I were

suddenly alone in our nook of the lavish lounge.

"Madame DePage does seem a terribly unlikely suspect," I said.

Miss Vance had shifted to the chair vacated by Marie DePage, to sit closer. "I would agree—and the time I've spent with her, which is considerable, only underscores that notion."

"Nonetheless, we had to have this interview."

"Oh yes."

"And we did learn some things."

It was at this point that I suggested Miss Vance investigate Dr. Fisher and his sister-in-law, Dorothy Connor, and Dr. Houghton, madame's male companion. She said she would wire Pinkerton to make what she called "background checks" on all of them—which she of course had already put into motion for the crew members Williams and Leach.

"What are these precautions to which madame referred?" I asked her. "What secrets are you keeping from me, Vance?"

She arched an eyebrow, and her half-smile dug a dimple in her left cheek. "After last night, Van, I would say precious few."

I did not blush. "If you don't trust me, well then . . . you don't trust me."

Miss Vance touched my hand. "I would be violating Pinkerton procedures."

"It's really none of my business. None of my concern."

"Don't pout! It's not manly. . . ." She leaned conspiratorially close, her tone shifting from quiet to near whisper. "Madame DePage has a steamer trunk in her suite. Inside is a locked strongbox in which one hundred and fifty thousand dollars, in cash, resides."

I frowned. "How is this a precaution?"

She shrugged in a matter-of-fact manner. "The bills are counterfeit."

I sat back, eyes wide. "What? But surely that's illegal. . . ."

"Not in this instance. In cooperation with the U.S. Secret Service, Pinkerton placed this fake money, as bait, in madame's possession. Should it be stolen, and the culprits not apprehended aboard ship, those counterfeit bills will lead the authorities to them. Lists of those bills will be distributed internationally."

"That is clever," I admitted. "And the real money is in safekeeping?"

"It's somewhere in my cabin," she said. "Isn't that enough information for you?"

It was. But I did have to wonder if it had been in her mattress—if so, I'd never been that close to so much money in my life.

Then it was time for the first luncheon sitting, though I stopped by the switchboard first—seemed we had appointments this afternoon with George Kessler, Charles Frohman and Elbert Hubbard . . . and the latter one would no doubt try my digestion.

TEN

Money Bags

Charles Frohman's suite was on the starboard side of the ship. With the exception of last evening's meal, Frohman had apparently not ventured out of his quarters since boarding; and he was not your typically blustery theatrical character, despite a propensity for surrounding himself with specimens of that obnoxious breed.

I was aware of him by reputation, vaguely at least—Frohman was one of the best-known and most beloved men in New York—but it was Miss Vance, that delightful actress turned detective, who prepared me for the interview.

"It's rather remarkable," she told me over luncheon, "that he agreed to see us at all."

"And why is that?" I asked.

"Well, the word is he's surprisingly shy, considering his profession—they call him 'the Silent Man.' He never solicits interviews and his celebrity is something he himself has never encouraged."

Charles Frohman, she explained with respect and even awe, was widely credited with raising the standards of the American theater, almost single-handedly dragging it out of the muck of disrepute, where fifty years ago John Wilkes Booth and his pistol had sent it crashing.

In an effort to see to it that the authors and actors he favored received proper exposure, Frohman bought theater after theater; he often had as many as eight new plays in rehearsal at once—and upward of five hundred companies touring. He became much more than just a business manager to these clients—he was friend, confident, father confessor and artistic adviser. This galaxy included Maude Adams, Ellen Terry, Otis Skinner, Ethel Barrymore, William Gillette and many more.

Frohman insisted on quality—mounting well-written plays, as intelligent as they were entertaining (Miss Vance said)—and employing actors whose talent was matched by private lives clean of scandal. Miss Vance felt that the American theater was now on an equal footing with its European counterpart, and acting would soon achieve a level of respectability equal to any of the professions.

I took in this information gratefully, along with the rest of my meal, and did not point out to her how ridiculous these last few assertions struck me. My silence may have been hypocritical, but even a man of letters knows when to shut up, around a woman of pulchritude.

Standing outside the door of Frohman's suite, Miss Vance and I exchanged smiles—the rather raucous strains of "Alexander's Ragtime Band" were bleeding through. I knocked several times—firmly, to be heard over Irving Berlin.

The music ceased, and in short order the door opened, and we were met by Frohman's valet, a slender, cheerful, rather effeminate young man in a dark gray suit. The valet showed us into the study of the suite, which was in the Colonial style.* A desk against the wall was piled with play manuscripts; an occasional table next to it bore an elaborate ship-shaped basket filled with flowers and fruit.

The frog prince of a producer was perched on a damask print settee by an open porthole—though he'd confined himself to his quarters, he could at least smell the sea air—and his squat frame was wrapped up in a burgundy silk smoking jacket, a script folded open and in his lap. His left slippered foot was on a padded stool, and his cane leaned against the sofa near his right hand. On a round table next to him was an array of dishes filled with various bite-size chocolate candies and salted nuts; and on a matching round table, on the opposite side of the settee, a gramophone rested with a stack of cylindrical discs— the source of that ragtime tune.

"I must apologize for not rising," Frohman said. His voice was a nasal, soft-spoken baritone, pleasant enough, but unsuited for the stage. "My rheumatism can be a de- manding travelling companion, when it's so inclined— and it is, this trip, I'm afraid."

I introduced Miss Vance, and myself, and shook hands with him—his hand was small, almost dainty, surprising for such a roly-poly fellow—and we took chairs on either side of him, pulled in to face him.

---

*The suites had been decorated by various well-known English firms in such styles as Empire, Georgian, Queen Anne, Sheraton, Louis XV, Louis XVI and Colonial, with panelling and furniture utilizing satin- wood, mahogany, sycamore and walnut. Suites and "special cabins" had modelled ceilings, ornamental lights and gilt fittings on doors and fur- niture.

Homely as he was—his head was as squashed as a Hallowe'en pumpkin—his genial, self-deprecating nature soon lent him an attractiveness of character that dispelled his physical shortcomings.

Almost immediately he put Miss Vance at her ease, winning her over entirely.

"I know you!" he said, eyes sparking. "Philomina Vance—I saw you in *East Lynne*, at the Chicago Theater!"

She touched her bosom. "I had no idea you were there, sir!"

"We won't have any of this 'sir' nonsense—my friends call me C.F. And I must insist we be friends . . . William! Ginger ales all around."

William had been sitting on the other side of the room, reading a magazine; he rose and fetched.

Frohman's cheeks plumped further as he beamed at Miss Vance. "You were quite wonderful—I know it was negligent of me, not to come backstage and meet you."

"How I wish you had . . ."

"We'd never been introduced, and I felt it would be a breech of etiquette."

"Sir . . . C.F.—in our business, such propriety is put aside! If you don't mind my saying, you're royalty, in the theater . . . and a king never has to stand on ceremony."

Still smiling, he shook his head. "My dear, ceremony is all a king has to stand on—not that I'm a king. A little success doesn't warrant abandoning good manners, or common courtesy. . . . It was my intention to have one of my agents call you, but shortly after that performance, you left the theatrical profession, I understand."

"I did," she said, "though if I'd had a call from Charles Frohman, I might *not* have!"

His interest seemed genuine. "And how is that you've become a journalist?"

"If I might interrupt," I said, "Miss Vance is not the journalist—I am."

He nodded. "And I understand, Mr. Van Dine, you're with Samuel McClure—which is why I consented to your interview. I admire the muckraking Mr. McClure very much."

"I'm sure he'll be delighted to hear that. . . . Miss Vance is a friend, helping me out, you might say."

"Such charming company is always a help," he said to me. Then to Miss Vance, he said, "Should you ever decide to return to the theater, my dear, let me know. You cut a commanding figure, on the Chicago stage, and New York needs to know of you."

Miss Vance was blushing from all this, and her delight was clear. "You're very kind, C.F. Very kind."

William brought everyone glasses of iced ginger ale.

"Help yourselves to the goodies," Frohman said, even as he was doing so with chocolate kisses from one of the bowls. "I'm afraid I have a fierce sweet tooth . . . and I've passed along my confection infection to William. . . . Isn't that right, William?"

"Yes, it is," William said with smile, regarding his employer with obvious fondness, before returning to his chair elsewhere in the room.

"We had a regular dessert orgy last night," Frohman chuckled.

I was beginning to wonder how chocolate had figured into that; but I was not here to pry into such things—I had several other agendas. I began with my duties for the *News.* . . .

"I understand you visit London twice yearly," I said,

"to scout new plays and discover acting talent."

One of Frohman's specialties was introducing American actors to English audiences—and English actors to American audiences.

"I'm afraid I've fallen back to once a year," he said. "These trips have become increasingly difficult for me."

The articular rheumatism had developed after a fall on the porch of his home at White Plains three years before; ever since, he'd been a virtual prisoner in a suite at the Knickerbocker Hotel in Manhattan. Travel might have seemed an escape, if it hadn't aggravated his condition so severely.

"That's why I booked passage on this ship," he said. "The *Lucy*'s the fastest ship on the Atlantic—and I can have the trip over and done with, as quickly as possible."

Miss Vance asked, "Have you ever considered sending one of your staff to go to London, to see the new productions?"

"I've been tempted—but, in truth, I don't trust anyone else's judgment . . . Whether a play works, or an actor has talent, that's something I feel here . . ." And he tapped his ample belly with a forefinger.

I asked, "Weren't you wary of this talk of U-boats?"

"Frankly, I was. . . . My friends at the German Club . . . Captain Boy-Ed and Colonel Van Papen . . . advised me, in rather cryptic fashion, not to sail on this ship."

This was an interesting wrinkle.

He was going on about the others who had tried to convince him not to travel on the *Lusitania*, which included many of his famous clients. Isadora Duncan and her dance troupe, and actress Ellen Terry, had cancelled their reservations on this ship to cross on the slower *New York*.

"The U-boat rumors are all about the *Lucy*," Frohman said. "And taking an American liner is probably safer than sailing on a British ship . . . but the faster the better, for me."

"Worth the risk?"

"Worth the risk. How can anyone take this German bluster so seriously? But so many people are."

"You're of German descent, obviously . . ."

He nodded, and frowned. "A German-American, yes. That doesn't make me pro-German. But it does make me pro-American."

"America isn't in this war."

"Yet. When we are, German-Americans like me will stand behind the Stars and Stripes. As a Jew, I know all too well of prejudice. . . . Now I see my fellow German-Americans already being viewed through a prism of bias."

I made sure to write that down—that was a nice turn of phrase: "prism of bias."

"For that reason, I'm producing a new play by the novelist Justus Miles Foreman. . . . I'll introduce you, he's crossing with us . . . that deals with this subject. Opens in Boston in two weeks. *The Hyphen,* it's called . . . and it refers to the hyphen in the term German-American."

I raised an eyebrow. "That would seem to be yet another risk you're taking."

He waved that off with a pudgy hand, right before it dipped back into the bowl of chocolates. "The arts . . . even the popular arts . . . must take a stand. I'm hoping to find a producer in Britain for the play, as well."

That seemed optimistic.

"Of course," he continued, "this trend to musicals and slangy 'mystery' plays threaten thoughtful drama, and the drawing-room comedy . . . though I'm not really worried about these so-called 'movies'—we won't live to see them become more popular than the stage."

I had enough for the *News*—it was time to reveal the role Miss Vance was truly playing. With a nod, I cued her.

"C.F.," she said, "you may have noticed that I'm travelling with Madame DePage."

He had.

She briefly explained her function as ship's detective, and his eyes widened—he was fascinated by this, and they spoke for perhaps five minutes about her departure from the stage to the Pinkerton Agency.

"We are concerned about a theft ring aboard," she told him.

He shifted, and pain tightened his face momentarily. "It's rumored Madame DePage is travelling with the funds she raised."

"I have heard that rumor," Miss Vance said with a smile.

"Which is why you are her devoted companion. I also believe George Kessler . . . an old acquaintance, if something of a blowhard . . . may be foolishly travelling with . . . well, that's not for me to say."

But it was for me to note, both mentally and literally.

Miss Vance sat forward. "Are you travelling with any valuables or a large amount of money? Sir, you can trust us . . . Staff Captain Anderson has already vouched—"

"It's 'C.F.,'" he said, "and as a matter of fact, yes, I am travelling with a considerable amount of cash. Normally, I would have funds in various English banks, but we had . . . there's no use trying to disguise the fact . . . some financial reverses. Last year was a bad one for my theater syndicate."

"So," I said, picking up on this, "you're taking along funds with which to buy new properties."

"Yes, if I'm lucky enough to find any. . . . There's fifty thousand dollars, in that bulging briefcase by my desk."

Miss Vance and I exchanged sharp expressions. I asked, "Has anyone approached you, aboard ship, trying to establish a new friendship?"

His eyes frowned, his mouth smiled. "To get into my confidence, and then my briefcase? Other than supper with my friends last night, in that Broadway show of a dining room, I've been entrenched in this suite, reading plays—I devour manuscripts like chocolates."

"What about last night? At dinner?"

He sipped his ginger ale and thought that over. "Well, that fellow Williamson . . . Vanderbilt's friend . . . said he'd like a meeting with me."

"Did he say why?"

"Yes—he's an art dealer. Vanderbilt is a client—apparently, Williamson recommends buying certain paintings as an investment, I take it. Lives mostly in Paris, I believe."

I jotted this down; Williamson was on our docket anyway—one of that elite half dozen who'd received threatening telegrams and been on Klaus's list.

As we took our leave, Frohman apologized for not seeing us to the door, and again reminded Miss Vance—as if a reminder were necessary—to contact him for theatrical work.

"And I intend not to be an antisocial animal for this entire trip," he said, with a salute of his ginger ale glass. "I'm having a party Thursday evening—and you are both invited."

We accepted his invitation, and thanked him for his hospitality.

In the hall, Miss Vance was glowing from the reception she had received. But I reminded her that, for now at least, she was more detective than actress.

The interview with George Kessler—the so-called "Champagne King"—would vary from the previous two in a significant way: Kessler had requested I meet him in that exclusively male haunt, the 'First-Class Smoking Room.' Miss Vance took the opportunity to return to the side of Madame DePage, who was in the 'Reading-and-Writing room' with her new friend, Dr. Houghton—someone we were interested in knowing more about, anyway.

The smoking room was aft on the Boat Deck, a large* chamber dominated by an enormous ornate wrought-iron skylight with leaded glass and inset panels. Walnut paneling framed furniture of the Queen Anne period—sofas, easy chairs, settees, writing desks and marble-topped tables—and the red carpeting and upholstery, in concert with the natural wood tones, created a rich masculine warmth at odds with the white and gold of so much of the rest of the ship.

The air was a smorgasbord of cigar smoke, making a cigarette man like myself feel something of a piker—and a pauper. This was, after all, the bastion of rail barons, shipping magnates, international publishers and millionaire businessmen.

George Kessler didn't know me, but I recognized him—his bushy black beard was hard to miss. He was seated

---

*Fifty-five feet by fifty feet.

in one of two angled easy chairs facing an elaborate, un-lighted fireplace, with a brown valise tucked under (and held in place by) his legs. A cigar smaller than a pool cue in the fingers of his left hand, the Canadian wine magnate was wearing a three-piece dark gray suit with lighter gray pinstripes, and reading an issue of *The Philistine*, the digest-sized magazine published (and largely written) by Elbert Hubbard.

I approached, introduced myself, he did not get up, we shook hands and I took the other easy chair.

"Are you a subscriber to that magazine?" I asked him.

"Hell no," Kessler said, with gruff good humor. "That eccentric ninny is passing these out all over the ship . . . though I must say he gives Kaiser Bill the devil in this article."

"You're no fan of the Germans?"

"I am not. Some men make money off wars, but for me it's a goddamned nuisance—restricts my travel, plays hell with my ability to entertain my friends and business associates."

"That's partly why I wanted to interview you, sir," I said, getting Mr. McClure's work out of the way. "These famous 'bashes' of yours. . . ."

For perhaps ten minutes the outgoing businessman re-galed me with tales of the extravagant dinners and par-ties—how he had once hired London's best carpenters, scenery painters and electricians to turn the Savoy Hotel's courtyard into a corner of Venice . . . including flooding it and serving dinner in a giant white gondola. At another event a mammoth cake was conveyed to guests on the back of a circus elephant, while Caruso sang. At yet an-other do (the Savoy again), he turned the garden into a faux North Pole, complete with silver-tissue icebergs and fields of plastic snow.

I had written all of this down, on the questionable assumption that any of the *News*'s readers would care, when Kessler paused to relight his cigar, which had gone out during his blatherings. As he did, he must have taken a closer look at me, because he blurted that he'd seen me earlier.

"Is that right?" I said.

"Yes! You were giving Anderson a bit of a bad time, on deck, and God bless you for it—I saw that pitiful excuse for a lifeboat drill! Ye gods, what a joke."

"It's less than reassuring, all right."

He shook his head and the thicket of black beard bounced. "These are wartime conditions—bunch of damned ostriches, heads in the sand. You know, I complained directly to Captain Turner."

"You did?"

"I did—the daft old bastard. I went right to his day cabin and bearded the lion in his den—said, 'I think it would be an excellent idea if each passenger was given a ticket listing the number of the lifeboat he's to make for.' "

"How did Turner take it?"

"He just looked at me—like a shaved walrus. I said, 'You know, Captain—just in case anything *untoward* happens.' Finally he told me Cunard had already considered this idea—it had come up after the *Titanic* disaster! But it was rejected as too impractical."

"I would imagine this response disappointed you."

"It did, and I told the old boy so! And he just replied that he did not have the authority to act on my advice—even if he wanted to! Bugger him, I say."

How I wished this could go into my *News* articles. . . .

"Do you know how Turner spends his time?" Kessler asked.

"Frankly, no."

"Tying fancy nautical knots, to impress his officers! Challenges 'em to top him. *They* think he's a fool, too. . . . There are women and children on this ship, goddamnit! Have you seen how many tykes are aboard?"

I, of course, had; but somehow I felt Kessler's prime concern was self-preservation.

"I have the feeling," I said, "that steamer travel does not suit your temperament."

"You're correct, sir—no voyage is too short for me. I get restless—even with that sea air and walks on deck, I have a cooped-up feeling. But it has its positive side— I've had numerous good business ideas; sometimes I feel my mind is whirling with new ways to make more money."

"And to spend it?" I said, with a smile. "Maybe turn the Savoy into the Taj Mahal?"

"Hell of an idea," he said. But his impatience even extended to me, and this interview. "Well, is that it? Did I give you what you needed? You got the spelling right?"

I told him the interview was over, and that I did indeed have the correct spelling of his name; but that I would like a few more minutes with him. He cooperated, and I explained about Miss Vance—whom he remembered from seeing her on deck with me ("Fine-looking woman!")—and our fears that a thievery ring might be aboard.

At mention of that, his face turned white. "It's a good thing I carry a gun," he said.

"Why is that, sir?"

He leaned closer. "I can speak only in strictest confidence. I would want this repeated only to the Pinkerton agent—so that she might help in a preventative manner."

I had no idea what he was talking about, but I nodded.

He stroked the nest of beard. "You might consider me as eccentric as that Hubbard character, in my own way."

"Why is that, sir?"

"Well. . . . I am of the belief that a man should not leave his possessions out of his sight." He tapped the brown valise over which his legs rested. "I have some transactions in mind, in London, that may demand fast financing."

So the valise must have contained a sizable quantity of cash—much as Frohman's briefcase bulged with fifty thousand dollars.

"I have two million in stocks and securities," Kessler said. "Having it so close by . . . well, it's much safer this way, don't you think?"

And he thought Captain Turner was a fool. . . .

ELEVEN

Ham Seasoned with Sage

Late that afternoon I again joined forces with Miss Vance. We met in the Reading-and-Writing Room (which was smaller* than the gentlemen's smoking lounge), a mostly female preserve offering rose-color carpeting that harmonized soothingly with walls panelled in cream-and-gray silk brocade, with finely carved pilasters and moldings. The etched-glass windows boasted embroidered valances and curtains of silk tabouret, and the inlaid mahogany furnishings included settees, easy chairs and writing chairs upholstered in the same rich silk, with a vast mahogany-and-glass book-crammed bookcase that consumed an entire wall. In what better setting could one hope to jot off a note on impressive *Lusitania* stationery?

I had just completed my interview with George Kessler, while Miss Vance—here in the reading room—had sat

---

*Forty-four feet by fifty-two feet.

chatting with Madame DePage and her friend Dr. Houghton.

"Houghton seems quite innocent," she said, beside me on a small sofa. Madame DePage and Dr. Houghton had departed to prepare for the first evening dinner sitting.

I frowned. "But they hadn't met prior to this trip . . . he sought her out, she said. . . ."

"Yes—they'd corresponded, however, and were in that sense old acquaintances. They spoke in detail about the hospital in La Panne . . . went on and on about a nurse named Cavell, in Brussels, from whom madame hoped Dr. Houghton could arrange a pass through German lines."

"That seems unlikely."

Miss Vance shrugged. "So Dr. Houghton told her—but madame naively clung to her belief that doctors and nurses 'transcend the national and the politic of war.' "

"Good luck to her with that view."

With a lifted eyebrow, Miss Vance said, "There well may be, as you suspect, a shipboard romance between them . . . madame is a passionate woman, in every respect . . . but if Houghton is not the genuine article, he's a masterful impostor."

"Still, you *will* check on him, with your New York office, I trust."

"Oh yes. And by Tuesday we should have preliminary reports on those crew members, Williams and Leach, as well . . . And what did you gather from your conversation with the Champagne King?"

I sighed, leaned back on the comfortable sofa. "Well, he's a loudmouth who likes to impress others by throwing his money around."

"Nothing more?"

"Nothing more than the two million dollars in stocks and bonds in that bag of his."

Miss Vance's eyes showed white all round. "Do tell! Well, his technique is working—I *am* impressed."

I gave her the details, such as they were.

She shook her head. "What a foolish ass . . ."

"Nonetheless, the purpose of those names in the stowaway's shoe becomes clear—it seems unlikely it's potential assassination targets. Rather, robbery victims."

Nodding, she said, "That would seem the common denominator—Madame DePage has her war relief funds, Frohman his money to buy new properties in London, and this oaf Kessler has his stocks and bonds in hand—to keep them 'safe.' "

I chuckled. "As if all this food weren't enough, the *Lucy* is a virtual brigands' buffet! Courtesy of a bunch of first-class idiots with their first-class purses full."

"And what of the Sage of East Aurora?"

She was nodding toward Elbert Hubbard, who sat at a handsome writing table complete with built-in mercury gilt lamp, near another such desk, at which his wife, Alice, perched. Both were intently applying ink to paper, bathed in afternoon sunlight filtering down through the leaded-glass dome almost directly above them.

"Well, it's time for our appointment," I said. "Shall we find out?"

Within minutes, introductions had been made, and we repaired to a pair of adjacent couches, Miss Vance next to me, with Hubbard at my left, his wife seated next to him. Plain but not unattractive people, the pair's shared shoulder-length hairstyle created a peculiar visual bond. Alice Hubbard wore a simple, unpretentious afternoon dress of blue serge. Hubbard wore a loose-fitting blue jacket that had certainly once been new, though perhaps not in this century; underneath was a white shirt and an oversize, floppy darker blue velvet tie, and on the floor next to him was a battered briefcase. . . .

Another briefcase! Was there a million dollars in it, I wondered, or perhaps several bags of diamonds? That would have fitted the trend, all right—although in this case, the "treasure" in that battered bag was more likely page after scribbled page of words of wisdom from the aphorism-spouting "homely philosopher."

I knew quite a bit about Hubbard already, having written several humorously critical articles about him (in one of which I'd termed him "the P.T. Barnum of the arts"). His career as an author—he was sort of a Mark Twain without the wit or storytelling ability—had not begun until his mid-thirties. A poor boy who'd quit high school to work as a travelling salesman, he had sold soap door-to-door, educating himself by devouring books in the dim light of dingy hotel rooms.

No one could deny that Hubbard had a gift for sales—had he not been so sincere about his beliefs, he would have made a wonderful confidence man. He had risen to a partnership in that soap company, which his admittedly clever merchandising ideas had turned into a multimillion-dollar enterprise. At the height of this success he walked out to enroll in college!

He chose Harvard, no less, where his writing teachers looked at his prose and advised a return to the soap business. Indignant, Hubbard left the campus, returned to his farm home in small East Aurora, New York, and began submitting his work to Manhattan publishers, who also knew soap when they smelled it.

Finally, finding no takers for his brilliance in prose,

Hubbard began to self-publish his magazine, *The Philistine*, a periodical whose homely little anecdotes and ham-on-wry quips attracted a following. His antiwar article "A Message to Garcia" caught fire and sold forty million copies, making him famous . . . and rich.

He had built an empire of sorts there in East Aurora, becoming a kind of benign cult leader to a group called the Roycrofters, who lived in a village he ruled. He invited people to come to learn to work with their hands, while, in their spare time, learning to use their minds. At the end of the work day, the Roycrofters would listen to music and read books. It was capitalism dressed up like communism.

The Roycrofters' chief source of income was printing and binding expensive editions of the classics as well as Hubbard's own writings (Alice's, too). In addition they wove rag rugs and baskets, and manufactured hand-modelled leather goods, brassware, pottery, and Mission-style furniture.

"I'm pleased to talk to you, Mr. Van Dine," he said. He had an undeniable warmth, and possessed a presence as compelling as his wife—who disappeared into the sofa—did not. "After all, one of my tiny claims to fame is pioneering the on-the-spot profile."

"Your 'Little Journeys,' " I said, with a forced smile and a nod, referring to booklets he'd published over the years in which he'd written articles based on visits with famous people. John D. Rockerfeller, Luther Burbank, Thomas Edison—one celebrity a month for fourteen years . . . all of the articles hero-worshipping tripe.

Though his face was almost childishly placid, his brown eyes had fire. "I presume you wish to speak to me about my article . . . Did you get a copy?"

"No, I did not, sir."

"How about you, young lady?"

"No, Mr. Hubbard," Miss Vance said.

He beamed and reached down and unlatched the bulging briefcase, withdrawing two copies of a digest-sized magazine with a rather plain cover. He handed a copy to me, and another to Miss Vance, with obvious pride.

The magazine's title—*The Philistine*—was in a sort of Gothic script, vaguely religious in aspect. It was subheaded: "A Periodical of Protest," and bore no cover illustration, just an aphorism between red bars: "NEUTRALITY: The attempt of a prejudiced mind to convince itself that it is not prejudiced."

A small design included the volume and issue number, and in a justified-margin square of type it said: "Printed Every Little While for the Society of the Philistines and Published by Them Monthly. Subscription, One Dollar Yearly. Single Copies, Ten Cents. October 1914."

"I'm anxious to read your article," I said, meaning it. "But I've already read many excerpts in the press."

" 'Who Lifted the Lid Off Hell?' has attracted more attention than anything I've written since 'Garcia.' " He was grinning like a monkey, and his wife was looking at him sideways, with her own smile, less the simian variety and more the madonna.

Miss Vance said, "I understand it's quite critical of Kaiser Bill."

"I like to call him Bill Kaiser," Hubbard said, and winked at her, as if this were an incredible display of wit.

"You called him a number of other things, too," I said. I had the magazine open, and quickly scanned the article that was considered the most scathing condemnation of the Kaiser to appear in any American publication to date, looking for examples. "Here you say he's 'a mastoid degenerate' . . . and here, a 'megalomaniac.' "

Hubbard was nodding. "Bill Kaiser's always speaking of God as if the Creator were waiting to see him in the lobby. He says God is on his side." He snorted a laugh. "Any man who believes the Maker of the Universe takes a special interest in him is clearly a megalomaniac."

He had a point.

I offered another example: "The Kaiser's a 'sad, mad, bad, bloody monster.' "

Again nodding, Hubbard said, "That's right. Oh, some have said Bill Kaiser has kept the peace for forty-three years . . . but he was just biding his time for this grab at world domination. And every male child born in those forty-three years, who can carry a gun, is being made to do that monster's obscene bidding."

" 'Caligula, that royal pagan pervert, was kind compared to the Kaiser.' . . . 'Nero, the fiddling fiend, never burned half as much property.' . . . And yet you expect the Kaiser to grant you an audience? An interview?"

He folded his arms, and that kindly face offered me a patronizing smile. "Mr. Van Dine, the only way to avoid criticism is to do nothing . . . and say nothing."

"But if you want the Kaiser to listen to reason, wasn't it a mistake to—"

"The greatest mistake you can make in life is to continually fear you'll make one."

How could you discuss anything intelligently with this human homily machine?

"Bill Kaiser," he was saying, "is just another of these self-appointed folk who rule us, who are unwilling to do unto others as they would be done by them . . . that is, to mind their own damned business and cease coveting things that don't belong to them! That's all war is, you know—a result of the covetous spirit to possess."

I didn't disagree with any of this, exactly, it just seemed obvious, as obvious as the way this character liked to hear the sound of his own voice.

But Miss Vance, surprisingly, seemed keenly interested, and asked him, "Why do you think the German people stand behind 'Bill Kaiser,' then?"

"The answer is easy," he said. "It's a matter of the hypnotic spell of patriotism . . . the lure of the crowd, combined with coercion. Look at Germany today! No private individual can operate an automobile. No bands can play in public parks. All savings banks are closed. Factories are closed. Colleges have been turned into hospitals—why not? All the students are at the front!"

I tried again. "Do you consider yourself anti-German, or just anti-'Bill Kaiser'?"

"Oh, my heart is with Germany! The Germany of science, invention, music, education, skill. The crazy Kaiser will not win."

"But you think he will talk to you."

"Even if I don't get any closer to the Kaiser than the Paris suburbs, I'll write of the war from an American point of view that's sorely needed—from Zeppelin raids over London, to the British viewpoint on American neutrality."

"But you've heard from the German government . . . ?"

"Yes—they say I will be allowed to observe conditions as they are. I will represent myself with a friendly nature and a quiet demeanor."

"What's the use of the trip, then?"

He grinned and tapped his skull alongside the flowing graying locks. "I intend to store all in my bean and in that way elude the censor. I'll give the truth to my readers, when I get back . . . if I get back."

"You have your doubts?"

He shrugged, and patted his wife's hand. They exchanged secret smiles. "I may meet with a mine, or a submarine . . . or hold a friendly conversation with a stray bullet in the trenches. Who can say?"

Miss Vance said, rather suddenly, "Mrs. Hubbard—why are you following your husband into harm's way?"

Her husband watched the quiet, seemingly meek woman, waiting with the rest of us for her response.

"If such a thing happens," she said, in a gentle second soprano, "Elbert and I will go down hand in hand."

This sobered Miss Vance and myself, but Hubbard beamed at his bride. Then to us he said, "I'm always considering what I would do, should this happen, or that. So nothing can surprise me—even death!"

Surprisingly, I was finding myself interested in this man's point of view—never had I encountered so cheerful a brand of fatalism.

Miss Vance asked, "Are you a religious man, Mr. Hubbard?"

"I'm familiar with the various religious beliefs and the ecclesiastical creeds and dogmas of the world . . . I've investigated and analyzed all the theological theories . . . and believe in none of them. My religion is the religion of humanity, which has its heaven on this earth."

I found this remarkably compatible with my own views, and asked, "Where do you think science fits in?"

He grinned. "Now that's the real miracle worker—the great philanthropist who freed the slaves and civilized the master. Science is our savior and our perpetual providence, the teacher of every virtue, the enemy of every vice and the discoverer of every fact."

"Some would call that blasphemy," I pointed out.

"Public opinion is the judgment of the incapable many," he said, "opposed to that of the discerning few."

He was falling back on the aphorisms again—for a while there the sage in the Buster Brown haircut had actually been discussing his views. Perhaps my frustration showed, because when he spoke again, the aphorism-spouting ceased, for a while anyway.

"Mr. Van Dine, I am a farmer, a publicist, a lecturer, a businessman and a writer. I do believe in a Supreme being, but my only prayer is, 'Give us this day our daily work' . . . though I suppose I pray, too, that I never meddle, dictate, or give unwanted advice. . . . If I can help people, I'll do it by giving them a chance to help themselves."

" 'Rest is rust?' " I said with a smile, invoking his most famous saying.

"That's right—and life is love, laughter and work. Not to mention, just one damned thing after another . . ."

Even if we were back to aphorisms, I actually laughed at that, as did Miss Vance.

He started to play to the receptive audience, saying, "I don't take it too seriously, life . . . None of us get out of it alive, you know."

His wife spoke up again. "As a great man once said, 'He has achieved success in life who has worked well, laughed often and loved much.' "

I did her the courtesy of writing that down, then asked, "And who said that?"

"Why, my husband, of course."

Shifting in my chair, I said, "These positive thoughts

are all well and good, Mr. Hubbard . . . but the fact remains, we are sailing toward a zone of war, and you were warned by telegram that this ship was targeted for destruction."

For the first time, Hubbard frowned, more in thought and surprise than in displeasure . . . though some of that was in there, as well. "How did you know that, sir?"

I shrugged. "I'm a journalist—I picked up that crumpled telegram you discarded. Are you aware five other prominent passengers on this ship were similarly warned?"

Still frowning, he nodded. "Staff Captain Anderson informed me. But he said not to worry."

"Did he, now. Tell me, when you published this inflammatory piece on 'Bill Kaiser,' what sort of reaction did you get from the German-Americans among your readership?"

His chin lifted and he seemed proud to report, "Ten thousand of them cancelled their subscriptions overnight." He shrugged and added, "This is nothing new—when I was critical of Brandeis, I lost many of my Jewish readers, despite my stand over the years against anti-Semitism."

"What did you do about these cancellations?"

"Well, over all, our circulation increased. . . . We've reprinted that issue in the hundreds of thousands, much as with the 'Message to Garcia.' And, of course, I wrote each of those who cancelled a friendly letter."

"You wrote ten thousand letters, yourself?"

He nodded. "It took some time—but they were my readers, after all."

His wife made one of her rare contributions to the conversation. "Elbert is too modest to say so," she began, and I thought, *modest?* "But before, after and during the controversy, seventy-eight German-American names were on the Hubbard payroll."

Ignoring this, Miss Vance asked Hubbard, "What about death threats?"

"My heavens, I've always had my share of those. I suppose I had thirty or forty, concerning the Bill Kaiser piece."

"Were they investigated by the police?"

"Of course not. Suffering such cranks is part and parcel of my role in life."

I exchanged glances with Miss Vance—she knew as I did that dismissing the possibility of Hubbard as an assassination target was not easily done, in light of all this.

"Do you think 'Bill Kaiser' might have this ship hit by a U-boat," I asked, "just to make an example of you?

His eyes danced at such a grandiose thought. "To be torpedoed," he said, "would be a good advertisement for my views, don't you think?"

I had heard him say much the same thing to the reporters, coming aboard the ship, and it indicated just how prefabricated his "off the cuff" remarks were. Still, the words—in light of German stowaways, sabotage and murder—had a new and chilling effect on me.

Miss Vance took this opportunity to explain her role as the ship's detective, and informed the Hubbards of the possibility of a thief or ring of thieves being aboard. She believed he might be a target. Had he brought any valuables along, or an unduly large amount of cash?

"By the standards of a Vanderbilt," Hubbard said, "I probably seem a piker—but I admit I did bring along some five thousand dollars in paper money."

"Why so much?" I asked. "I can't imagine you and

Mrs. Hubbard giving yourselves over to extravagance, even on a European trip."

"Mr. Van Dine, I'm more than just an idea garage, supplying spare parts, lubricating oil and mental gasoline to my fellow human beings . . ."

I managed not to groan.

". . . I am also a businessman. My Roycrofters are expert in fine bookbinding, and creating craftworks in wood, metal, copper and leather. A secondary mission of this trip is to seek quality materials, in particular Spanish leather for our bindery."

Was every briefcase in first class crammed with money?

We inquired if he'd spoken to any strangers on the ship, if anyone had tried to strike up a conversation, and make a friend of him. . . .

"Why, certainly. *Everyone* I've encountered—scores in these two days. They are, after all, my species!"

"Your species," I said numbly.

"Yours, too! Mr. Van Dine, the fact that you are a human being brings you near to me—it is a bond that unites us! Often in life, all we need is the smile or hand-clasp of a fellow human being, and perhaps a word of good cheer, to get us through a rough day."

Miss Vance tried to cut through this Pollyanna blather, asking, "But has anyone pressed too hard? Perhaps, approached you for business reasons?"

"No."

I asked, "Have you observed anything suspicious? A steward, perhaps, whom you came onto in your quarters, but who had scant reason to be there?"

He glanced at his wife, who met his eyes with a shrug.

"No," he said.

"Would you consider," I suggested, "removing your rose-colored spectacles, for the duration of this voyage, and report to Miss Vance or myself anything suspicious you might observe?"

Miss Vance added, "There may be physical danger, either to you and your wife, or risk to your possessions . . . specifically, your business funds."

Seeming to take no offense at my "rose-colored spectacles" remark, Hubbard smiled and nodded. "More than happy to cooperate. Do you agree, Alice?"

She nodded, too. "More than happy."

That seemed to sum them up for me: more than happy . . . moving well past joy into the realm of ignorant bliss.

Right now Hubbard was studying me—perhaps sensing my cynicism, though little I'd said revealed as much. He asked, "Mr. Van Dine, have you heard of Mr. and Mrs. Isador Straus?"

"The names are familiar, but . . ."

"They died on the *Titanic*—Mr. Straus was a wealthy man, in the department store trade; he and his wife had been married a very long time. They chose to stay aboard and meet their fate, rather than be separated, when Mrs. Straus could easily have found a seat on a lifeboat . . . 'Women and children first' being the law of the sea."

"I do remember," I said.

He looked heavenward. "They knew how to do three great things, the Strauses—how to live, how to love and how to die." He turned his gaze fondly on his wife, and she returned it; they were holding hands, and I suppose I should have found it trite, but there was something genuine and even moving about it, much as I despise cheap sentiment.

Hubbard said, "To pass from this world, as did Mr. and

Mrs. Straus, is glorious—happy lovers, both. In life they were never separated, and in death they are not divided."

The hambone was nothing if not a showman, and without another word—not even an aphorism—he rose, as did his wife, and they nodded their good-byes and made their exit.

TWELVE

The Art of Friendship

The next morning, Monday, found the great ship off the Grand Banks, basking in sunshine, riding a gentle swell. According to one of our fellow first-class passengers, Charles Lauriat—a Boston bookseller who considered himself an amateur expert on matters nautical—the *Lucy* was doing a good twenty knots, maintaining a long, easy stride, though occasionally pulsating in brief spasms from the sheer force of her steam turbines.*

As was the usual case on a lengthy ocean voyage, the reassuring routine of shipboard life had quietly asserted itself. Passengers plopped into deck chairs with novels (that many were reading Theodore Drieser's new one, *The Financier,* was an encouraging sign in such culturally bar-

---

*Lauriat—who played in the daily ship's betting pool—was keenly interested in the ship's progress; his approximation of her speed was correct, though he was surely unaware that at twenty knots, the *Lusitania* had hit her top speed, due to the reduced number of boilers in use.

ren times). Away from their sedentary situations, middle-aged men strode the decks like athletes, their stomachs tucked in, their chests thrust out, sucking in the fresh sea breeze, cleansing their city-soiled innards. The sharp, salty air seemed to egg on the appetite, making possible the consumption of the endless cornucopia of food; and people you might ignore on dry land seemed not only tolerable company but witty, worthy cohorts.

Miss Vance and I did not spend all of our time engaged in investigation. Now and then, on an evening, we could be found doing the tango or the foxtrot, and well. Often, however, we were not available, spending time privately in either her or my quarters, and what was exchanged between us is not germane to this narrative; besides, even I am too gentlemanly to go into detail, however wonderful it might be to record such vivid memories.

We also on occasion attended the ship's concerts, where an array of talent performed, ranging from the world's finest to numerous self-proclaimed artistes with more audacity than ability. Nonetheless, in our self-indulgent, overfed mood, we were inclined to find all of them entertaining, even if not in the way intended; like cattle being fattened for the slaughterhouse, Miss Vance and I were part of a contented lot.

Perhaps we had become distracted by shipboard foolishness, or lulled into complacency by the knowledge that the stowaways were indeed deceased and nothing further of a suspicious or dangerous nature had transpired, since their passing. In our defense, the final interviews of individuals on Klaus's list were arranged not at our convenience, but at that of the interviewees.

Alfred Gwynne Vanderbilt was, after all, the richest man on the ship, probably the *Lucy*'s most important passenger, with the possible exception of Elbert Hubbard. We were fortunate that Vanderbilt consented to see us at all, as he had no love for the press, which had been rough on him from time to time.

But Staff Captain Anderson was able to convince the millionaire to receive us—Vanderbilt was a frequent Cunard guest, crossing two or three times a year—and the interview (with Vanderbilt and his friend Williamson) was scheduled for Monday afternoon.

The remaining interviews, of course, were with crew members Williams and Leach, but Miss Vance wanted to wait for the reports from Pinkerton on the pair. She knew questioning them at all would be delicate, considering the defensiveness of the two captains; better to limit it to one round of informed interrogation.

So on Monday afternoon, a few minutes before the appointed time of three o'clock, Miss Vance and I made our way to the starboard side of the promendade deck. There, Vanderbilt occupied the second of the two so-called Regal Suites, the other on the portside of the ship—our side of the ship—being filled by Madame DePage and Miss Vance herself.

We were approaching the door to the suite when a figure emerged from within, and seized our attention, to say the least. Suddenly we were face-to-face with a brown-haired, blue-eyed young man whose complexion rivaled a fish's belly for paleness—none other than Steward Neil Leach.

"Mr. Leach," I said. "Good afternoon."

"Mr. Van Dine," he said, with a nervous nod. Then he smiled a small, polite, canary-color crooked-toothed smile to my companion, saying, "Good afternoon, Miss Vance."

My tone pleasant, conversational, I said, "We haven't

seen you since the unfortunate events of Saturday night."

"No." He shook his head. "Terrible. Just awful."

Miss Vance said, "Having all of that happen on your watch . . . must have been distressing."

"Oh, it was. It was."

With a sweet smile, as if commenting on the nice day, she said to him, "You may have been the last to see them alive."

His eyes widened. "How is that, ma'am?"

"Well, you must have delivered their supper. I would think that would, at least, make you the last crew member to see them before . . . the unpleasantness."

"I did serve them, yes."

Now, that was an interesting offhand admission, considering the likelihood of the cyanide having been introduced into the dead men's systems, in that manner.

"But," he was saying, "I'm fairly sure Mr. Williams looked in on them, later . . . if you'll excuse me, ma'am . . . sir."

He began to move off but I touched his arm. Gently. "Mr. Leach, may I ask why you were in Mr. Vanderbilt's suite?"

"Delivering a Marconigram, sir."

"I see." I nodded in dismissal, and moved toward the door of the suite, poised to knock.

"Sir!" Leach said.

Miss Vance and I looked back at him—he appeared even whiter than usual.

"I'm not sure you should be bothering Mr. Vanderbilt," Leach said, "if I'm not overstepping saying so . . . He's had some bad news."

I frowned. "The Marconigram?"

Leach nodded. "It's the second he's received today,

sir—the other came this morning, and I delivered that one, too. This new 'gram was confirmation of the earlier one."

"Well?" Miss Vance asked, with an edge in her voice.

"I believe a friend of Mr. Vanderbilt's has died . . . a close friend. . . . If you'll excuse me."

And Leach hurried off, apparently having had enough of this awkward encounter.

I glanced at Miss Vance, as we stood in front of the white door, and my eyes asked her what we should do.

"We have an appointment," she said. "We received no word of it having been cancelled or postponed. . . . It would be rude not to keep it."

She was right, of course—she so often was—and I knocked.

A valet in full butler's livery answered, a tall, distinguished-looking character whose expression conveyed instantly how troubling it was to him, having to share the planet with the likes of me.

I announced myself and Miss Vance and told the imperious valet that we were expected—we had an appointment. We waited in the hallway while he checked; then, less than a minute later, we were shown in.

This was the drawing room of the suite, panelled in sycamore, decorated in the Colonial Adam style with inlaid satinwood furniture, the walls draped with tapestries, the windows shaped and curtained as in a private residence, or perhaps in the private apartment atop the Vanderbilt Hotel on Park Avenue. We were shown to a brocaded settee where we sat, and waited.

I knew something about Vanderbilt, though unlike Hubbard, he had not served as the subject of my writing; but my employer Rumely had provided a file on several of the prominent potential interviewees, and Vanderbilt

had been among them. Like anyone in America who occasionally read a newspaper, however, to me Vanderbilt's
story was well-known.

Alfred Vanderbilt was heir to the world's greatest fortune—estimated at one hundred million dollars—and
head of that fabulous empire of shipping interests and rail-
roads forged by the notorious tycoon Commodore Cor-
nelius Vanderbilt, Alfred's great-great-grandfather.
Though he'd long been a familiar figure at resorts and
spas frequented by the wealthy of the world—and especially a habitue of sporting events—Vanderbilt had in recent years developed the reputation of a near recluse.

As a younger man, he had been the typical playboy,
whose love of fast cars and faster women was legendary—
a dashing young man with assorted polo ponies and
countless memberships in exclusive clubs, but no interest
at all in the fantastic enterprise his forefathers had built
and his father had passed along to him. He preferred instead to race his thirty-thousand-dollar sports car over
Florida beaches like a man demented; or to join with cro-
nies to flee the family's country home at Oakland Farm
in taking wild trips in mixed company.

Yet Vanderbilt had not grown up into the standard-
issue extroverted, partygoing, cigar-in-one-hand-drink-in-
the-other lout of his privileged class. He was said to be
shy, painfully so, avoiding crowds and reporters, hating
being pointed out. He was by all accounts happily married
to his second wife, Margaret Smith Hollins McKim—the
Bromo-Seltzer heiress—and devoted to their two sons.
Many said the breezy young millionaire had matured into
a responsible adult.

Others said that he was suffering from the pall cast over
his life by the tragedy that followed the dissolution of his

first marriage. In 1901, when he married tall, titian-haired society beauty Elsie French, the wedding cake had been baked in the shape of a trolley, each slice of which contained a precious item of jewelry, so guests would have keepsakes. But within seven years, the trolley of wedded bliss was off its tracks—Elsie had divorced him on grounds of misconduct with one Mary Agnes O'Brien Ruiz, wife of the Cuban attaché in Washington, D.C.

Vanderbilt had gone on with his life, and he and the Bromo-Seltzer heiress began a courtship which led to marriage only a few years after the expensive divorce. But Mary Ruiz made a nuisance of herself, in the press, in the courts, a spurned mistress who was embarrassingly persistent in her refusal to just go away.

Then, one day, finally she did—by committing suicide in London. The details of the inquest into Mary Ruiz's death "by her own hands, while of unsound mind" (off her trolley?) were never revealed to the public; attempts by the press to secure the records of the proceedings were blocked, and hush money had reportedly been lavished on both friends of Mrs. Ruiz and certain officials.

This was why Alfred Gwynne Vanderbilt shunned the press, and the spotlight; the Ruiz suicide was a matter he had never publicly discussed.

A man entered from the bedroom, but it was not Vanderbilt, or the valet, either (who had politely disappeared): This was Charles Williamson, slender as a knife in his dark suit with a dark red bow tie, a dark-haired fellow whose keenly intelligent blue eyes were the most distinct of his otherwise blandly regular features.

I knew little of Williamson, though Miss Vance said he was an art dealer who advised Vanderbilt and other prominent moneybags in the purchase of paintings, sculptures and assorted objets d'art.

He introduced himself, making clear that he knew who we were, and we stood, and I shook his hand. We sat again, but he remained standing before us, his hands behind him, and he frowned, rather like a displeased schoolmaster.

"You had no way of knowing," he said, and his voice was a hoarse tenor, "but Alfred has received tragic news. A Marconigram this morning from Mrs. Vanderbilt arrived, saying Alfred's closest friend, Frederick Davies, has died, suddenly."

We made the proper murmurs of sympathy and shock, though I knew only vaguely of the man—he'd been a prominent New York builder.

Rocking on his heels, Williamson said, "A second 'gram just arrived, from a business associate, confirming the sad fact of Freddy's passing."

I rose. "Well, we certainly won't impose on—"

A hand raised in stop fashion. "No. Alfred seems intent on fulfilling this obligation. He promised Staff Captain Anderson he would help you out, on this article of yours."

"We could reschedule for another time, another day . . ."

"No, he would like to receive you. I think he feels the activity might take his mind off the tragedy. But I would ask you to make your stay a brief one, and to avoid any subjects that might be . . . bothersome."

"Anything in particular," I asked, "that should be avoided?"

Williamson twitched a humorless smile. "You certainly know, even in more unclouded circumstances, that the Ruiz affair is off-limits . . . strictly."

I shrugged. "I had no plans to make any such inquiries."

Williamson smiled again—this one of a patronizing variety. "Good. . . . I'll see if Alfred is ready."

"Mr. Williamson," Miss Vance said, good-naturedly, "are you normally Mr. Vanderbilt's social secretary?"

His frown seemed an overreaction. "No. I'm his friend, his close friend."

"And a business associate?"

The frown deepened. "Out of our friendship, a certain amount of business has arisen."

"You're an art dealer?"

"Miss . . . Vance, is it? Do you make a habit of asking questions to which you already know the answer?"

She smiled beautifully. "No—sometimes I seek confirmation of what I have heard . . . I seldom accept hearsay as fact. To do so can often be destructive, even in seemingly innocent instances."

His expression was blank, as he processed this; then he half-bowed, and said, "Yours is a most wise and gracious approach, Miss Vance. . . . I am an art dealer, adviser, commissionaire and connoisseur."

"Most impressive," she said.

"I merely share my views, my tastes, with my wealthy friends who wish to invest in art. And then I share my connections, so that these properties can be purchased."

I said, "I always considered art something more emotional and instinctive than 'properties' in which to invest."

He seemed both interested and amused. "You know something of art, Mr. Van Dine?"

"Yes . . . I'm somewhat of a . . . connoisseur, myself."

Williamson cocked his head, folded his arms. "Have you written anything on the subject I might have read?"

I retreated behind my pseudonym: My extensive body of criticism had been published under my real name, of course. "No—my interest in art is strictly as one who loves it. My writing for the *News* is rather more prosaic, I'm afraid."

"Too bad. Perhaps some day you'll honor us with your views on the subject. What is your chief area of interest?"

"Modern art, I would say."

"Fauvism, perhaps? Or Cubist works? Picasso? Braque?"

"Actually, I prefer the Syncromists."

He frowned, almost if I'd said something distasteful. "Really? Well, to each his own . . . I much prefer the Orphist color abstractions of the Delaunays, if such things are to be taken seriously at all."

"I prefer Synchromism," I said rather stiffly.

"Well, perhaps the work of that fellow Morgan Russell could be said to have merit. But that hack Stanton MacDonald-Wright . . ." And he shuddered.

The artist he had just insulted, of course, was my own brother . . . but what could I—that is, S.S. Van Dine— say?

So I echoed his own statement: "To each his own." And hoped my irritation didn't show, though I could a feel a flush in my cheeks.

"At any rate," he said, "it's a pleasure to have even a brief discussion of art with another devotee. . . . Now, if you'll excuse me . . ."

He had turned back toward the bedroom, when I called out gently, "Oh, Mr. Williamson . . ."

He turned, his patience clearly tried. "Yes, Mr. Van Dine?"

"Would you mind sitting in on the interview? I would

appreciate your presence, both as a calming one for your friend, and to ask you the occasional question about your views on this ship, and the voyage."

He nodded another sort of bow. "Certainly. That would be my pleasure."

When he had disappeared into the bedroom, Miss Vance turned to me with a grin and glittering eyes. "Nicely done."

"How so?"

"Getting Williamson to stay. We need him just as much as we need Vanderbilt."

And this was true, of course—Williamson had also been on the late stowaway's list.

When Vanderbilt entered, followed by his art dealer friend, he was obviously not at his best. His complexion seemed gray, his eyes laced with red, and the expression he wore when introductions were made—and I stood to shake his hand—seemed fraught with melancholy, despite his polite smile.

"Forgive my informal attire," he said, referring to his brown silk dressing gown.

He and Williamson were in chairs facing us as we sat on the comfortable settee.

"We understand you've received sad news," I said, "and we would like to express our condolences."

"Oh, yes," Miss Vance said, sitting forward, hands clasped. "We would certainly understand if you wished to put this interview off—"

"No," the millionaire said, raising a hand in gentle interruption. "The distraction is a welcome one—and I'm sure you'll make pleasant company . . . more pleasant than I, I'm afraid. I beg your patience."

"Not at all," I said. "Would you like to say anything

about Mr. Davies, for the readers of the *News*?"

"You may quote me that I have known no finer, kinder man." His eyes looked into memory. "We were classmates at Yale . . . travelled extensively together. He and my sister Gertrude were almost married . . . but that's not why you came."

"Nor do we mean to pry," I said, and I began with unoffending queries about the *Lusitania*, and what it was about the ship that made it a favorite of his. I scribbled this pap down into my notebook, dutifully, for perhaps five minutes, before venturing into more significant waters.

"I take it you're making a point of it," I said, "travelling to attend the International Horse Show Association meeting in London . . . despite the war, I mean."

"You may be misinterpreting my actions," he said patiently. "This war is a very real thing—we can't pretend that our lives can go on, unaffected."

"I understand last year's annual meeting was cancelled, due to war concerns."

"Yes. Last year's show was cancelled, also, as you may know. But the general feeling over there, now, is that the war is going well enough to resume the fall event."

"You must agree with that view, if you're attending, sir."

"I respect it." He paused, and seemed to be mulling something over; then he glanced at Williamson, who shrugged. "As a favor to my friends at Cunard, I could give you a small piece of news . . . if you would agree not to wire it home, until after the association's meeting next Tuesday."

"Certainly."

He drew in a deep breath. "I will be announcing, at the

annual meeting, that I will not be racing this season.
There's a war on, after all—and while perhaps giving up
four-in-hand racing doesn't compare to the sacrifices of
some, it is a symbolic gesture I can make."

I nodded, and put on an expression of admiring seriousness; but in truth, I felt him a silly ass—how typical
of the rich to take their petty passions so seriously as to
think giving up horse racing had any significance to either
the average man or the war effort itself.*

"This of course hardly compares to my sister Gertrude's
contribution," he admitted. "She's really a tireless philanthropist, Gertrude is. At her urging, we've established a
hospital unit in France, to care for wounded soldiers. . . .
Miss Vance, I believe you're travelling with Madame
DePage—she can confirm my sister's contribution to the
Allied cause."

Miss Vance nodded, indicating she already knew of
this.

But I said, "Doesn't that put you at risk, Mr. Vanderbilt,
travelling to Europe through the war zone?"

He frowned. "How so?"

"If the Vanderbilts are aiding the Allies, mightn't the
German side wish to make an example of you?"

Vanderbilt snorted a laugh. "I could not care less. Let
that bunch of damned Huns try."

Glancing first at Miss Vance, and then back at him, I
said, "Mr. Vanderbilt, we are here for two reasons."

---

*Van Dine's somewhat snide opinion aside, for Vanderbilt this was a
meaningful act. The millionaire always exhibited his horses at Olympia,
and had transported twenty-six horses, sixteen coaches and a team of
grooms and assistants across the Atlantic.

Another frown. "Really?"

I explained Miss Vance's role as ship's detective, and our concern for the prominent passengers who had received warning threats via telegram at the dock.

"That would include you as well, Mr. Williamson," I said to the art dealer.

Williamson said, "My reaction is the same as Alfred's—those telegrams were the work of a jokester."

"A jokester with damned poor taste," Vanderbilt put in. Then to the lovely Pinkerton agent he said, "You'll forgive my deplorable language, Miss Vance."

"Understandable in these times," she said, "and in your personal situation."

Vanderbilt thanked her for this consideration, and asked me, "You don't think the Germans would target this ship for destruction simply because *I'm* on it? To make an example out of me?"

Well, it seemed to me to make more sense, as symbolic gestures went, than a millionaire quitting horse-racing; but I kept this thought to myself, saying, "Perhaps not you alone, Mr. Vanderbilt. But we also have Elbert Hubbard aboard . . . you're familiar with his widely published anti-Kaiser article?"

"Oh yes," Vanderbilt said. "And I suppose Madame DePage, as well, could be viewed as a personality associated in the public's mind with the Allied cause."

"Yes. And the *Lusitania* herself has potential military applications—has even been rumored to carry munitions—and certainly could be viewed as a symbol of Britain's supposed mastery of the seas."

Vanderbilt was smiling, a little, nodding, too. "You have a sharp mind, Mr. Van Dine. I must say I admire your intellect."

"Thank you, sir. . . . You should also be aware that Miss Vance and I have reason to believe a band of thieves may have boarded the ship, as well."

Williamson sat forward. "Thieves? Does that even make sense? Where could they run, how could they hide, in such an enclosed space as this? How could they hope to take their booty off the ship with them?"

"They might go over the side," I said, "in a lifeboat."

Vanderbilt said, "Well, these potential robbers will find precious little in these quarters to make their efforts worthwhile."

Miss Vance's brow was knit as she asked, "You're not travelling with valuables of any kind?"

"Not in particular, no."

"What about money? Understand, sir, I ask this in strictest confidence as a representative of the line."

The millionaire shrugged. "A few hundred pounds. No need for more—I maintain a residence in Park Lane, an apartment, and a furnished houseboat at Henley. So I have bank accounts to draw upon, for time I spend there."

Williamson offered, "I'm not travelling with valuables, either."

I asked him, "How about paintings or art objects for clients?"

"No—and I, too, maintain a London residence. I'm travelling with less than a hundred pounds."

Miss Vance was clearly trying to reckon with this shift from pattern, but I felt I knew the answer. "Mr. Vanderbilt, the thieves would *assume* you have money. . . . Mr. Williamson, they may well assume you have art objects."

The art dealer's air of superiority was nowhere to be seen now. "Should we be concerned?"

We asked them if they had observed anything suspicious—either a steward who didn't seem to be where he belonged, or overly friendly strangers among the passengers, seeking to create an "in" with them.

Neither man could recall anything of that nature.

"I appreciate your interest," Vanderbilt said, "and we will stay alert, and report to you anything suspicious we might observe ... but as to this German threat—why worry about submarines? The *Lucy* can outdistance any submarine afloat."

Shortly after that, we took our leave, and Vanderbilt walked us to the door, a gracious and friendly host whose melancholia had diminished as we had been drawn into our conversation and these other matters of import.

Before we left, Williamson said to me, "We must have a drink, and talk art at more length."

In the corridor, as we walked back to our side of the ship, I asked Miss Vance what she had made of all that. She said she was still troubled by the fact that Vanderbilt and Williamson did not fit the motif of the others on our list.

"Unless they're lying," she said, "and are carrying cash and, perhaps, valuables from the world of art."

"I don't know, Vance," I said, as we strolled into the Promenade Deck's Grand Entrance area. "Vanderbilt seems straightforward enough."

"What about Williamson?"

"He's a patronizing bastard, but otherwise ..."

"There's something you don't know about him." She glanced about, and several other passengers were waiting in the wicker-dominated entry area, for the elevators. "Let's go to my room, Van ..."

That was an invitation I hadn't yet turned down, on this

voyage; but as we sat on the bed, making love was not on the beautiful detective's mind.

"I trust you are aware of the Ruiz incident," she said, "which Williamson referred to—saying it was off limits for questions?"

"Of course. Vanderbilt's mistress who committed suicide in London."

"That's open for debate. The Pinkertons were investigating that matter, for one of the late Mrs. Ruiz's relatives . . . but the case was dropped, when client funds ran out."

"It was not a suicide?"

"That may never be known. What we do know is that Charles Williamson was also a friend of Mrs. Ruiz—had apparently been something of a go-between in the years of the affair. It was Williamson who closed up her house on Grosvenor Square, after her death; it was he who took charge of her belongings and dismissed the servants. It was he who paid fifteen thousand dollars to a pair of reporters to spike their copy about the night of her death . . . the night Williamson discovered the body of Mary Ruiz."

THIRTEEN

A Tinge of Blue

Mid-morning Tuesday, Philomina Vance and I requested a meeting with Captain Turner and Staff Captain Anderson. This elicited little enthusiasm from Anderson—apparently anticipating even less enthusiasm for the idea from Turner—but Miss Vance was insistent.

"We have important new information to report," she told Anderson, when after breakfast we had caught up with him on the starboard side of the Promendade Deck, where he'd just concluded another of his ineffectual crew-members-only lifeboat drills.

The morning was warm and bright, the sea smooth and free of whitecaps. The throb of the engine, the swish of water, the ship-sea smells, were lulling; but we would not be lulled.

"I know he'll be available in his dayroom at ten-thirty," Anderson said, mildly frowning. "But I must warn you, Miss Vance, to Captain Turner, this affair is over."

"Then I must warn you, Mr. Anderson," Miss Vance

said crisply, "that your captain is misinformed."

And she was not bluffing or even boasting—Miss Vance had received significant new information by cable from her home office. The Pinkerton agents in New York had come through for us splendidly.

So it was, at just after ten-thirty, that we had reconvened in the captain's white-walled, oak-wainscotted dayroom. We sat again at the round maple table, Turner and Anderson, in their blue gold-braided uniform jackets, seated opposite each other, with Miss Vance—typically fetching in pale blue linen with white Bulgarian-embroidered trim and, as was frequently her wont, no hat—seated across from me. I must have been wearing some suit or other.

"I suppose you have that fingerprint information for us," Turner said gruffly, and incorrectly. He had a pipe in his right hand, and the fragrance of its smoke seemed to me singularly unappealing.

"Actually, no," Miss Vance said, with the sweetest smile. "That knife—our murder weapon—was stolen from my room."

Anderson sat sharply up. "What?"

Jaw jutting, eyes hard, Turner demanded, "When was this?"

"That first night—or I should say, Sunday morning, in the wee hours, after we first met here in your quarters, Captain Turner."

Through his teeth, Turner asked, "And why have you not reported this before?"

"The only person who could have taken it," she said, lifting an eyebrow, "was a crew member. For that reason, I felt it only judicious to keep the information to myself, for the time being."

Anderson seemed less irritated than Turner, but he too was unhappy with her. "Your implication is insulting, Miss Vance—we have said before that we stand behind the integrity of our crew."

I said, "You've also said before that you scraped the bottom of the barrel to find them."

The staff captain's eyes flared at me. "I won't put up with that, Mr. Van Dine! You are here at our discretion and under our sanction, I must remind you."

Straightening, Turner said, "A passenger might have got hold of a key somehow—either a spare room key, or a passkey. You seem quick to impugn the integrity of our staff."

Anderson shifted in his chair. "We'll conduct a search of the ship for that knife, immediately."

I said, "Why waste the effort? It was surely tossed overboard, long ago."

Neither captain had any reply to that.

"Absent fingerprints," she said, "I do have new developments to share. Mr. Van Dine and I have successfully completed our interviews with those passengers named on the stowaway ringleader's list."

"We believe that several of them," I picked up, "may be identified strongly enough with the Allied cause to inspire assassination attempts."

"In particular," Miss Vance said, "Madame DePage and Alfred Vanderbilt are involved with aiding the Allied wounded. And Elbert Hubbard's inflammatory anti-Kaiser position makes him particularly vulnerable."

"On the other hand," I continued, "we can see no reason why the German secret service would single out Charles Frohman, George Kessler and Charles Williamson for punishment. Frohman is producing a pro–German-

American play, Kessler is simply a businessman who views the war as an inconvenience and Williamson is an art dealer of less prominence than these other celebrated passengers, included among them chiefly because of his close ties to Vanderbilt."

Turner was listening, but his eyes had that blankness one sees in a dog monitoring human speech for the word or two he recognizes—"bone," "outside."

"So the scrap in the stowaway's shoe," Miss Vance said, concluding this phase of our presentation, "would not seem to be a list of potential assassination targets."

"However," I said, "we have learned that a majority of these passengers are in possession of disturbingly large amounts of money or negotiable stocks. Elbert Hubbard has five thousand dollars with him, to purchase leather and other materials for his arts-and-crafts colony. Frohman has much more than that, with which he intends to secure theatrical properties. Madame DePage, of course, has one hundred fifty thousand dollars in war relief funds. And Kessler—I'm glad you're sitting down, gentlemen—carries around two million in stocks and bonds in that briefcase of his."

Turner and his staff captain stared across the table at each other in wide-eyed disbelief at this unbridled foolishness among such supposedly superior human beings as their first-class passengers.

"As for Vanderbilt and Williamson," I added, "they do not seem to have undue amounts of cash or valuables with them . . . both men maintain London residences . . . but it would be a reasonable assumption on the part of thieves that such men would be worth robbing."

"Then the stowaways were a robbery ring," Anderson

said, eyes narrowed, nodding slowly. "Their purpose was plunder, not sabotage."

"They may have pursued a dual purpose," Miss Vance said, reminding them of a theory she had proposed earlier. "Stealing Allied war relief money is a blade that cuts two ways, after all—and if these stowaways had planned to do their robbing late in the voyage, they would probably have fled to Ireland . . ."

Anderson, nodding more quickly now, said, "You mentioned previously the possibility of IRA involvement."

"Suppose near voyage's end," she said, "an explosive device were detonated somewhere off the coast of Ireland. In the confusion and commotion of passengers seeking lifeboats, these robberies could have been accomplished by the stowaways in stewards' garb, and the thieves could then have been picked up by boat by IRA accomplices."

"It seems far-fetched to me," Turner said, shaking his head.

I asked, "More far-fetched than finding three German stowaways with a camera in one of your pantries? More outlandish than their murders?"

"Moot point," Turner huffed. "Falling-out among thieves, simple as that. Dead men can't steal or for that matter kill, can they? I'm damned if I know why we're giving this matter any further attention . . . I have a ship to run!"

Turner began to rise.

Miss Vance glanced at me; I nodded—we'd discussed this, prior. Then she said to them, "I'm afraid I withheld another key piece of evidence . . . or at least potential evidence."

Turner, now standing, exploded. "Good heavens, woman, what?"

Anderson merely stared at her, aghast.

"The condition of the two dead men locked within their cell indicated they had been poisoned, and that the stabbing was a postmortem ruse designed to suggest that 'falling-out among thieves' conclusion you reached, Captain."

Turner plopped back into his chair as the Pinkerton operative explained the evidence of cyanide poisoning, from the blue-tinted skin tone to the whiff of bitter almonds.

"I would not hold your physician accountable for his poor diagnosis," she said. "He is young, and not trained in criminal forensics."

Anderson's expression was grave. "And you assume the two stowaways were poisoned by a crew member."

"Yes," she said curtly. "My chief suspects were Master-at-Arms Williams, Steward Leach . . . who admits to having served them their final supper . . . and, frankly, Staff Captain Anderson, yourself."

"*I* am a suspect?" Anderson said, his expression mingling alarm and bitter amusement.

"You had easy access to the stowaways in the brig," I pointed out, "and who better than yourself to sneak them aboard in the first place?"

"Further," Miss Vance stated in her business-like way, "you have ties to Mr. Leach, having hired him as a family friend, which opens pathways to further conspiracy."

The usually affable staff captain was trembling with anger, his cheeks flushed. "This is an outrage. . . . I am a loyal ship's officer, and I served with the Royal Navy! To suggest I am a German collaborator—"

"I suggest no such thing," Miss Vance said. "You've been accused of nothing. We merely point out that certain circumstances and facts place you on a list of suspects."

"A damned short list!" he blurted.

"That is accurate," she said. "But we have narrowed it, considerably. You see, gentlemen, I have received information from the Pinkerton agency, which points the finger away from you, Mr. Anderson . . . your record of service to Cunard and for that matter your country is not only clean, but exemplary . . . and from Master-at-Arms Williams, as well."

"Williams also has an excellent history of service to your company and to the Royal Navy," I added.

"Then . . ." The flush had left Anderson's cheeks. ". . . you obviously suspect Mr. Leach. Would that not implicate me, as well?"

"You would certainly be questioned by the authorities ashore," Miss Vance admitted. "But Mr. Van Dine and I are of a mind that you were, frankly, manipulated into hiring Mr. Leach, because of those family obligations."

"Manipulated," Anderson said, rather distastefully.

"Poor judgment," I said, "is a far lesser 'crime' than treason, don't you think?"

"You have a peculiar sense of humor, Mr. Van Dine," Anderson said. "Not at all appropriate."

"Never mind that," Turner said brusquely. "Young woman, what do you have on this man Leach?"

Without referring to the lengthy cable she'd received, Miss Vance rather impressively recounted the new information. Neil Leach—whose father indeed was a lawyer, practicing in the West Indies—had majored in modern languages at Cambridge, with an emphasis on German.

"Good Lord," Anderson said. "Then he could have spoken to the stowaways, and would have understood anything they said!"

"Yet he never volunteered his services," Miss Vance said, "as a translator, after their capture."

"Remember," I said, raising a professorial forefinger, "when we entered the pantry, the ringleader said, *in German,* 'About time.' "

"He was expecting someone," Turner said, making the simple deduction.

"Yes—someone on the crew . . . someone who had given the stowaways stewards' uniforms."

Miss Vance continued with her briefing on the background of Neil Leach, who in 1914 had taken up a post as a tutor to the son of a German industrialist. When the war broke out, he was briefly held, then paroled—probably recruited as a spy—and sent to America on a German ship.

"In an interesting turn of events," she said, "on the ship he became friends with a German steward. Since mid-April, Leach and the steward have lived together in a boardinghouse on West Sixteenth Street that is regarded as a hotbed of German activity—Captain Boy-Ed, the German naval attaché, keeps a room there, as do a number of suspected German espionage agents."

"Why isn't something done about it?" Turner asked crossly.

I shrugged. "America is not at war with Germany."

Miss Vance continued: "The couple who run the boardinghouse, named Weir, are vocal supporters of the German cause. And a young German woman, in the same boardinghouse, frequently spent time with Leach, and told one of our agents that 'Neil' had been excited about an appointment he had at the German Consulate on Broadway—she said Leach spoke of 'financial opportunities.' "

"Charles Frohman is an acquaintance of this fellow,

Boy-Ed, as well," I commented. "We doubt this implicates the producer in any way, although it's certainly an interesting coincidence."

Miss Vance looked from one captain to the other. "Boy-Ed may have known Frohman's intention to travel with cash to invest in theatrical properties. . . . In any event, these circumstances may not be damning, but it's clear Leach has suspicious affiliations with German sympathizers and even espionage agents."

Anderson, perhaps relieved that no fingers were pointing at him (at the moment), asked her reasonably, "What should be done, in your opinion?"

"We would like to question Mr. Leach," Miss Vance said. "But moreover, we feel he should be held in custody."

"On what charges?" Turner asked. "What real evidence have you?"

"Hold him on suspicion," she said with a shrug. "Hold him for questioning by the British authorities."

"For the safety of the ship," I said, "putting him in the brig, or at least confining him to his quarters, would seem prudent, don't you think?"

Turner's gaze settled on his staff captain. "Your opinion, Captain Anderson?"

Anderson was thinking, though there was nothing brooding about it; the facts Miss Vance had presented seemed to have won him over to our side. His words, finally, confirmed as much: "Sir, I'm in accord with our ship's detective. Young Mr. Leach's association with the enemy in time of war is quite sufficient reason to take him into custody."

Turner began to nod slowly, then he said, "That's good enough for me. . . . And I may owe you people an apology. You've done damned fine work, and you have the ship's best interests at heart and in mind."

"Thank you, Captain," she said.

"Thank you, sir," I said.

A knock at the door interrupted this meeting of our newly formed mutual admiration society.

"Would you?" Turner asked Anderson, who nodded and rose to answer it.

A familiar male voice from the doorway said, "Is the captain in, Mr. Anderson? Might I have a word with him?"

The voice was Alfred Vanderbilt's!

"Certainly, sir," Anderson said, and ushered the millionaire—sporty in a navy-blue pinstripe with a lighter blue bow tie and a jaunty gray cap—inside the day room.

Vanderbilt greeted all of us, acknowledging first Miss Vance, then the captain, then myself. He seemed surprised and even pleased to see us.

"Now this is a coincidence," he said. "Captain, I've come because of the warning your ship's detective and Mr. Van Dine gave me yesterday. . . . They instructed me to report anything I might see that struck me as suspicious."

"That's a wise policy," Turner said.

Miss Vance asked, "What have you witnessed?"

He shrugged. "Perhaps nothing—but I had just met up with my friend Mr. Williamson, whose cabin is on the portside . . . where I believe yours is, Miss Vance, and yours Mr. Van Dine . . ."

"That's right," I said. I had left my cabin (and telephone) number for him yesterday; and of course he knew Miss Vance was staying with Madame DePage in the ship's only other Regal Suite.

Vanderbilt was frowning. "That steward . . . I believe his name is Leach . . . was coming out of your cabin, Mr. Van Dine. He looked rather . . . alarmed, when I noticed him. He hurried off, and I knocked on your door . . . but there was no answer."

"Because I was here," I said, with a nod.

"I know that, now—but what was that steward doing in the unattended cabin of a passenger? Stewards don't make beds or clean rooms, do they?"

"That's certainly not Mr. Leach's job," Anderson said.

On the *Lusitania*, as on most ships, stewards tended to matters of food service and other passenger needs.

"Well," Vanderbilt said, "both Mr. Williamson and I found it damned questionable."

Miss Vance said, "Yesterday we observed Mr. Leach deliver a Marconigram to Mr. Vanderbilt's suite—Mr. Anderson, has he been assigned to the wireless shack?"

"Stewards or bellboys deliver those messages," Anderson said, "depending on their availability."

Vanderbilt seemed embarrassed. "I hope I'm not making a mountain from a molehill."

"No, sir," Anderson said. "This is useful information. Thank you!"

Vanderbilt smiled, and took his leave.

"I would suggest," Miss Vance said, "prior to questioning Mr. Leach, a thorough search of Mr. Van Dine's cabin be made. . . . You have no objection, Mr. Van Dine?"

"None, Miss Vance," I said. "In fact, I quite insist. . . ."

Captain Turner returned to the bridge, and left us in Staff Captain Anderson's hands. We took the elevator down to the Promenade Deck, and Anderson himself assumed charge of the inspection of my cabin, which was

too small for us to join in. Miss Vance and I waited in
the hallway, leaning against the mahogany railing, ex-
changing (to be frank) smug expressions. It felt quite good
to have been so right.

Within minutes, our vindication cranked up a further
notch.

"Ye gods," Anderson said. He was on his knees, looking under the bed, as if a cuckolder might have been hiding there from a vengeful husband. He withdrew an
object, holding it up for us to observe.

Though I had never seen one before, I felt quite convinced I knew what the object was.

But Miss Vance breathlessly confirmed my opinion: "A
pipe bomb!"

Exiting my cabin gingerly, Anderson held the thing out
at arm's length—a half-foot of lead pipe, plugged with
reddish brown wax at either end.

"I really should examine it for fingerprints," Miss
Vance suggested, though her tone was tentative.

"I'm afraid we will have to forgo such detective work,"
Anderson said, making a preemptive decision, and he
moved quickly aft, heading toward the Grand Entrance
area, and the nearest access to the sheltered deck and the
open air.

Miss Vance unhesitatingly followed behind him,
though he said several times, "Keep back, both of you!
Stay away!" Against my better judgment, I ignored his
advice, and followed Miss Vance and her example.

When we reached the deck—passengers were lined up
along the rail, enjoying the sunshine and the view of the
quiet sea, others in deck chairs, reading or napping—Anderson yelled, "Make way! Make way!"

And as the burly staff captain ran up to the rail, a space

was cleared for him by wide-eyed passengers, who looked with wonder as Anderson drew his arm back like a base-ball pitcher, and hurled the lead pipe toward—and into—the sea. He had a good arm, the staff captain, and the object flew a good three hundred feet before the greedy water swallowed it with a gulp.

Miss Vance, her expression perplexed, approached Anderson, who was catching his breath. "That was evidence, you know," she said.

"It was also . . ." And he glanced around at the curious faces of passengers, to whom he smiled, nodded, saying, "Nothing of importance! As you were . . . back to your, uh, enjoyment of this fine day!"

The passengers received this awkward statement with the skepticism it deserved, and milled and murmured amongst themselves; but no mutiny emerged—they simply, grudgingly, returned to their relaxation.

And as Anderson stalked back in the direction from which he'd come, we fell alongside him, on his either arm, and he said tightly to Miss Vance, "That was also, quite likely, a bomb."

Neither of us argued with him; what else could it have been? A joke in—to quote Vanderbilt, the other day—"questionable taste?"

"What now?" I asked.

"I'm going to collect Mr. Williams," he said, referring to the master-at-arms, "and request that he get his revolver."

Miss Vance, keeping pace with the staff captain's stride quite nicely—we seemed to be headed toward the elevators—asked, "May I assume you're heeding our advice, and taking Mr. Leach into custody?"

"You may. But I would prefer you leave this matter to me."

"Mr. Anderson," she said, "don't talk rubbish—we're accompanying you. I'm the ship's detective, and Mr. Van Dine is my assistant."

So I was Watson after all!

Within minutes we were on D deck, so far forward we were in the very nose of the ship, where—past the mess-hall-like Third Class Dining Room—a number of the stewards kept their quarters. Leach and another fellow shared a tiny cabin on the starboard side. Many of the stewards roomed together in dormitory-style areas another deck or two down, known as the "gloria."

But Leach, friend of Anderson's that he was, had been assigned one of these coveted cubicles. He had not been at his work station—he should have been busy with food service matters, involving the children's dining room—and Anderson was checking the man's quarters, accordingly.

Master-at-Arms Williams had the revolver in hand, to the right of the door, while Miss Vance and I were lined along the wall, down a bit, to the left. Anderson knocked.

"Mr. Leach!" he called.

Nothing.

"Mr. Leach!" Anderson called again.

Still nothing.

So the staff captain, backed up by the revolver-ready master-at-arms, used his passkey, and swung open the door.

They went in and we waited.

We heard a muttered, "Jesus Christ," apparently from Anderson.

"Miss Vance!" Anderson called. "Come in here, please."

She squeezed in; though not officially invited, I followed.

Leach was on the lower bunk, as if taking a snooze; but this was no nap: His posture was not one of repose, rather an ungainly sprawl that looked not a bit restful. His eyes were open, seeing nothing; his mouth was open, saying nothing.

And his skin bore a noticeable tinge of blue.

FOURTEEN

Party of Two

A cup of tea, two thirds of which had been consumed, the remaining third of which displayed the telltale aroma of bitter almonds, was found on a small wooden table near the bunks in Steward Neil Leach's cabin.

Anderson declared the death an obvious suicide, and I will spare the reader the detailed redundancy of our next meeting with Staff Captain Anderson and Captain Turner, in the latter's dayroom, in which the matter was declared once and for all finally closed.

"With the discovery of the pipe bomb in your quarters," Anderson declared, "the purpose of the stowaways, and their crew member confederate, is established clearly as sabotage . . . not theft, however much money some of our first-class passengers may have been foolish enough to bring along with them."

Miss Vance seemed to have her doubts, but she did not express them to the two captains; from the tightness around her eyes, I could sense she had determined the uselessness of any effort to continue. She did request—a request that was granted—that she be allowed to take the late Leach's fingerprints, and compare them to any prints found on the cup of cyanide-laced tea. This procedure, however, revealed only the dead man's hands.

The following morning, Wednesday, we sat in the Verandah Cafe, enjoying the sparkle of the sea, the lullingly monotonous drone of rushing water, and glasses of iced tea (with lemon, sugar, but no cyanide). We had both received formal invitations to two parties Thursday evening: Theatrical producer Charles Frohman was throwing one in his suite, and wine magnate George Kessler would be taking over the Verandah Cafe itself for his do.

Traditionally, such end-of-the-voyage parties would have been held closer to . . . the end of the voyage; but Staff Captain Anderson—to whom such social concerns had been relegated—had organized the ship's final concert for Thursday night. The *Lucy* would be arriving in Liverpool early enough on Saturday that reserving Friday evening for packing and other disembarkation preparations seemed prudent.

We were just discussing the parties, when Charles Williamson—out enjoying the fine day, spiffy in a gray suit, and as hatless as Miss Vance—stopped by to inquire about the same subject.

"Will you be attending the Frohman affair?" he asked cheerfully, after we had invited him to pull up a chair and join us.

"Yes," I said, "and probably the Kessler one, as well."

The breeze ruffled his dark hair. "He's a beastly character, this Kessler . . . but he's invited me, so I suppose I shall do the polite thing and attend."

Miss Vance asked, "How is your friend Mr. Vanderbilt

today? Is he recovering from his personal blow?"

Williamson frowned, shaking his head. "He's quite
melancholy, frankly. But I did manage to get him to take
his meals at the dining room yesterday, and he's agreed
to attend the Frohman party."

"It will be good for him," I said.

"He's quite a fan of Mr. Frohman and his theatrical
ventures. The night before we embarked, I accompanied
Alfred and his wife to a Frohman production."

"*A Celebrated Case,* perhaps?" Miss Vance asked.

The production at the Empire Theater was a particularly
popular one.

"Yes—excellent show." The handsome, slender art
dealer glanced at the sea, the blue of his eyes a darker
shade than the waters. "Hard to believe this trip is almost
over."

"Such voyages seem forever," I said, "and in an instant
they're gone."

Williamson grinned wolfishly. "Now you're sounding
like that fellow Hubbard."

"Please! No insults."

Again he shook his head. "And we haven't had a
chance to really talk art yet—we have a debate ahead of
us, on Synchromism, I feel."

I returned his smile, saying, "Perhaps we do."

"Maybe at the Frohman party," he said, rising, nodding
to us. "Or the Kessler. . . . Miss Vance, good morning."

"Good morning, Mr. Williamson."

He disappeared off down the deck.

"He's in a pleasant mood today," she said.

I ventured a smirk. "Maybe that's because we didn't
bring up the Ruiz 'suicide.' That fellow can smile all he
likes—he's a scoundrel."

Her own smile was amused, but the twinkle in her eyes seemed different, this time. "Do you think so?"

"Certainly. He either arranged a murder for Vanderbilt, or took it upon himself to kill the discarded mistress, and he's wormed his way into his very rich friend's life and pocketbook, ever since."

Miss Vance was beaming at me. "Why, Mr. Van Dine—I believe you're exactly right. . . . We don't really think this investigation is over, do we?"

"No. Leach had an accomplice in first class, who spiked the poor bastard's tea with cyanide, so the dead steward could take the full blame."

She sipped her harmless tea. "Well, Leach was in it to his navel, no question—this was the work of a party of two. Leach got the stowaways aboard, and the plan was to disguise them as stewards . . . probably in plain sight."

"Giving them simple duties, you mean?"

Nodding, she said, "Possibly hiding the Huns when they weren't gathering espionage materials, seeking to show the ship has munitions and other contraband aboard."

"So they were, in your view, saboteurs."

"Yes—but they were discovered too soon . . . before they could talk at length with Leach, and meet their confederate in first class, for full instructions." Her smile outsparkled the sea. "You caught them, Van, ants in their pantry—speaking German with a camera in their hot little hands."

"And Mr. Leach panicked, with the stowaways taken into custody. . . . Two of the Germans seemed anxious to talk, to make a deal, which would have meant the end for Mr. Leach."

"So," she said, picking up my thread, "he fed them a

cyanide-spiced dinner . . . but only two of them. Their ringleader was loyal to the cause, and went along with Leach's improvised plan, to stab the corpses, and (he hoped) cover up their murder by cyanide."

Now I picked up her thread. "Leach then accompanies Klaus to first class, where they meet with their confederate. . . . But why was Klaus stabbed? He had complied with Leach's murder of the other two, after all."

Her eyes stared unblinkingly into her thoughts, which she collected for several long moments. Then she said, "I believe their ally in first class saw no use for Klaus—the plan was now defunct, after all. Our first-class conspirator would recoil at the suggestion that Klaus be hidden in *his* room! The German was of no further use, and eventual questioning of Klaus in Britain by the secret service might well expose the conspirator's aiding and abetting of sabotage."

"A capital crime," I said, with an arched eyebrow and a nod. "So . . . after Leach escorts Klaus to first class, a discussion ensues in the hallway . . . an argument?"

Miss Vance shrugged. "Possibly Leach and his accomplice offered Klaus the opportunity to take a lifeboat into the sea. But Klaus may have objected—without a U-boat waiting, that was near certain death. Or possibly Klaus was a good German, and wished to finish his mission of sabotage, before departing, however much danger he put them all in."

"Then we were wrong that this was a matter of robbery."

She shook her head forcefully. "No—we were right that this is about *both* sabotage and robbery. Leach's accomplice in first class—the brighter of the two by far, possibly a criminal mastermind—was in this only for the money."

"What *was* their plan, do you think?"

She leaned back in her chair, eyes narrowed. "It was much as we've speculated, I should think: Near journey's end, a bomb goes off, off the Irish coast, and in the confusion, stewards loot the key staterooms . . . the names on that list from the stowaway's shoe."

I considered that. "Or they might have used tomorrow night's parties, as an opportunity."

Now her eyes widened; she nodded. "Good, Van! That's an interesting line of thought. . . . Go on."

Like a puppy whose master had patted his head, I tried further to please. "Every potential target on Klaus's list will be at one of those two parties tomorrow night—two of the names on the list are throwing the affairs! This, of course, assumes that our accomplice knew of these parties in advance."

"A reasonable enough assumption. Invitations to both affairs had been printed up beforehand. . . . Go on."

"If their accomplice is indeed one of the prominent names on that very list, he or she could have kept an eye on the robbery victims at the parties, keeping them busy, paving the way for plunder by his co-conspirators."

Now she seemed doubtful. "But the robberies would be discovered."

"Ah, but this is a big ship . . . plenty of places to hide the loot. It's doubtful, this close to the end of the voyage, that the ship would be searched in any rigorous fashion at all. Remember, we're talking millions, here, in cash and securities."

Now I had her again; she was smiling, nodding. "Yes . . . yes. The authorities at Liverpool would seal off the ship, no passengers would be allowed to leave, until the booty was found . . . and every suspect on the ship questioned, all twelve hundred of them!"

But that had me doubtful, suddenly. "Would Cunard put up with such an embarrassment?"

She waved off my uncertainty. "They would have no choice. It's a matter of law enforcement . . . and stir into the soup the presence of enemy agents during wartime, and you can bet the passengers would be stuck on this vessel for days—the closest to dry land they could get would be looking out a porthole!"

And of course the band of looters/saboteurs could not withstand what would await them at Liverpool. . . .

"So," I said, "now we're back to a bomb."

"To a bomb," she said with a nod. "Before the ship reaches an English port, our saboteurs-in-stewards'-clothing set off another of those pipe bombs—just off the coast of Ireland . . . and you know the rest."

As the crew hustles passengers into lifeboats, during the commotion and perhaps the panic, the villains retrieve their booty and go over the side, picked up by pro-German accomplices. The first-class conspirator most likely stays aboard, and receives his share at a later, safer date.

"And a good plan it was, too," she admitted. "Either version. . . . Only, they've been interrupted in their efforts."

"Death *can* be rude, at times . . . but what if you're right, Vance? What if the accomplice in first class is something of a criminal mastermind? Perhaps the crooked chef who cooked up the twisted recipe in the first place?"

Again her eyes narrowed. "You mean . . . our first-class felon might continue improvising?"

I jerked a thumb toward the ship. "He . . . or she . . .

shows every sign of such an inclination, starting with Klaus's murder, and that pipe bomb deposited in my cabin, yesterday. . . . Or was that Leach's independent handiwork, d'you think?"

She shook her head. "I believe not—I think your first instinct is correct. I think we have a murderous thief aboard who will likely try to gather his millions, yet."

I studied her—studied her like a modern art painting I was trying to fathom. "You . . . you *know* who it is, don't you?"

Her smile was tiny and smug; so was her shrug. "Yes—don't you?"

I admitted I didn't.

She leaned forward, locked her eyes with mine. "Think for a few moments, Van, and you will. You have all the clues you need."

"Really! Such as?"

She ticked them off on her pretty fingers. "First, the threatening telegrams—what was their real purpose? Second, the sequence of the names on the list in Klaus's shoe—is it truly random? Third, the planting of the bomb in your cabin yesterday—why was that done, and at that particular moment? Finally, why did Klaus die on the portside of the ship?"

I confess my mind was reeling, but as we continued to discuss the matter, the clearness of it—the sheer obviousness of it—did present itself . . .

. . . as did our best course of action, which most certainly was not to present our findings to the two captains.

Instead, we would go to the two parties—that is, cocktail parties, thrown by Frohman and Kessler, tomorrow evening. She would go to one, and I would go to the other.

And before the final concert of the voyage, we would have our thief . . . our murderer . . . our answer.

By Thursday morning, when Miss Vance and I were strolling the Boat Deck's open-air promenade, the *Lusitania* had experienced a change, however subtle. During the night, the ship had crossed into the war zone, signalling new precautions—we could see that the lifeboats had been swung out in their davits; and stewards were rigging more elaborate blackout curtains over doors and portholes.*

Visibility was splendid, and the morning foretold a day as lovely as the previous several—sunshine, cool breezes, with the promise of a crisp evening. By the time evening arrived, however, I admit my nerves were on edge. We had spent the day in typical shipboard tomfoolery—food and strolls and even some time behind closed doors. But the task ahead was one for which a Pinkerton operative— even one as beautiful and feminine as Miss Vance—was far better suited than a man of letters.

Both cocktail parties began at six P.M. Approximately ten minutes past that hour, I dropped Miss Vance off at the Verandah Cafe, where Kessler was entertaining in the cool, open air, dusk painting the sea a shadowy shade of blue. Among the attendees were ship-builder Fred Gaunt-

---

*In addition Captain Turner had tripled his lookouts, aware he was fast approaching dangerous waters, and needing to take a fix on his position as soon as land was sighted, to begin working out the course and speed to port at Liverpool. Because of her size, the *Lusitania* could only cross the mouth of the Mersey at high tide . . . and if he missed that, he would have to spend twelve hours steaming back and forth, a virtual target for prowling U-boats.

lett, the would-be nautical expert Charles Lauriat, the paranormal enthusiast Miss Pope and her young Friend, and several dozen others, most notably Madame DePage and her shipboard companion, Dr. Houghton.

Staff Captain Anderson had dropped by to represent the officers of the ship—Kessler was still giving him a bad time about the lifeboat drills—and I nodded hello to him. I scattered a bit of small talk around the cafe for perhaps five minutes, making sure to shake the Champagne King's hand and thank him for the invite.

Miss Vance positioned herself near the bar, where we knew she would have easy access to the telephone.

"Good luck to us," I said, and kissed her cheek, boldly.

Her eyes were glittering again. "Good luck to us," she repeated.

I paused, my hand on her arm. "You love this, don't you?"

Her smile was as enchanting as it was wide, the breeze catching the dark blonde tendrils and doing wonderful acrobatics with them. "Very much. . . . It's better than opening night."

Five minutes later, I was a floor below, on the starboard side of the Promenade Deck, in a suite where Charles Frohman was entertaining a slightly larger, even more star-studded group. The chubby frog prince of Broadway beamed as he moved throughout the crowd, leaning on his "wife" (that ever-present cane of his), seeming in less pain than before. The genial host was decked out in a dark suit with scarlet tie under a stiff white collar—formality and theatricality at once, a Napoleonic ring on his little finger to add a dash of Broadway flamboyance.

Everyone was dressed for dinner—men in formal wear, women in décolleté gowns—but few were likely to bother with the dining saloon this evening: Generous trays of canapés were on the occasional tables, and Frohman's girlish man William (as if having to keep track of Master-at-Arms Williams and Charles Williamson weren't enough!) continually threaded through the room keeping Champagne glasses brimming. And the Champagne saw to it that the drawing room stayed alive with laughter and banter.

Vanderbilt and Williamson stood sipping Champagne, but the millionaire seemed gloomy, in the aftermath of his friend's death, if not outright depressed. The art dealer was talking to everyone who happened by, full of personality, as if feeling the need to make up for his subdued friend.

Among the well-dressed, even glamorous crowd were Frohman's theatrical entourage, including the actresses Josephine Brandell and Rita Jolivet, and the playwright Justus Miles Forman. In the midst of these fashionably dressed guests, an oasis of gauche, were the Bard of East Aurora and his bride; Hubbard was his usual floppy-tied self, in a tuxedo no respectable rental firm would let; his wife looked modestly attractive in an off-white silk gown appropriate for a wedding, circa 1900.

Right now Hubbard had found his way over to Williamson and Vanderbilt. The millionaire was staring into space, sipping his Champagne; but—judging by the snippet I heard—the art dealer had engaged Fra Albertus in a discussion of their common interest.

"You must not over-intellectualize art," Hubbard was saying, and it frightened me to hear that view, because I agreed with it. "There is in most souls a hunger for beauty, just as there is a physical hunger."

"But art is an intellectual process, too," Williamson argued. "It must engage the mind as well as the heart."

Hubbard shook his head. "Beauty speaks to the spirit through our senses—harmony as set forth in color, form and sweet sounds."

"Art is a more complex thing than that, surely!"

The bard snorted a laugh. "Art is not a 'thing'—it is a way."

Back to aphorisms—but that, I had to admit, was a pretty good one.

I moved on, and suddenly I was facing my smiling host—homely as he was, his good nature made him appealing. "And where is your lovely friend . . . Miss Vance?"

"She is, I'm afraid, representing us at the Kessler affair."

"Well, I hope she'll stop by and eat some of my food, and drink some of my Champagne."

I smiled. "If Kessler doesn't fill up his guests with bubbly, something's wrong."

"True enough," he laughed. "Now, I want to make sure Miss Vance knows my interest in her thespian abilities is quite sincere. Will you be staying in London for a while?"

I shrugged. "Perhaps a week."

"Splendid. I would like you and Miss Vance to be my guests, and accompany me to James Barrie's new play, *Rosy Rapture,* at the Duke of York's Theatre, Saturday evening."

"Mr. Frohman, that's very generous!"

He raised a small chubby forefinger. "None of that—C.F., remember. C.F.!"

"Well, C.F., I accept your gracious invitation on both our parts."

Before long I had managed to reach my goal—I meant

to position myself near the desk, where the phone hid behind that enormous ship-shaped basket of flowers and fruit. Those flowers were doing fairly well, for as many days as had passed; I noted the card was signed by Maude Adams, the famous actress Frohman had discovered.

I nibbled canapés, but didn't overdo the Champagne, chatting with whomever happened by. There was a great deal of war talk . . . fairly optimistic, however: Allied advances on the Western front and in the Dardanelles, with the prospect of Italy joining the Allied cause.

Captain Turner himself came by, in a rare sociable mood. Several guests asked him about the new shipboard precautions—everyone had noticed them—and Frohman asked, "Are we in any danger, Captain?"

"In wartime there's always danger," Turner said. "But no cause for alarm. . . . I *would* request that those gentlemen who are fond of cigars refrain from lighting them on deck."

Whether that was intended as a joke or not, it got a laugh that rippled across the suite, just as a bellboy was entering, to hand the captain a wireless message.* Turner bid some hasty good-byes and took his leave.

Shortly afterward, Williamson took his leave as well, thanking Frohman, saying he needed to drop by the Kessler party, out of politeness; C.F. understood. And Vanderbilt was left behind, with his Champagne and his doldrums.

"This war," Hubbard was saying, a group of theatrical

---

*The telegram read, "Submarines active off south coast of Ireland." Thinking it might be part of a longer message that was broken up, Turner wired for details; the same message was repeated.

types gathering around a ham greater than themselves, "will progress from horror to horror. . . . Art, science, invention, man has lifted himself to the Matterhorn of Hope . . . and now this."

I used the phone, calling the Verandah Cafe, asking for Miss Vance, who soon came on the line; we spoke briefly. Then I wandered over to Vanderbilt.

"Mr. Vanderbilt," I said, nodding.

"Mr. Van Dine."

"If I might risk rudeness, I would like to ask a rather personal question."

He looked at me curiously; an eyebrow lifted. He was a little drunk.

I asked my question. "You didn't actually see that steward, Leach, come out of my room, did you?"

His eyes tightened. "Whatever do you mean?"

"Your friend Williamson saw it, but asked *you* to report it. Do you know why?"

Vanderbilt's defensiveness vanished; he shrugged. "He told me what he'd seen, and that he was concerned— asked if I would go to Captain Turner about it. He was afraid to."

"Afraid?"

"Well, he knew Turner wouldn't turn me away—that I'd be taken seriously."

"I see," I said, as if that made sense.

The phone's ring was almost lost in the cocktail chatter, but I heard it, and went to answer; but Frohman's valet, William, reached for the receiver before I got there.

I said, "That will be for me."

He made a face and said, "I'm sure . . . Frohman suite!" He listened, then turned to me with surprised confusion, handing me the phone, saying, "It is for you, sir."

"Mr. Williamson has arrived at the party," Miss Vance's voice said into my ear, over the sound of festivities on her end of the wire. "He's making the rounds—no one will miss the fact that he was here."

"Time for you to leave."

"Yes it is."

I hung up, because it was time for me to leave, as well. Making no good-byes, I slipped out, and I reached the door to Madame DePage's suite just as Miss Vance arrived, looking fetching in her low-cut green silk gown, a small purse in hand.

We did not speak. She used her key in the door—these were her quarters, as well as madame's, after all—and we went in to wait in the lavish suite, with its Louis XVI decor and walnut panelling, its residence-like windows covered in black.

We did not have long to wait.

Dressed in a steward's uniform, Charles Williamson—a large satchel in hand—entered the suite's living room; he had just begun to search when I emerged from where I'd crouched behind a green settee, and said, "You look good in white—but you'll look better in stripes."

His eyes hardened—he was frozen in the middle of the room—and his hand dipped into the satchel, which was unlatched, and emerged with a revolver . . .

. . . but another revolver, a smaller but no less deadly one (compact enough for a purse), had inserted its snout in the back of his neck, before his own gun could become much of an issue.

"As ship's detective," Miss Vance said, "I'm placing you under arrest, Mr. Williamson. . . ."

I took the gun from his right hand and, from his left,

the satchel—in it were Mr. Kessler's stocks and bonds, and Hubbard's five thousand.

"I suppose C.F. Frohman's cash would have had to wait," I said, "till his party was over and he was off attending the concert."

He made no denials. His blue eyes flicked from one of us to the other, his lips curled in something between a smile and a sneer.

"If you don't mind my asking," he said, hands raised, "how did you know?"

"Klaus had a list in his shoe," Miss Vance said accommodatingly—training her gun on Williamson, as I covered him with his own weapon. "Your name was at the top of it—and the names below were in alphabetical order. Quite straightforward, really—the stowaways' contact first, followed by a listing copied from a passenger's register, provided by your friend, the late Mr. Leach."

"And you knew, from that? No court would accept such thin evidence."

"No court has to—you're nabbed red-handed, sir. But there are other matters—your inclusion among those who received warning telegrams, for example. You are hardly worthy of inclusion on such a celebrated list—why would a mere art dealer be included among the prominent likes of Hubbard, Vanderbilt, Kessler, DePage and Frohman?"

The sneering smile settled in one corner of his mouth. "Why indeed?"

"*You* sent those wires—you or your associates. A fairly venerated ploy, the villain hiding amongst his victims . . . giving himself access to all the famous personages on that list, by becoming one of them. We asked your intended victims if any stranger on the ship had gone out of his way to make a friend of them. . . . Your name came up, but only once . . . yet you no doubt got next to *all* of them—though they didn't think of you as a stranger. No, not Vanderbilt's friend—you had something in common, after all . . . you were part of the group warned with those threatening telegrams!"

His smile had begun to fade.

I said, "You planted that bomb in my room—Vanderbilt admitted to me that you asked him to report seeing Leach do it, to Captain Turner. You meant to distract us, while you gave your accomplice a friendly drink of cyanide-laced tea; and in creating his 'suicide' you also meant to further cement in our minds Leach as the culprit. . . . Staging suicide is a specialty of yours, isn't it?"

Now he frowned.

"Your cabin is just down the corridor," Miss Vance pointed out sweetly. "On the portside of the ship . . . the hallway where you stuck a knife into your cohort's back."

His laugh was hollow. "Why do you care? He was just a German—they were all just a bunch of damned Hun spies, and I took care of them. I deserve a medal."

"Perhaps," I said, "but not a satchel of money."

"Alert the master-at-arms," Miss Vance said to me. Then to Williamson she said, "You're checking into new quarters—the brig."

Williamson only smiled. "I hope they've cleaned it out. That blood can get sticky."

Chilled, I used the telephone.

FIFTEEN

Sinking Feeling

I suppose I have been frank enough about our relationship to reveal that Miss Vance and I spent Thursday night together in her cabin. After our shared exploit, we craved each other's company in the manner of adults of free will and progressive thinking. We were happily and snugly slumbering in each other's arms in a bed designed for one when the bellow of the ship's foghorn rudely awakened us—and I damned near fell off the bed.

There was no getting back to sleep—the foghorn was simply too insistent—and, after I'd returned briefly to my cabin to freshen up and dress, we joined the DePage group at the first breakfast seating. Only Madame DePage herself had been informed of last evening's melodramatics, largely because, after all, they had been staged in her quarters. Captain Turner himself had told Vanderbilt of his friend's transgressions, and what was said between them I do not know—the millionaire made himself scarce, and I did not see him at all until much later that Friday.

Otherwise, a cloak of confidentiality as thick as the morning fog enveloped the ship.

Jaded, at this time, by the *Lucy*'s embarrassment of gastronomic riches, neither Miss Vance nor myself ate what could be called a hearty breakfast—tea and scones with marmalade being about the extent of it. Perhaps we felt that letdown that follows any great adventure—Miss Vance even commented that she was reminded of the day following the closing of a play's successful run.

A walk on the Boat Deck's open-air promenade presented an experience both surreal and ghostly, the air chill for May, the view past the railing one of swirling mist. The *Lusitania* might have been the *Flying Dutchman*, a specter ship at home in dense fog—perhaps I should have run this theory past the paranormally inclined Miss Pope. And even a landlubber like me could tell we'd slowed— the engine's deep thrum had shifted significantly in amplitude and tempo.

Again we sat in the Verandah Cafe, sipping hot tea, saying little, wrapped up in an ambience that was both eerie and strangely restful.

Out of the fog, down the deck, emerged Staff Captain Anderson. He brightened upon seeing us, and strode over.

"Just the man I was looking for," he said to me.

"Really?" I replied, surprised. "Please join us."

He sat, removing his cap. "I have a request. I feel somewhat abashed, asking . . . since in retrospect you and Miss Vance were right about so much, and I was so wrong."

"Nonsense. What is it?"

He shifted in the chair, still uneasy. "Well, all attempts to question Williamson have failed. He won't give us any sort of statement, much less admission, despite being caught in the act."

"Won't talk," Miss Vance said, between tea sips, "without his solicitor."

Anderson nodded. "Nearly his very words."

The Pinkerton operative shrugged; she wore a gray linen morning suit and, of course, no hat. "Common among criminals of all classes."

"You see," the staff captain continued, "we're concerned about the sabotage aspect of this affair . . . that there may still be some sort of small but deadly explosive device tucked away somewhere."

"You've got him locked up," I said. "Surely if such a device had been planted, he'd be in as much danger as the rest of us."

Anderson sighed. "Or he might feel he could make his escape in the resulting tumult."

"Locked away as he is?"

"He might hope for release. That would be the humane thing, in such a case."

I decided not to offer an argument on the merits of letting the fiend drown in his cell, and instead asked, "Could a pipe bomb, such as the one you found in my quarters, really do a ship this size much damage?"

"That depends upon its placement. You see . . . and Mr. Van Dine, I am trusting your discretion—what I am about to reveal is not for publication, you understand."

"Certainly."

He spoke softly and deliberately. "We do have a small cargo of what might be considered munitions aboard— four thousand-some cases of rifle ammunition . . . some five million rounds . . . and over a thousand cases of three-inch shrapnel shells, along with their fuses."

"Might be" considered munitions?

At last I had fulfilled my mission for my employer Ru-

mely: discovered the presence of contraband aboard the
Lusitania. But somehow I felt no sense of victory.

"How much of a danger does that present?" Miss Vance
inquired.

"Well, that's fifty-one tons of shrapnel alone. I would
say a bomb, even a small one, might ignite a larger explosion. We've searched that area of the ship, but . . . I
still have a certain trepidation about what Mr. Williamson
and his conspirators may have done."

"I can understand that," I said, with a dry sarcasm that
Anderson may have missed.

"In addition," he said, "we are near the end of our voyage, and our coal bins are nearly empty . . . a coal dust
explosion is another possibility, should such a device be
ignited."

"You haven't made your request as yet," I reminded
him.

With a world-weary sigh, Anderson shook his head and
said, "The bastard . . . excuse me, ma'am . . ."

"You may call the son of a bitch a bastard if you like,"
Miss Vance allowed.

"Thank you, ma'am—the bastard says he'll talk to you,
Mr. Van Dine . . . and only you. And in private."

That set me to blinking. "Why, in heaven's name?"

"That," Anderson said, with a puzzled shrug, "he will
not reveal. Are you willing to speak to him?"

I responded with my own shrug, more resigned than
puzzled. "With iron bars between us, I am willing—
though Lord knows what he might want of me."

And so it was that I came to stand in the ship's brig,
staring into the smug face, and the intelligent and dare I
say evil blue eyes, of Charles Williamson . . . like the late

and unlamented prisoners before him, still attired in his purloined stewards' smock.

He had been stretched out on the lower bunk, and now walked over to me, and stood—in traditional prisoner style—grasping the bars with both hands and staring at me through an opening between them . . . displaying a disturbingly self-possessed smile.

"What do you want with me?" I asked, impatiently. "I have no particular interest in finally getting around to our discussion of art, if that's what you have in mind."

Half a smile carved a hole in his left cheek. "Are you sure, Mr. Wright?"

For a moment, it went right past me—then I realized: *He had just called me by my right . . . Wright . . . name!*

"*Of course* I recognized you," he said to me, with a haughty laugh. "We have been at several functions, though we were never introduced. But everyone in art circles in New York City knows of the astringent Willard Huntington Wright. Don't you have a new book on art theory coming out or something?"

I said nothing—I admit I was shaken.

"Can you really be so thick?" he asked patronizingly. "Didn't you know I was needling you, when I criticized your brother's work? Did you really think that was a coincidence?"

"So you know my real name. So what? I'm travelling under a pseudonym, in order to interview people who might not grant me an audience, if they knew my real identity."

"Like Hubbard—whom you have skewered in print, several times, I believe."

I shrugged. "Perhaps . . . and how does this make a private audience with me a desirable thing, for a goddamned murderer and thief like you?"

He took no offense, merely laughed, and dropped his hands from the bars. "Have you a smoke?"

I removed the cigarette case from my inside jacket pocket, handed him a Gauloises—and lighted it up with a match. He inhaled the rich tobacco greedily, waiting long moments to exhale a blue-gray cloud.

"I know your politics," he said. "Everyone does, in our world. . . . You're a prolific one, aren't you? *Two* books coming out . . . one of them on Nietzche, I believe."

I said nothing to confirm the undeniable correctness of his statement.

"You're as pro-German as I am," he said suddenly, the smile gone, the eyes flashing.

So that was it!

"I should think you're chiefly pro-Williamson," I said.

His eyes tightened, and his smile was small yet satanic. "I can be a valuable ally."

"Can you."

"Just don't forget about me, down here."

"What's that supposed to mean?"

"Should anything untoward occur, in these treacherous waters . . . just remember your fellow pro-German down in the brig. That's all."

I stepped closer, my nose near the iron bars. "Is there another bomb somewhere on this ship?"

He backed away. "I didn't say that. I merely point out, we're in the war zone. Should we fall prey to a U-boat, I shouldn't like to go down with the ship, trapped behind these bars—I would find dying on a British vessel most distasteful."

I sneered at the rogue. "Just because *my* tastes run to

Wagner, Goethe and Schopenhauer, don't assume I wear a photo of the Kaiser in a locket near my heart."

He shrugged, wandered over to the bunk, stretched out on it again, arms winged behind his head, cigarette bobbling in his lips as he said, "That's all I have to say . . . Mr. Wright. I'll keep your silly little secret, too . . . as a show of good faith."

In the corridor I was met by Miss Vance and Staff Captain Anderson.

"What did he want?" Anderson asked.

I snorted a wry laugh. "The fool thinks this Kaiser Wilhelm beard of mine suggests a pro-German heart beating in my chest."

Miss Vance frowned. "And that's all?"

"He asks that I not forget him, down here in the brig . . . should a U-boat try to sink us."

Her frown tightened. "He could mean, if a bomb goes off."

"Yes, he could . . . Captain Anderson, I would suggest you redouble your efforts to search the ship for such a device."

Glumly, Anderson nodded. "That's good advice . . . and we'll take it. But a vessel this size has many a nook and many a cranny."

Miss Vance was shaking her head. "He must be bluffing," she said. "He must be. . . ."

"I'm sure he is," I said.

Neither of us, however, seemed terribly swayed by our own argument.

By mid-morning, the fog had burned off and the weather turned clear and warm, revealing a flat lake of a sea, disturbed only by the lazy roll of a ground swell from where the shore should be. Land took its time revealing itself, the direction of the coastline offering nothing but a gathering flock of filthy gray seagulls flapping alongship the ship, heads turning greedily from side to side.

Then just before noon, the murky shadow of land teasingly materialized off the port beam. From the rail where the lovely Pinkerton agent shared her binoculars with me, we watched it grow, becoming more distinct, revealing itself as a rocky bluff. Around one-thirty, the coast took on a more definite configuration—trees, rooftops, church steeples, sweeping by. Miss Vance and I exchanged relieved expressions that the crossing had been safely made. What if a saboteur's bomb *were* to explode? The shore was so near.

Oddly, the flat, blue-green waters seemed to belong to the *Lucy* alone—no other vessels, commercial ones or warships either, presented themselves. Where was the Irish Coast Patrol, for one? Hadn't we been promised protection from the British Admiralty?

We returned to the Verandah Cafe for a rather late and light luncheon—both Miss Vance and I had decided the dining saloon with its endless food and mawkish orchestra could wait till this evening—and, by two o'clock, had finished our little crustless sandwiches and a dessert of assorted petits fours.

Sitting idly, enjoying the view of the bright blue sea, I noticed a white-gold glimmering swirl of sunlight on the water's dimpled skin.

"Is that a porpoise?" I asked, pointing.

Miss Vance sat up and squinted toward the sunny sight. "I'm not sure. . . . They usually leap."

"Whatever it is," I said, "it's spreading . . . coming closer. . . ."

"That's a torpedo, isn't it?" Miss Vance asked, frightfully calm.

I stood, looking toward the forward end of the ship. "Have they noticed it on the bridge, I wonder? Can't be a torpedo . . ."

Still deadly calm, she said, "I think it is."

The handful of other passengers in the cafe had noticed it, as well, and were making similar comments—no one panicking, everyone strangely still, as if waiting for that foamy, frothy wake, arrowing inexorably toward us, to reveal its intentions.

Which it did: The shock of the impact was surprisingly mild if distinct, making a heavy, somewhat muffled roar, the ship trembling momentarily under the blow's force. Miss Vance was on her feet, and in my arms—we were holding each other tight when a second, more severe explosion rocked the vessel, and all of us, the deck itself seeming to rise, then settle.

Instinctively, we looked toward the explosion's source, and a geyser of coal and steam and debris erupted between the second and third funnels, a skyward shower of deck planks, boats, steel splinters, coal dust and water, quickly followed by the hard rainfall of gratings and other wreckage clattering and scattering on the decks and splashing into the sea, forward of us.

Grabbing on to Miss Vance's shoulders, I pulled her back deeper into the shelter of the cafe, as wreckage descended on the deck like ghastly hailstones. The canvas awning, stretched across the cafe's entrance, sagged under the weight of water and ruins, and seemed about to split apart.

Taking her by the hand, I dashed out onto the littered

deck, the rain of rubble apparently over, and away from the cafe, heading forward.

"That second explosion . . ." I began, over the hissing of ruptured steam pipes.

"The son of a bitch *had* planted a second bomb," she said through her teeth. Her pretty face was freckled with soot. "And that U-boat torpedo detonated it!"

"We should gather our belongings," I said, "and get our life jackets, and find our way to a lifeboat."

She agreed, and we continued forward along the deck, among other passengers who were displaying a surprising and altogether admirable lack of panic. Perhaps, despite all of the denials, everyone had suspected the ship might be hit, even expected it, and now reflex action had taken over, and passengers were moving in a fairly orderly manner up toward the lifeboats.

Near the entry to the deck's Grand Entrance area, we were startled to see Elbert Hubbard and his wife; standing at the rail, the husband's arm around the wife's waist in an affectionate fashion. They seemed frozen, or perhaps dazed.

I knew their cabin, like mine, was a deck below, on that same portside corridor, and I said, "You need to get to your stateroom, and get your life jackets—straightaway!"

In a soft, almost placid voice—barely audible above the hissing and clamor—Hubbard said, "There may not be enough boats. Someone must sacrifice."

I grabbed on to his arm. "Spout your aphorisms another time, you fool—this is life and death!"

That the boat was already listing seriously to the right was all too apparent.

He jerked his arm away and glared at me—the only

time I'd ever witnessed any expression on that face that evinced anything like anger—and he said, "Mind your own business."

"Is that the best you can do for your famous last words?" I asked bitterly.

The hell with him. Taking Miss Vance by the arm, I headed into the Grand Entrance, which was thronged with people moving up the stairs and out onto deck. Signs of a gathering frenzy were now indeed in evidence, and understandably.

The elevators were out of the question—the electricity had gone, and the lifts were trapped halfway between floors, filled with passengers coming up from lunch. They were screaming down there, trapped like rats, rattling their cage.

At the top of the companionway, I suggested she wait for me, here.

"No! I'm coming with you."

"No need—give me your key, and I'll fetch our life jackets. What else of yours is vital?"

Reluctantly, she was accepting my decision, handing me her room key. "My passport's in the top drawer of the bureau. . . . Nothing else."

I held her by her arms and kissed her on the mouth; she returned the kiss with desperate enthusiasm.

"I'll be back," I said.

"I'll be here," she said, as frightened passengers, many soot-smeared, rolled by in a human tide.

As I took the stairs, many more were coming up than going down, a swarm of hysterical second-class passengers surging up from belowdecks, lacking the outward composure of those of the first class who were resolved not to be caught up in a sordid stampede. I had to lower

myself to their level and elbowed my passage with no
thought of common courtesy. At the bottom of the stairs
a steward was urging passengers to be calm, and handing
them life jackets—many ignored both his good advice and
valuable gift.

I suppose I could have worked my way over to him,
and snatched up two of those life jackets, but I had
enough sense of decorum and decency to realize I should
fetch the ones I knew to be in our cabins. The passageway
was jammed with fleeing passengers, mostly second-class
I would venture, and I could only imagine the sheer panic
of the lower decks—third class and, God help them, the
"dirty gang" down in the boilers.

The starboard list was unmistakable but not extreme,
and, other than pushing through the crowd, I had no trouble making my way to the forward portside corridor.
While many were heading for the deck, a few other self-
composed first-class passengers were doing as I was, seeking their valuables and life jackets in their cabins.

The torpedo's impact must have affected the structure
of the ship more than was readily apparent, for I discovered my cabin door was badly jammed, and it took three
swift kicks to rudely open it.

With the ship's electricity gone, and no porthole, my
cabin was as dark as a cave. I lighted a match, and quickly
found my life jacket on its shelf in the wardrobe, and from
the nightstand gathered the leather pouch with my passport, various other papers and folding money. The list of
the ship had increased, in this short time, rather alarm-
ingly.

It was necessary to kick open Miss Vance's bedroom
door, as well—it occurred to me a great deal of money
was somewhere in this bedroom, but I did not know where

. . . nor had she requested it. Perhaps Madame DePage and her friend Houghton had already retrieved the funds—or abandoned them, if the bulk made such impractical. Using another match, I recovered Miss Vance's passport from the bureau and her life jacket from its wardrobe shelf.

As I exited, the ship lurched further starboard, a severe tilt now, and the sounds of chaos on the decks above, trampling feet, excited voices, betrayed an absence of discipline, to say the least. The passage was now empty, and dim—the only light filtering in from way down the corridor, at the Grand Entrance area, adjacent to the portside and starboard promenades. The starboard list was so extreme, in fact, that I as walked toward the entry light, I had one foot on the floor and the other on the wall.

Moving along the dark passageway, clutching close to me the pair of bulky, fiber-filled life jackets, I noted that— down some of the cross passages, leading to staterooms— the portholes were gaping open . . . and the water was eagerly lapping at those portals, like the tongues of hungry beasts. Soon the sea would come rushing in, in all its inexorable coldness. The ineptitude of Turner and, yes, Anderson was outrageous—that these had not been closed and sealed, as we steamed through the war zone. . . .

When I reached the Grand Entrance, the wicker furniture overturned, crushed, discarded, potted plants spilling their soil on the linoleum, the mounting horror unequivocal. Passengers down in those stalled elevators were shrieking, beating desperately on the grille gates; the water would have them soon. Panic-stricken, white-faced third-class passengers were streaming up the companionways, scrambling up the stairs, climbing over one another with no compunction.

A well-dressed woman and her daughter were standing

to one side of the wide but human-clogged stairway, tucked against the slanting wall, the child saucer-eyed and clinging to the dark-haired, blue-eyed mother, whose chin was high.

"Is there anything I can do to help?" I asked the woman.

"No, thank you," she said proudly. "There is nothing you can do. . . . We will wait for these . . . *people* . . . to pass, before taking our turn."

"That's probably wise," I said, with a movement of my eyes that was meant to convey to the mother that her child would not fare well in that struggling mob.

"The captain says the ship cannot sink," she said, like a Christian convinced of Heaven. "We have no intention of becoming alarmed."

I was standing there—the incline so steep now that I had to work to regain my balance, especially amid all the jostling—like a boy waiting for the right moment to hop a carousel. Only a few seconds had gone by when a bloody-faced figure in stewards' whites stumbled into me, coming up from the shelter deck, and I grabbed on to him, because he seemed barely conscious, and would otherwise have fallen and been trampled.

It was Williams, the master-at-arms!

I dragged the sturdy fellow from the crowd, and positioned myself against the wall, supporting him. He'd suffered a terrible blow or had taken a fall, his forehead bloody, one of those thick black eyebrows badly cut, and streaming blood.

"Get your breath," I said, "and we'll get you up to the Boat Deck."

"Mr. . . . Mr. Van Dine . . ." he said, eyes wide with

recognition and . . . what else? Humiliation? "I was a fool, a damned fool!"

"Williams, what—"

"I tried to do the right thing, sir, the humane thing . . . but the bastard took advantage! Jumped me, goddamn him!"

I asked, but I already knew. "Who did this?"

"That bastard Williamson—he was my responsibility, and I couldn't leave him to drown, could I?"

"Of course not," I said, though I could have, easily.

"That's not the worst of it, sir! He . . . he's got my revolver!"

Time was too precious for recriminations, so I merely hauled the bloody fool up the companionway; he seemed to have regained a clear enough head, and his balance, and he disappeared off toward the deck, muttering that he would find "the blighter."

The Boat Deck's Grand Entrance area, like the one below, had its furniture and potted plants upended; but the passengers were no longer thronging the area, having found their way to the decks.

And then my heart sank, because there was no sign of Miss Vance—I had been gone too long, apparently, or she had been swept up in the melodrama.

As I looked around, I saw something that at first struck me as quite absurd: Alfred Vanderbilt and Charles Frohman were seated side by side in wicker chairs, and they were surrounded by a pile of life jackets and five wicker baskets filled with slumbering babies! They were tying the life jackets to the baskets, and Frohman was bending to do so, and his discomfort must have been considerable.

I was not surprised to find Frohman staying aloof from the mass of hysteria—with his severe rheumatism, how could he hope to survive? But what in the hell were they up to? As I went over to them, Vanderbilt's imperious valet, still in full livery, materialized with a basket in either hand, a slumbering infant in both.

"This is the last of them, sir," the valet said.

"Good—now see what other kiddies you can round up, and we'll help them into the lifeboats."

"Very good, sir," and the valet again disappeared.

I stood before this preposterous tableau—amazingly, not a child was awake and squalling!—and asked, "What in God's name are you up to, Vanderbilt?"

"Ah," Vanderbilt said, as casual as if he were attending a race at Ascot, "Mr. Van Dine—I've had my man Ronald raid the nursery. Moses' baskets—they should float nicely."

"Gentlemen, I don't believe this steamer could be far from her final plunge—"

The millionaire stayed at his work, tying a life jacket to a basket. "Mr. Van Dine, it's a wonderful irony, isn't it? I have a white marble swimming pool at my farm, but I've never been in for a dip. All my time's gone to my horses, and of course the ladies. . . . Never did learn to swim."

"Let me help you get these out kids out on deck, and we'll get you into a lifeboat, then."

"No, Charles, Ronald and I can manage—we need to keep this precious cargo away from that rattled rabble out there . . . when the water comes up, we'll drop the wee ones in."

I turned to Frohman. "C.F.—can I help you onto deck?"

"No, I prefer to stay with my friend Albert," he said, grunting as he worked. "This will be a close call—we'll have a better chance here than by rushing to the lifeboats."

I had no time to argue; such choices were for each man to make for himself. "Have you seen Miss Vance?"

"Why, yes," Vanderbilt said. "A lot of these fools had their lifebelts on incorrectly—heads through armholes, upside down around their waist and the like. Last I saw her . . ." He pointed toward the starboard exit onto the deck. ". . . she was helping as many of them as she could, in putting them on correctly."

"Some," Frohman said, "scurried away—must have thought she was trying to *take* their life jackets! Cowards."

"You have enough for yourselves?" I asked, meaning the life jackets, feeling somewhat guilty bearing a pair of them myself, for Miss Vance and me.

"Certainly," Vanderbilt said cheerfully. "Good luck to you, man!"

"Mr. Frohman—C.F.? I can help walk you along—we are moments away from . . ."

He smiled up at me, that homely face a beautiful thing. " 'Why fear death? It is the most beautiful adventure in life.' "

"What's that, a Hubbardism?"

Frohman seemed a little offended. "Hardly! James Barrie—*Peter Pan*."

And the froggy producer returned to his slumbering infants in their Moses' baskets, who unknowingly awaited far worse perils than mere bulrushes.

Disturbed though I was to have lost track of Miss Vance, I had confidence in her competence—her cool head and professionalism would rise well above the mad scramble. Or so I told myself, to hang on to hope and sanity. On the promenade, however, the rush was over, confusion replacing panic—people were milling, thronging the deck waiting for a discipline or order to be imposed upon them ... which seemed unlikely to be provided.

The Hubbards were nowhere to be seen—they had vacated (or been pushed away from) their position at the rail. In the undiscriminating mix of passengers from all three classes, I saw the occasional familiar face. Miss Pope and her Friend dove from the deck, choosing not to get involved with the lifeboats at all. Madame DePage, I noted, was bandaging the wounded with strips of cloth torn from her own dress; Dr. Houghton was aiding her. No sign of Miss Vance, though.

The lifeboat situation was hopeless.* Crewmen and male passengers were striving without luck to lower the boats, and were placing women and children into them. Horror-struck, I realized these boats would never be cleared, and would go down with the steamer ... which surely would make her final plunge any second now. Better to leave these poor souls on the deck, where they might have a chance, might find a piece of wreckage to use as a makeshift raft, a table, a deck chair, a wooden grating.

A bit aft of the main entrance, a lifeboat filled with women and children—Miss Vance not among them—waited patiently for help that would probably never come. No one was even attempting to free the craft from its davits. With the steamer sinking so rapidly, the boat

---

*The severe and steadily increasing list of the ship made safe loading and launching of the lifeboats an impossibility. Boats on the portside had swung inward, many smashed to kindling; starboard, they swung out too far to safely mount and lower.

would have to be cleared at once, if they were to be saved.

Staff Captain Anderson—in his shirtsleeves, his affable manner replaced by a tense grim demeanor—was doing his best to supervise the ill-advised launching of the boats. I went to him and suggested that the ship was sinking so fast, they might be better off waiting till the water reached the ship's keel, and simply cut the ropes, and simultaneously knock the snubbing chains loose.

He was ahead of me; he pointed to a boat nearby where seamen were poised to do exactly what I'd suggested.

And at this moment a man in white who was not a crew member approached one of those seamen, and was speaking to him.

"Christ!" I blurted. "That's Williamson!"

Anderson's gaze flew to the man, who was snarling at the seaman, *"Launch this boat, now!"*

Williamson obviously planned to leap inside the craft.

"Can't do it," the seaman said, a young blonde lad. "Captain's orders."

And Williamson thrust a revolver toward the seaman— that gun he'd taken from the master-at-arms—and said, "To hell with the captain—*do it!*"

I stood frozen—all this ship needed right now was a madman shooting off a gun! But Anderson was edging forward, moving closer to Williamson, whose back was to the staff captain.

The young seaman complied with Williamson's demands, freeing the snubbing chain.

Freed of its restraint, the boat swung inward like a pendulum and smashed into Williamson, squashing him like a bug against the boat's gunwale. Any cry of his was obscured by the screams of passengers as the lifeboat crashed to the deck, sliding forcefully into a waiting knot of crew and passengers, Anderson among them. I plastered myself against the wall, the boatload of terrified women and children narrowly missing me, but sweeping the others with them, the unconscious staff captain, too, down the deck and into the rising sea.

Around me screams of horror followed the stunning display of brute stupidity—the author of which, one Charles Williamson, lay a crushed open-eyed corpse beneath the blood-smeared gunwale.

In moments the sea would come up and wash me off the deck, too; so I beat the bastard to it, and dove in. The coldness was a shock, yet somehow bracing, even invigorating, and I swam, despite the bulk of the life jacket, swam a good hundred feet away from the ship before turning, and treaded water. I wondered if anyone, perhaps from that crashed lifeboat, was following, and needed a hand.

I also wanted to see the steamer's final plunge. The bow already buried beneath the sea, the ship's fantail loomed a hundred feet into the placid blue sky, revealing four huge propellers, barely turning, and an immense rudder, sunlight glinting off their steel. Sliding into the blue waters, the ship suddenly, bizarrely, froze—the nose of the great ship, its eight-hundred-foot length deeper than the sea, had hit bottom!

A terrible clash and clatter echoed across the water as everything within her collapsed and scattered itself, as if a giant box of broken glass and spare metal parts were being shaken by a playful, nasty god.

Hundreds were mountain-climbing the slanted deck, seeking handholds, some falling into the sea, as the dying beast that was the *Lusitania* made its final agonized death cries—a boiler exploding, a funnel crashing, one last great moan of tortured steel.

Then she was gone—slipping under the water with no significant suction, no boiling vortex, foam flecking the last glimpse of her superstructure and decks, a few boats still swinging like toys from their davits . . . a finger snap, and the big *Lucy* had disappeared.* She left behind a wide white ring glimmering on the surface of an otherwise smooth sea in the afternoon sun. Within that ring was a snarl of floating wreckage and bodies, on and under the surface, some of them alive, gaggles of men and women and children twisting like flies on some giant fisherman's hook.

For a while I swam around and helped those I could by pushing pieces of wreckage to them, to which they might cling. After some fifteen minutes of this, I was getting tired, and cold, and was just realizing I was in trouble, when arms hauled me up out of the water and into a collapsible boat, a shallow thing with its folded canvas sides up.

The boat was filled with people—twenty or more, men enough to row but mostly women and children. A voice called out my name to me, and either I was dreaming a sweet dying dream, or had unpredictably enough gone to heaven.

Because the voice was Miss Vance's, and I was soon, half-conscious, sheltered within the embrace of her damp but wonderful arms.

---

*The *Titanic* took four hours to sink; the *Lusitania,* by some accounts, as little as fifteen minutes.

"I hope Williamson drowned in his cage," she said, sometime later.

"Oh," I said, "it was much better than that."

Not much else is worth the telling. Our lifeboat had a good crew, which included that fellow Lauriat, and we might have headed for land but instead stayed out and, for two hours or so, picked up those who seemed in the most helpless of conditions. I will spare you the tragic images, involving women and children, particularly mothers and their babies. Some of the babies in their nursery baskets, thanks to Vanderbilt and Frohman, were retrieved from the sea.

When we had as many aboard as we dared—thirty-two was the final count, I believe—we finally rowed toward shore, but first encountered a fishing smack. Though they had already taken on two boatloads of survivors, they made room for us, as well.

The old fishermen gave us the blankets from their bunks, started a fire and made us tea; it was a wretched vessel, slippery with fish scales and the filth of fishermen, and no man or woman could wish finer accommodations. The steamer *Flying Fish* took us to Queenstown, where the rest of this tale is well-known and would only serve to depress the reader, and the book's author.

Suffice to say, of the key figures involved in the mystery, only Miss Vance, George Kessler (minus his briefcase) and myself survived. The psychic Miss Pope also came through, and Dr. Houghton; so did Captain Turner, who on the rescue ship *Blue Bell* was bitterly chastised by a mother who had lost her child.

I suppose I would sound like Elbert Hubbard if I were to point out that a disaster brings out the best and the worst in us. The millionaire and the theatrical producer died bravely, helping the helpless; so did the noble doctor's wife who had sought to raise money for hospitals. The Bard of East Aurora and his bride apparently went down to their cabin to die together, whether to make room for others in lifeboats, or to glorify themselves, who can say? Miss Vance, the heroine of the piece, was rescued in the midst of aiding others.

And the villain died, as he'd lived, a villain.

"It is what we think, and what we do," Hubbard once said, "that makes us what we are."

Perhaps, by that sweet fool's yardstick, all I am is a survivor . . . but we need survivors, don't we? Who else would tell the tale?

A Tip of the Captain's Hat

As in the previous novels in what others have called my "disaster mystery" series, I have in this book combined the factual with the fanciful. Unlike the first of these books, *The Titanic Murders* (1999), the mystery herein relates directly to the disaster itself, tied as it is to the political and historical context of the tragedy, and its causes. Nonetheless, some liberties have been taken, though precious few; and what may seem to some readers mistakes may be a reflection of the sometimes contradictory source material.

Before discussing the sources of my research, I would like to share a few historical afterthoughts that I did not feel appropriate to the body of the book.

Contrary to popular belief, the sinking of the *Lusitania* did not lead to America's participation in World War One. Of the approximately 1,200 men, women and children lost in the sinking, only 124 were Americans—not enough to go to war over, but plenty to turn sentiment in the U.S.

against the German side, undoubtedly paving the way for this country's entry into the conflict.

Numerous theories have been posited as to the nature of the second—and far more damaging—explosion that followed the undoubted single torpedo that hit the ship, courtesy of the German submarine *U-20*. Among these are munitions (specifically gun cotton) blowing up, the boilers exploding, coal dust combustion, a second torpedo or even a British sub sinking the ship, to prime the war pump for Winston Churchill. This novel proposes yet another possibility, based upon the factual presence of German saboteurs on the *Lusitania*.

Captain Bill Turner, incidentally, suffered through several *Lusitania* investigations but still was given a new command—he lost that ship to torpedoes, as well, and wound up sailing a desk. Whether he was a scapegoat or just an idiot remains a point of conjecture, and—like the reason for that second explosion—a subject much discussed in the reference sources I used.

The cast of characters in what I intend as a traditional, closed-environment mystery—somewhat in the Agatha Christie manner—consists primarily of real people. (Only Philomina Vance is fictional, and she takes the place of a real detective aboard the ship, one William Pierpoint of Scotland Yard.) The background material about all of these characters is as accurate as possible, though in some instances, with minor figures—Staff Captain J.C. Anderson, for example, or Master-at-Arms Williams—precious little is known.

Warning telegrams were in fact sent to Frohman, Vanderbilt and a number of other prominent passengers. Although in reality they were not murdered, the three German stowaways existed, as did Neil (sometimes

"Neal") Leach, who several authorities believe had been in league with these probable saboteurs and other German agents.

Charles Williamson, of course, was not in real life their murderer—since these murders happened only in my imagination—but he was indeed involved in the suspicious "suicide" of Alfred Vanderbilt's mistress, and did seem to have blackmailed the millionaire with art investment as a front. Williamson seemed, then, fair game to be this novel's villain. The incident of a passenger with a gun trying to force the launching of a lifeboat, only to be crushed by it, did happen—sources vary as to the identity of that passenger.

I have again used a real-life writer of detective fiction as my protagonist. Unlike Jacques Futrelle (*The Titanic Murders*), Leslie Charteris (*The Hindenburg Murders*), and Edgar Rice Burroughs (*The Pearl Harbor Murders*), S.S. Van Dine was not a favorite author of mine. I did read his Philo Vance novels as a young man—when I was devouring any mystery that wasn't nailed down—and was fascinated by the pseudo-reality of his memoir technique, including his use of footnotes to achieve verisimilitude; the style of this novel has, in that regard at least, been an attempt to present a pastiche of his work. I reread one Vance novel in preparation for this novel—*The Benson Murder Case*—and, while the writing itself seemed highly competent, could not remember encountering a more irritating or less appealing detective character than Philo Vance.

Van Dine has always fascinated me, however, because of his rise and fall—that he was a spectacularly popular mystery writer who, within ten years of his prime, was largely forgotten. The eccentric egotist behind the pseudonym, Willard Huntington Wright is the subject of *Alias S.S. Van Dine* (1992) by John Loughery, a compulsively readable biography that I wholeheartedly recommend. Loughery's portrait of Wright was the chief influence on my portrayal of S.S. Van Dine, although I turned to numerous references in the mystery field as well, including *Encyclopedia of Mystery and Detection* (1976) by my friends Otto Penzler and the late Chris Steinbrunner, and *Twentieth-Century Crime and Mystery Writers*—Second Edition (1985) by John M. Reilly. Wright was not on the final voyage of the *Lusitania,* but he did sail three months prior, bringing his artist brother, Stanton, safely home; this real-life connection to the *Lucy* inspired his use in this novel.

My two longtime research associates came through for me in a big way—the sinking of the *Lusitania* made for a particularly challenging and exhausting research job. George Hagenauer read every book on the subject he could find, and pointed me to the best and most pertinent material; in addition, he spent hours on the phone and in person with me, discussing which real people on the voyage would make interesting characters, probing the historical issues and ramifications, and generally "spitballing" the plot. George in particular helped examine the complicated figure of Elbert Hubbard, a man who was a household name in his day and is largely forgotten now (not unlike S.S. Van Dine). He also helped develop the backstory of Pinkerton agent Philomina Vance. I always thank George for his work, but this time I really couldn't have done the job without him—he dug into ancient newspapers and magazines, and prepared files on a dozen *Lusitania* passengers, and prepped me beautifully for this voyage.

Lynn Myers—a real-life Pinkerton agent himself, if not as attractive a one as the fictional Miss Vance—did an incredible job for me, too, finding articles and books, and in particular leading me to (and locating a copy of) the single most important source—*"Lusitania": The Cunard Turbine-driven Quadruple-screw Atlantic Liner,* a 1986 reprint of a 1907 Cunard volume that features deck plans, photos and detailed descriptions of everything on the ship. Introduced and expanded upon by Mark D. Warren, this book was an indispensable tool, as most books on the *Lusitania*—unlike those on the *Titanic*—tend to focus less on the ship and the voyage and more on the sinking and the politics.

Four other books provided the bulk of the information I drew upon, and all are quality works, any one of which would be worthwhile for a reader who'd like to know more about this subject (most also tell the story of the U-boat that sank the *Lusitania,* which is absent from this novel): *Exploring the Lusitania* (1995), Robert D. Ballard with Spencer Dunmore; *The Last Voyage of the Lusitania* (1956, 1996), A.A. Hoehling and Mary Hoehling; *The Lusitania* (2000), Daniel Allen Butler; and *Seven Days to Disaster* (1981), Des Hickey and Gus Smith.

Also useful were *Lost Liners* (1997), Robert D. Ballard, Rick Archbold and Ken Marschall; *The Lusitania* (1972), Colin Simpson; *The Lusitania Disaster* (1975), Thomas A. Bailey and Paul B. Ryan; *The Lusitania's Last Voyage* (1915), Charles E. Lauriat, Jr.; and *The Military History of the Lusitania* (1965), Louis L. Snyder. Of these, Simpson's book is probably the best known and most widely circulated, and provided me with information about Leach and the stowaways, as well as some nice details about the sinking. Some of Van Dine's movements during the sinking are drawn from Lauriat's experiences.

I also viewed two documentaries, *Sinking the Lusitania* (2001), written by its director John Booth with David Davis; and *National Geographic: Last Voyage of the Lusitania* (1994), directed by Peter Schnall and written by Patrick Prentice. The latter follows Robert Ballard's exploration of the shipwreck, which dispelled some theories about the cause of the sinking. Both documentaries were helpful.

My portrait of Elbert Hubbard drew upon *Elbert Hubbard of East Aurora* (1926), Felix Shay; "Elbert Hubbard: Warrior with Words," an article by Norman Carlise in the April, 1955 issue of *Coronet*; and various Roycrofters publications, in particular issues of *The Philistine*. Much material on Hubbard is available on the Internet, including several pages of his aphorisms. Most of what Hubbard says in this novel comes from his writing and speeches and other quoted sources; his feelings about Mr. and Mrs. Isador Straus, the tragic couple who died on the *Titanic,* are from an article he wrote, rather presciently. Alfred Vanderbilt material was drawn in part from *Who Killed Society?* (1960), Cleveland Amory, although Vanderbilt—like Hubbard—was covered in detail in various *Lusitania* books. Ideas for period apparel were aided by Maryanne Dolan's *Vintage Clothing 1880–1960* (1987). The material on S.S. McClure and Edward Rumely came from Loughery's Van Dine biography and the excellent *Success: the Life and Times of S.S. McClure* (1963) by Peter Lyon.

The government opened postwar reparations hearings that enabled businesses and individuals to make claims for losses caused by Germany's actions during the war, including the *Lusitania* sinking. Various government publications of the United States and Germany Mixed Claims Commission and other reparations tribunals served as perhaps the most useful source of information on *Lusitania* passengers. Here we found the information on Charles Williamson's shady deals, which came to light when his relatives made claims on papers of his describing art and other assets that, under investigation, proved not to exist.

Also used were various issues of *The New York Times* from right before and after the tragedy. *Times* coverage provided the background on Madame DePage and the dock scandal that grew out of the German blockade.

This was a difficult novel for many reasons, not the least of which was my writing much of it in the aftermath of the September 11, 2001, tragedies. Such an event calls into question the value of entertainment—and for a number of days, I did not feel much like playing the role of entertainer—and proved particularly troubling to a writer in the process of creating a confection based around another tragedy of war.

That the *Lusitania* prefigured so much of the September 11 tragedies—one of my references reported a survivor comparing the swift sinking of the ship to "the collapse of a great building on fire"—made this task both more distressing and, finally, rewarding. Through the distance of history, in the guise of entertainment, I could explore some of the same issues that plague us almost a century later. I hope I have provided not only escape, but a morsel or two of food for thought, and that this mystery novel is in no way disrespectful to the gravity of such dire events.

I am grateful to my editor, Natalee Rosenstein of Berkley Prime Crime; when I was drowning in research materials, Natalee—who had in the first place suggested the *Lusitania* as a "disaster mystery" subject—threw me a life preserver by extending my deadline. My friend and agent, Dominick Abel, lent his usual support, and also helped buy me valuable time. And my wife, Barb—in a stressful period—was as always the best first mate a skipper could hope for. Unlike Elbert Hubbard's wife, Alice, however, she always had plenty to say.

About the Author

Max Allan Collins has earned an unprecedented eleven Private Eye Writers of America "Shamus" nominations for his historical thrillers, winning twice for his Nathan Heller novels, *True Detective* (1983) and *Stolen Away* (1991).

A Mystery Writers of America "Edgar" nominee in both fiction and nonfiction categories, Collins has been hailed as "the Renaissance man of mystery fiction." His credits include five suspense-novel series, film criticism, short fiction, songwriting, trading-card sets and movie/TV tie-in novels, including *In the Line of Fire, Air Force One* and the *New York Times*–best-selling *Saving Private Ryan*.

He scripted the internationally syndicated comic strip *Dick Tracy* from 1977 to 1993, is co-creator of the comic-book features *Ms. Tree, Wild Dog* and *Mike Danger*, has written the *Batman* comic book and newspaper strip, and the mini-series *Johnny Dynamite: Underworld*. His graphic novel, *Road to Perdition*, is the basis of the

DreamWorks feature film starring Tom Hanks and Paul Newman, directed by Sam Mendes.

As an independent filmmaker in his native Iowa, he wrote and directed the suspense film *Mommy,* starring Patty McCormack, premiering on Lifetime in 1996, and a 1997 sequel, *Mommy's Day.* The recipient of a record five Iowa Motion Picture Awards for screenplays, he wrote *The Expert,* a 1995 HBO World Premiere; and wrote and directed the award-winning documentary *Mike Hammer's Mickey Spillane* (1999) and the innovative *Real Time: Siege at Lucas Street Market* (2000).

Collins lives in Muscatine, Iowa, with his wife, writer Barbara Collins, and their teenage son, Nathan.